A Novel by G S JOHNSTON

www.gsjohnston.com

Follow on twitter@GS_Johnston

the SKIN
of WATER

Published by MiaRebaRose Press

First published electronically 2012

This edition published 2014

Györgynek, aki egy csodálatos történetet mesélt nekem egyszer...

CHAPTER ONE

At the height of the Hungarian summer of 1943, Zeno Czibula saw a woman in the forest.

She strode along a trail edging the sheltered verge of Lake Balaton. Even at this distance, her white diaphanous dress stood out against the deep forest. Diamond light bounced from the silver lake, picked out the dress flowing behind her slight frame, a dress not built for walking in forests. Zeno guessed she was staying at The Hotel Hungary.

She stopped. He held his breath. She looked right, left, over her shoulder. She may have seen him, sensed a set of eyes piercing her solitude. He moved behind a tree. He felt a small stick beneath his left foot and feared it would snap, echoing in the forest's damp quiet. So he stood, one foot raised, peering out from behind the tree. Then he did what he always did: lifted his Cine Kodak Eight Model 20 to his eye, released the wound mechanism, and began to film.

A nervous gazelle, she tilted her head this way and that. She looked down at her shoes and scuffed them off, kicking them clear. She stood facing the path towards the hotel. Her brown hair, straight and strong, bounced about her shoulders. She'd return to the hotel. He moved his lens in that direction and she slipped from his view. She'd hesitated.

The camera's mechanism clanged in the quiet forest. He should reveal his vantage. If she caught him spying he'd be fired and despite being only seventeen he needed this job. As he stepped from the tree's cover, the camera still to his eye, the stick snapped under his left foot. Nearby turtle doves took fright and flight, fluttering across the camera's field of vision. Through the lens, he saw her begin to run—away from the hotel, a sprinter from the blocks, barefoot now.

He switched off his camera and left it at the base of the tree. Once his legs began to race, following the narrow trail, the heat and humidity took hold. Sweat gathered on his upper lip and under his arm pits. He picked up pace anyway, his foot sure but silent. He found her abandoned shoes at the side of the path and scooped them up. The leather was soft, the slender heels not made for running.

The path led to a small bluff at the lake's edge. If he left the path and cut through the forest, he'd beat her there but alert her to his presence. He decided to follow her unnoticed, staying on the path. Her bare feet made no sound. He followed blind.

As the path rose, he stopped. He could hear nothing save the lake's low lapping and the drone of a distant powered boat. His senses sharpened. Was she now in hiding, watching him? He scanned the dappled forest but saw no trace of her. Perhaps he'd lost her. Or she him. No birds called. He breathed deeply, as if the air were robbed of oxygen. He shouldn't have followed a guest this deep into the forest.

He heard a sound, thin at first, then stronger, insistent with a timpani finish. A body hit water. He scampered up the remains of the path. Her dress lay discarded on the earth. On the western side of the lake, the afternoon sun glistened back at him, scorching his sight. No ripple, nothing broke the surface. He counted. One. Two. Three. Four. His heart pumped harder. Why had she not surfaced? His eyes darted about. She wasn't there.

He dropped her shoes, threw off his own along with his shirt and shorts, leaving only his underwear. He scanned the surface. Nothing. He dived, a grace-filled arc. As he descended those five metres, arms outstretched for balance, he glimpsed something breaking the surface. He hit the water, blessedly cool. His downward momentum dissipated and he pushed his arms up towards the light.

Once at the surface, he ran his hands over his face to clear the water and that flop of dark golden hair that hung down over his forehead. She was swimming, freestyle, away from him, her stroke firm and regular.

"Hey! Are you all right?"

She stroked on. He started strong freestyle strokes, his body a plane on the water. He could hear her limbs beat ahead of him, see her ruffle the water. He swam alongside her, slowed to her rhythm. And then she stopped, abruptly, as if she refused competition. He stopped, his legs caving in below him.

She brushed her hair from her face. Her pink nipples and small breasts blinked in the water. He couldn't look lower. Aware of his gaze, she glared at him, her hyacinth-blue eyes cold and penetrating.

"What do you want?" she said.

She was older than he expected, perhaps even in her mid 30s. Like her shoes, her accent was foreign and soft and expensive. Working at the hotel, he'd taught himself to mimic these accents of wealth.

"I was worried about you."

"There's no need."

"But you were swimming out into the lake."

"I didn't know this too was forbidden."

She was French, her accent light but noticeable.

"Well…" He was out of his depth. "I'll leave you, then."

He lingered a moment but she said nothing. He turned towards the shore, poised to swim.

"Young man, are you a guest at the hotel?"

Shit! A bellboy on his day off was forbidden in this part of the forest, reserved for paying guest. She could report him.

"Yes," he said.

"Then I'd appreciate you don't mention any of this." He nodded. "To anyone."

"Of course." He trod water. He should be away from her. "Enjoy your swim."

"And you yours."

He reached his arm again towards the shore.

"Your shoes…" he said, immediately regretting it.

"What of them?"

"I left them by your dress."

She raised her right eyebrow and nodded.

Slowly he turned away. He dug his hands hard into the water but as he began to plane, the turbulence caused his underwear, tied to his hips by string, to slip, then slide into the dark, dark water. He panicked, caught between escape and exposure. He couldn't stop. He continued his strokes towards the shore, slipping easier, his round buttocks white and glistening in the late afternoon sun.

With no difficulty at all, he hauled himself up on to the rocks and looked back at her over his shoulder. He hoped she'd resumed her swim but she was stationary, about seventy-five metres from the shore, treading water and staring in his direction. For a moment, neither of them could turn away.

He was sure she continued looking as he climbed back up the side of the bluff to his clothes, abandoned near hers, but he couldn't look while she was looking at his bare ass.

After he'd dressed, he made his way back to the hotel, slowed by the heat and the lack of underwear. How embarrassing. It could've been worse if he'd chosen to keep an eye on her and backstroked away. And what else could he have done except keep swimming? Stop? Duck-dive around her looking for his smalls? What a grand sight that would've been.

And he'd lied. He'd have to avoid her. The hotel was large, over five hundred guests. He could just avoid her room. But in order to do this, he'd need to know her name.

As he reached the end of the path, the Hotel Hungary rose seven stories out of the surrounding gardens. At this time of day, that breathless afternoon hollow, even the main building looked sleepy, the window box plants drooping, the eaves seeming to sag, quiet, no laughter, no signs of the activity soon to erupt as the hotel guests lurched towards cocktails, dinner, and dancing. Indeed, no hint of the war raging across Europe to which, through part good management and part good luck, Hungary had remained immune. German troops had marched through Hungary's streets and roads to the north and the south but no bombs had fallen, nothing had torn open its jewel, Budapest.

Something twinkling at the side of the path caught Zeno's eye. It was an ornate golden chain, fine weave, caught in the twigs of a low shrub. He knelt down and carefully pulled. As if he'd caught a fish, a weight resisted at the end of the chain, small but heavy. A sturdy gold crucifix. With great care he unraveled the chain and held it in his palm. Not really beautiful, plain flat surfaces, no Art Nouveaux curves. What should he do with it? He was no judge but thought it was gold and worth a fortune. Turn it in to the concierge? He heard voices. Two women, guests of the hotel, were coming. He clutched the crucifix in his palm and stood aside.

"Lord only knows where she's got to," one of them said.

They were looking for the woman. Should he go back and warn her? How stupid! He wrapped the chain around the cross and placed it in the button-down pocket of his shorts, the metal through the fabric cold against his skin.

The employees' quarters were at the rear of the hotel buildings, a group of small chalets scattered at a discrete distance. Zeno's roommate lay on his single bed, enervated and naked as usual.

"Hey," Zeno said. "I didn't think you'd be here."

"They want me to work again tonight."

Tibi was a deal older that Zeno, already twenty-five, blond hair with a film star's looks: a strong lantern jaw, full lips, fine blue eyes. His body, like Zeno's, was all chest and lung and broad shoulders. Listless by nature, he lived in Budapest but each summer came down to the lake to work.

Zeno pulled off his soaked shirt.

"Do you know a woman—"

"I know many women."

"Listen. She has dark hair. Slim. In her thirties? A hotel guest."

Tibi face soured. "It could be any of the women staying here. Why this one?"

"I saw her in the forest, near the lake."

Tibi sat up on the edge of his bed. He pulled a towel over his groin, took up a box of cigarettes, and lit one.

"But why would this old woman attract you?"

"Attract?"

"She's stirred something up in you."

"She seemed…"

Why had he started this? He didn't want to tell Tibi, the joker, how he'd embarrassed himself.

"I might have known you'd go for someone older," Tibi said. "You're such a sly, silent type…"

"Just because I don't paint my conquests across the sky."

"Exactly."

"She just seemed unhappy."

"And Zeno, the swashbuckling hero, must swoop in and rescue her." Tibi laughed, then said, "Does she have a foreign accent?"

"French, I think."

"And wearing a white dress with a faint leaf pattern?"

"Yes. Yes, she was."

"Steiner. It's Catherine Steiner. Very rich. What time did you see her?"

Zeno sat on the room's other single bed and faced Tibi.

"An hour ago…"

"This afternoon I took drinks to a table of women on the terrace. She left abruptly and said nothing."

"What'd happened?"

"That's it -- nothing. She just stood and left."

"What had they been talking about?"

"Same as usual." Tibi stubbed his cigarette in the ashtray and lay back down on the bed, arranging the towel and placing his hands together behind his head. "What was in fashion, what wasn't. Nothing. After she left, the women talked about her. That something had upset her."

A sharp knock at the door heralded Kovács, the head waiter of the hotel's restaurant.

"Zeno," he said. "I was hoping you'd be here. We need you to work tonight in the restaurant."

Zeno sighed. He was only a bellboy but twice before in emergencies he'd been pressed to help wait tables. The war stayed out of Hungary but it had robbed the hotel of staff, especially of the itinerant workers on which it was so dependent for the busy summer period. Zeno hadn't really enjoyed waiting tables, embarrassed by his inexperience. But the money was better and the tips could be good.

"Tibi can partner you," Kovács said.

Still Zeno hesitated.

"It's Thursday night," Tibi said. "The men are all in Budapest working. It won't be so busy."

Both Tibi and Kovács looked at him. Zeno wanted to move to Budapest and he needed extra money. He nodded.

"Good," Kovács said. "Both of you, get ready. I'll send up a uniform for you."

Kovács nodded in his military manner and left the room, closing the chalet door behind him.

"You'll do fine," Tibi said. "Don't worry."

"This war will kill me."

"Better to die as a waiter at the Hotel Hungary than on the Russian front."

Perhaps he'd be okay as a waiter. But first he needed to wash off the day's sweat. He walked over to his dresser and removed his shorts.

"Why aren't you wearing underwear?"

Zeno blushed, covering himself with his shorts.

"Long story."

Tibi raised an eyebrow and lay back on his bed.

Zeno and Tibi walked from the kitchens into the restaurant, smooth in their white dinner-suit uniforms complete with white gloves. The restaurant was empty of guests. In the hotel's bars, the sculpted guests took bitter aperitifs to stimulate their appetites. Kovács, already busy, merely inclined his head towards the pair.

"Just don't be seen for a while," Tibi told Zeno. "Stand over there and wait."

Zeno stood alone near the kitchen servery window while those more qualified buzzed about. The restaurant curtains were drawn apart. The open higher case windows above the line of French doors that looked onto a large terrace allowed something of the evening's cool to enter the room. But the humidity persisted. He felt it on his skin. The very last of the day's sunlight glistened on the darkening lake. One by one, the room's two dozen electric chandeliers ignited, but the room still felt dark, a side effect of the dark wood-paneled walls. A violin player drew a bow across strings that were quickly tuned. The trio sprang to life for a few bars, then rested.

"All this fuss," Tibi said, as he passed by Zeno. "These pigs will never even notice."

Zeno followed Tibi. He thought it was fine no trouble or fuss was spared. Did it matter no one noticed? The dinner guests began to file in. His stomach gurgled with first-night nerves. The whole staff breathed in together, became individual cogs in one machine. Quite quickly, the restaurant swarmed with the hum of conversation and peals of mirth. The trio played Schubert's String Trio in B Flat but the heat zapped all the brightness from the piece. Over two hundred people to be fed.

Kovács came towards them.

"The entrees are ready for table ten."

Tibi and Zeno and four other waiters took up six plates from the servery window. As they approached the table, Zeno's nerves jangled—three men and three women, one of the men a German SS Officer who'd stayed at the hotel before, a lieutenant colonel Müller whose round face looked generous until he curled the edges of his mouth in something of a snarl as he spoke.

The officer was seated next to László Fehér, a man Zeno also knew only by sight. He was a local member of the Arrow Cross Party, the Hungarian fascists, a rotund little man, always at the hotel for dinner and always with guests who seemed to outstrip his rank. Next to him were György Földes and his wife. Zeno had taken their luggage to their room and received a hefty tip. Földes was an industrialist from Budapest, a neat, quiet man.

Two women, both weekday widows, completed the party, seated together like maiden aunts, their backs turned towards Zeno, facing the magnificent view of the lake. The taller, Ilona Rákóczy, the wife of a big industrialist, sat on the left. The other was Catherine Steiner, her dark hair now dry and shiny and straight. Zeno, panic-stricken, moved as if he were an automoton.

"And where's your husband tonight?" the officer Müller asked her.

"He's in Budapest," she said. "He's working."

She drew out the second sentence. The officer smirked. The waiters moved to their places around the table.

"Such a large factory must never sleep," the officer said. "You're not Hungarian."

Zeno was close enough behind to hear her breath.

"At what point," she said, "does one cease to be something and become something else?"

"Mrs. Steiner is French," Földes said, bowing his head towards the officer.

"I was born in France," Mrs. Steiner said, "but I've lived here for over twenty years."

Zeno carried her soup. He positioned himself at her left side. He took a moment, to survey the setting, anticipate any sudden change.

"Steiner…" the officer said suddenly.

Zeno began to lower the plate, slowly at first.

"They're an old Hungarian family," Földes said, his tone firm. "They converted to Christianity in the late days of the empire."

"I think Herr Müller has me wrong. I am a French Catholic." Swiftly, Catherine lifted her left hand to her chest, fumbling in the folds of fabric. Gripped by a kind of seizure, Zeno shook, just enough to cause a little soup to spill to the side of the under plate. The other waiters perceived this tremor and halted their advance. Like a magician, Tibi produced a cloth and removed the droplet. Zeno breathed out.

"That was a liberal time for such things," Müller said.

"One has to wonder," Fehér said, "how much conversion was sincere or forced or simply pragmatic."

"What rot are you talking?" Földes said. "The Steiners are a model Christian family. They maintain The Lady of Charity Orphanage in Budapest. They've received the Pope's benediction."

Without shaking, which required strenuous effort, Zeno lowered the plate to the table. The other waiters lowered theirs. Catherine Steiner made no acknowledgement. Zeno stepped back.

"Vichyssoise," the SS officer said. "You remain true to your cuisine, at least."

"You misread me yet again," Mrs. Steiner said. "The soup may be French but the coolness is an American touch. The evening is warm."

The waiters withdrew to the side servery.

At that moment, Kovács motioned. Food was ready for other tables. While he delivered these meals Zeno worried about returning to serve Catherine Steiner. But what choice did he have? And after all, she'd not noticed him. She was occupied in countering the officer. It was worth the risk. He'd say nothing to Tibi.

His serving at other tables was without fault, and with each plate his confidence rose. And when he returned to Mrs. Steiner's table, he did what was required without incident. She never looked at him. The table's conversations were inconsequential, talk of the opera in Budapest, of some marriage scandal, of the war. The officer defended Germany's dwindling position in Russia, especially since the January fall of Stalingrad.

"The Hungarian Second Army suffered terrible losses," Földes said.

"There'll always be troop losses," Laszló Fehér said.

"The Soviets crushed the remainder at the Battle of Voronezh."

Müller breathed deeply. "You must realize the loss of Hungary's troops is our own loss. New machinery, modern machinery is needed." He looked directly at Catherine Steiner and she returned the intensity of his gaze. "There are moves to secure these things. Perhaps your husband would be interested in such contracts?"

Catherine glared at him. "Perhaps."

"Perhaps we could discuss this, later this evening?"

Catherine looked quickly at the others. "I'm sure there's nothing we can't discuss here. My husband will return at the weekend. He'd be happy to meet with you."

"How ironic!" His open palm struck the table. "I must return to Budapest at the weekend. To work." He roared with laughter and returned his eyes to Földes. "Once this work is completed, the war will proceed as the Führer intends."

When the waiters approached later with desserts, no one was speaking. Ilona Rákóczy's stern expression turned into a welcoming smile. Földes banged his hand hard on the table and argued that Hungary had taken considerable action.

"Then why has Regent Admiral Horthy so resisted deportation?" Müller said.

"The men are working in labor camps. For years, we have restricted the number of Jews in different areas of business. They are completely forbidden from government office. And we have made this tighter by defining a Jew as more than one grandparent of Jewish extraction. They are a race, not a religion. And we've legislated against marriage between a Jew and a non-Jew. Any such intimacy is illegal."

"Then why not deport them as we have asked?"

The dessert plates were lowered to the table.

"They're restricted," Földes said, "identified and controlled."

Catherine Steiner stood, abruptly pushing back her chair. She turned to leave the table, turning directly towards Zeno.

He'd no time to retreat. She looked into his face. Both froze. He felt his heart fall away. Her blue eyes flared violet, remained impassioned but not, he thought, with recognition. All eyes at the table were on her, but as this standoff extended, the eyes drifted to him. He stepped sideways. She looked down, away, and began to walk.

The fleet of waiters peeled from the table. All Zeno had to do was fall in line. As he moved back into the depths of the restaurant, he saw Catherine Steiner, her step brisk over the restaurant foyer. She'd bid no farewell, no explanation. She'd just left, much as Tibi said she had earlier that afternoon.

CHAPTER TWO

Zeno arrived for work at 6 a.m. in the reception area, comfortable again in his bellboy uniform. The concierge moved about, put his half glasses on, read something, took them off, and moved about some more. He barked a command at his assistant, sending him into a similar flurry of motion.

"What's the matter?" Zeno asked.

"Catherine Steiner has lost a gold crucifix."

Zeno froze. The concierge took off his glasses and glared at him. The crucifix. God damn it. And damn his inattentive memory to hell. It was lying on the floor in his shorts pocket. Zeno closed his mouth, tried to brush his expression clean.

"She thinks it's been stolen," the concierge said.

Damn, damn, damn.

"We must go to the Steiner suite," the concierge said, "and see if we can find this thing."

"But I can't."

The concierge swung back around to him. "You can't?"

"Someone should work here." He waved his hand at the reception desk. "There are people checking out this morning. Someone should be here."

"You don't seem to realize the gravity of this situation." The concierge's voice hissed on the "s" in the last word. "If it can't be found, Steiner will call the police and we'll all be under suspicion. Move it!"

The Steiner suite was on the top floor of the hotel, seven stories up, five bedrooms, a lounge and dining area, a large balcony with an uninterrupted view across the hotel grounds to the lake. The entrance hall had parquet floors, the lounge a higher ceiling and larger chandeliers, the furniture was plumped with a little more down than counterparts on lower floors.

Already a fleet of black and white uniformed maids fluttered about the room, the drapes pulled back, the weak sun spilling onto the floor. The apartment's electric lights were still turned on. A maid, Magda, who normally worked on a lower level of the hotel, rolled her eyes as she passed Zeno.

Catherine Steiner was seated on a sofa, wearing only a long sky-blue silk dressing gown pulled in hard at the waist. With her was Ilona Rákóczy, also in a robe and looking as if she'd just been pulled from bed to this drama. Despite the panic he felt, Zeno stared at Catherine. She wore no makeup. Her face, although still handsome, bore no trace of a girl and yet no real trace of age, no undue creases, the skin lucent despite her time at the lake. Her dark hair carried no gray. As she looked about the room, her eyes flashed. She was beautiful. He knew it then, as he'd suspected at the lake -- beautiful beyond any face he'd ever seen.

"It was a recent gift from Sándor," she said. "Thank God he's not here to witness all this."

"You're not here to stand," the concierge said, sotto voce, to Zeno. "Help György lift the furniture."

"I remember wearing it yesterday afternoon," Catherine said. "I put it on before I left."

"What time was that?" Mrs. Rákóczy asked.

The concierge motioned Zeno close to Catherine to help lift an armchair.

"I don't know…. When we met for a drink, in the afternoon."

"Around three, then?"

"I imagine so."

Mrs. Rákóczy thought for a moment.

"I believe I saw you wearing it. I think I saw it. But you left us. Where did you go after that?"

Despite his heart rate, Zeno glanced at Catherine. Her face darkened. Did she now think of her swim at the lake? Imagine the crucifix at the bottom of the lake? Did she now think of him? His bare ass. He turned his back on her.

"Where did you go?"

"I walked in the forest -- "

"But we looked for you there."

As they stooped to lift the armchair, the quick motion caught Catherine's eye. She looked first at the chair then directly at him. He could feel her gaze. His face burned. Magda ducked down under the chair, twisted, and looked up into the underlying springs and lining.

"I… noticed it was missing, last night at dinner."

"At dinner?"

"I hadn't put it on."

Shouldn't he end this silly game, this waste of time? No. He couldn't speak directly to Catherine Steiner. He'd lose his job for that alone. He looked at the concierge. He couldn't trust him, and anyway, she'd sworn him to secrecy.

Magda found nothing in the springs of the chair. She stood up, looking at Zeno.

"What a farce," she said quietly.

Zeno and György lowered the arm chair and lifted another for Magda to inspect. The fruitless search continued for an hour, every item in every room moved, turned, parted, shaken, or pulled apart. Once it was clear nothing could be found, the hotel manager, who'd arrived halfway through the search and taken control, asked Catherine what she wished.

"I'd just like it found. Perhaps I dropped it in the hotel grounds."

"Of course. Now there's good light, I'll instruct a thorough search of the grounds." The manager looked towards an assistant and nodded. He left the room. "Would you like tea brought up?"

"No," she said. "Perhaps it has been stolen."

"If you'd permit us to search the grounds, before we contact the police..."

"Yes. Yes, of course."

At the manager's instruction, the workers drained from the rooms. Zeno made his way back to reception, the area completely unmanned and the lobby empty of patrons or staff. He ran to his chalet.

The room was dark save for a shaft of sunlight, the air close and warm. Tibi was still asleep, his naked back turned to Zeno, the bed sheet pushed to the base of the bed. Zeno closed the door. In the dark, he fell to his knees and patted his hands on the floor, searching for the discarded shorts.

"Are you looking for this?"

Tibi rolled over, cocooning himself in the sheet. He pulled his hand free. The gold crucifix rested in his palm, the chain laced between his fingers.

"Why have you got it?"

"Stubbed my toe when I went to relieve myself." Tibi frowned. "Where'd you get this?"

"I found it in the garden. It belongs to Catherine Steiner."

Tibi bounced the crucifix in his palm. "Why didn't you hand it in?"

"I forgot."

"You forgot to hide it?"

"I forgot about it till I got to work and everyone was looking for it."

Tibi looked at him, pulled his mouth sideways.

"This must be worth six hundred pengő. How much will you earn this summer?"

"Four hundred."

"We could sell it."

"That would be dishonest."

"You're not convincing me. What's going on with you and her?"

"Nothing."

"Yesterday evening you asked about her. Last night at dinner you were nervous around her. What are--"

"Nothing happened. They're searching the grounds. Fast. Help me find it in the garden, will you?"

"These bourgeoisies have too much already."

"I have to give it back, dammit."

"Don't swim out of your depth." Tibi allowed the crucifix's chain to unravel from his hand. It fell to the bed. "If there's a reward, I want half."

The hotel grounds swarmed with maids and butlers and gardeners and any other spare set of hands, arse-up in flower beds, hedges and potted plants, others picking about in the well-tended hedgerows like workers in a field of tea. The Italian, Giovanni, waded in the murky waters of the main fountain, his trousers rolled up knee high, laughing and flicking water at one of the maids.

"I'm sure Catherine Steiner didn't swim there yesterday," Tibi said. "Where did you find this?"

"Over there." Zeno motioned with his eyes. "At the path."

At the entrance of the path, two maids half-heartedly brushed aside the bushes.

"We should go there," Tibi said.

"But they'll see us."

"You can't find this where she wasn't. Unless you know somewhere else?"

"Shut up. What about on the terrace?"

"You said that woman saw her leave with it."

"Right."

Tibi was right. It had to be found somewhere credible to her, some place she wouldn't dispute. Zeno breathed deeply. They walked towards the start of the path. Unobtrusively, they mixed with the others. How long should he wait? What was a fair time to search? He made his way towards the exact spot, but there were so few shrubs in which to hide it, really only the ones in which he'd found it. He held the crucifix in his palm. The maid, Magda, stood up in front of him, searching the same spot. He rammed the crucifix back into his pocket.

"Nothing there," she said. "Not that it's any great surprise."

She moved off to another area. He looked over at Tibi, who nodded to him to advance on their plan. Zeno began to act. He looked at those around him and tried to reproduce their slightly heavy brows, their eyes moving quickly, side to side, up and down. He checked if anyone was near and slipped the crucifix from his pocket and allowed it to fall. The chain caught in the branch. And there it hung, entangled, the sunlight catching on the gold. For a moment he thought he should just leave it for someone else to discover. But how long could this whole charade continue? What if no one found it? And what if someone did discover it and didn't turn it in and the police were called?

"I've found it," he said. No one but Tibi looked at him. How would a voice sound in such a situation? Elated? Surprised? Relieved?

"I've found it," he yelled, with all three qualities entwined in the words. Bodies straightened, heads and faces appeared from all manner of positions. Tibi ran to his side.

"Well done," Tibi said, squatting down to unravel the chain from the bush. People congregated around them.

"Thank God," another maid said. "Now we can all go back to work."

A senior worker arrived, took the crucifix from Tibi's hand and walked back towards the hotel. The other workers dispersed.

"What were you worried about?" Tibi said. "They only want the crucifix. Now they're satisfied. There's no scandal. No questions asked. No reward."

"Back to your places," a duty officer announced.

"But I searched here," Magda said. "I didn't find it."

She looked at Tibi and Zeno and then again at Tibi. Zeno shrugged his shoulders slightly and looked away.

"What one eye misses," Tibi said, "another sees."

"But I looked here."

Her eyes were determined.

"And you didn't find it," Tibi said. He screwed up his face at Magda and tapped Zeno on the back to make him walk.

The other bell boys were already in the reception area, the concierge back in place and working at a decidedly smoother pace. The morning proceeded. Bags and guests arrived and were processed with speed, dispersed to the various corners of the hotel. And from these corners bags were collected and brought back to the foyer, out to the waiting army of taxis and cars. Amongst all these comings and goings, there was no sign of Catherine Steiner. She must have stayed all morning in her apartment. Zeno could melt away again.

"Which one of you found the crucifix?"

Zeno blushed. It was the hotel manager.

"I did," he said.

The manager glared at him as if he wasn't capable of such a thing.

"Then you must smarten yourself and come with me."

"Why?"

The manager spun with great gusto towards him.

"Because Catherine Steiner wishes to thank you. Personally."

CHAPTER THREE

From the Steiner suite's entrance hall, Zeno breathed in the room.

"Wait here."

The manager walked down a corridor off to the left. The room's stillness and and the close scent of roses enticed him. So beautiful in its balance, the height of the ceiling to the length of the wall, the pattern of the cornice echoed in the carving of the skirting board crowned by a bold expanse of window. The vertiginous view of the lake drew him forward until he heard the manager's returning footsteps.

"As much as protocol demands that I should stay," he said, "Mrs. Steiner wants to see you alone." He came closer. "You won't speak to her or answer her. You'll say nothing. You'll accept no reward. Is that clear?"

Zeno nodded. The manager studied him for a moment, then left the suite. Zeno stood but the room beckoned him. He ventured forward to the wall of windows.

"The view of a bird."

The day was old now, the sun drawing down. Glare silvered the lake's surface. Small sail boats turned about only for an evening's joy. He followed the line of shore villages, Balatonudvari, Fövenyes, Balatonakali, and Zánka, but then they were lost in the day's haze. The hotel would have to be fifty stories high to see his home in the hinterland of the southwestern shore. He wished he had his camera with him. In a few months when he moved to Budapest, he'd miss the lake. A slow pan of this view would be something.

Someone coughed discreetly. He spun around. She stared at him, her eyes still and withdrawn as if to limit her view. Her small frame gave her proportion a sense of height but she was shorter than he'd expected, than he remembered, despite another pair of fine heels she wore. He'd never seen such skin, white and translucent and without flaw. She wore a gray suit, cut tight to her figure, most unlike the flowing dress she'd abandoned the previous evening. The gold crucifix nestled between the folds of a cream blouse. The thought of her naked breast, even now, aroused him. He steeled his eyes to hers.

"I thought it may have been you," she said. He dropped his eyes. "Come now, there's to be no pretense, no feigning lack of recognition." He looked up, and she smiled. "Where did you really find it?"

"Where it was. I thought you threw it there, like your shoes."

"Not at all."

"I found it yesterday evening, when I was returning from the lake...." Now the lake lay between them. "I forgot until this morning."

"I see." She scowled. "I'm most grateful. It's a recent gift from my husband. He'd have been... quite upset if it were lost."

"I see."

She walked towards a small desk at the rear of a large sofa and from the drawer took an envelope.

"Take it. Please."

"The manager said I can't."

She lowered her outstretched hand. He could smell her perfume, no hint of rose or lily or any other flower, yet bold to the point of cloying.

"Why did you lie, yesterday?" she asked.

"Lie?"

"You served me at dinner last night. You're a bell boy today. Are you a jack-of-all trades? You're not a guest at the hotel."

"There's a shortage of staff this summer, because of the war. I was called on to--"

"Why did you lie?"

"I can't afford to lose my job."

"Lose your job?"

"The forest's reserved for guests."

"I see. But you're young. Why are you so dependent on this job?"

"I send money to my mother and younger sister."

Catherine considered this. "Where's your father?"

"He left us."

She looked at him for a moment. "If so much was at stake, why were you in the forest?"

"I like to walk in the forest." He paused. "I had my camera with me."

She considered this. "So you're a photographer, as well as everything else."

"A movie camera. I was filming."

"Then what were you filming?"

The word "'you" formed and rolled along his tongue until he clenched his teeth.

"Whatever caught my eye." He warmed to her interest. "I need to learn so much, framing, proportion, tracking…." He stopped. "I forgot where I was."

"What would happen if you'd been caught there?"

"In normal circumstances, I'd be sacked. As they're so short of staff, I'd be reprimanded, offered less work. Please don't tell anyone."

Mrs. Steiner turned away from him and walked further into the recesses of the room. He couldn't imagine living in rooms with so much space that an article of furniture could be positioned and walked around.

"Then we *are* linked," she said, a new lightness in her voice, "by two secrets."

"I... I'm sorry?"

"You witnessed my... actions, yesterday at the lake. They were reckless. And I witnessed your trespassing."

She paused and looked him in the eye. He breathed deeply. She waved the outstretched envelope in a small circle.

"Buy yourself some film. Send it to your mother and sister. I won't tell the manager."

He stepped two paces towards her and took the envelope from her hand. Despite not touching, he felt her warmth. When she released the envelope, he lowered his own hand.

"Thank you, again," she said. "I must go. My husband's arriving this evening from Budapest. I wish you a good evening. I'll pray for you and your plans."

She turned to leave the room but stopped.

"I don't know your name?"

"Czibula," he said. "Zeno."

"Zeno? That's unusual. Are you a paradox?"

He breathed deeply, unnerved by this woman's intelligence and perception.

"It would seem my mother thought so."

For some moments, she observed him, moments he wanted to stretch and stretch. Her expression gave no more away. Then she turned and left, as if there was nothing else to say.

Outside the suite, he tugged at the envelope's wax seal but a chambermaid came from the elevator and made her way down the hall towards him. He pushed the envelope into his pants' pocket. They smiled at one another and he rushed to catch the elevator. The envelope felt remarkably fat, but he resisted opening it in front of the elevator driver. They were all gossips.

In the foyer, the other bellboys milled around the concierge area. On Friday evenings, a train brought the working men back to the lake. The staff called it the Bull Train. In the next few minutes a wave of up to a hundred men would descend on the hotel, and things needed to run smoothly.

Zeno exhaled. He was tired. He'd worked late last night and started early that morning. He just had to concentrate on the next few hours, then he could sleep.

The first of the taxis came up the hotel's meandering drive. Three men alighted. Zeno and another bellboy, Ferenc, a tall string of a boy, unloaded the luggage.

"It's a rest to be here for the weekend," the first man said. "My wife's far less demanding...."

"Summer in Budapest keeps you young," the second said.

"Worn out, but young."

And so began a frantic hour: luggage piled onto trolleys, into elevators, along corridors, into rooms, onto racks, tips accepted, then back down to the lobby to start again. At around six in the evening Zeno and Ferenc returned to the foyer, hoping the last had arrived, just as an Adler 2.5 litre limousine cruised through the hotel gates.

"It's practically a train," Ferenc said.

They stood and watched it wind up the driveway and ease to a gentle stop. An attendant stepped forward and opened the rear door. While Zeno and Ferenc made their way to the trunk, a single man alighted. He was at least in his late 40s, his tailor expensive, his body was strong, the frame lean and cared for. The car's trunk carried just a few smaller pieces of thick leather luggage. With no returning glance, the man walked out across the foyer towards the elevators, his gait relaxed, neither in a hurry nor tarrying. The bags were someone else's concern.

A taxi pulled in behind them.

"Isn't this going to finish this evening?" Zeno said quietly.

Zeno and Ferenc took the cases from the trunk of the Adler and loaded them onto a trolley.

"They look so silly on such a big trolley," Zeno said.

Ferenc pushed him in the ribs. Behind them, a young woman had alighted from the taxi. She was dressed in a powder blue woolen suit, the shoulders cut square, the skirt tight around her hips and the hem just below the knee. Her hat, a black round pillbox, seemed out of place, gaudy despite its color. She was only twenty-three at the most and made her way quickly to the reception area.

"Look at that," Ferenc said.

Like Tibi, whenever he could, Ferenc peppered the working summer with liaisons. Zeno watched. Her high heels and tight skirt and quick step made her buttocks move in a most appealing way.

"That's not something you see everyday around here," Ferenc said.

A young woman on her own, at this busy time of year when every room was booked in advance, was a rare sight.

"These are to go to the Steiner suite," the concierge said.

Zeno looked again at the luggage. Of course that man was Catherine's husband. He had that indifferent air of great wealth. And the car. And the clothes.

"You can take them up," Zeno said. "There's not many and I've had enough for the day."

Ferenc smiled. If there was a tip from Mr. Steiner, he'd garner the whole. Zeno didn't care. He left the hotel and dragged himself back to the chalet. Tibi was already in the final stages of preparing for work.

"Did you get a reward?" he asked.

He'd completely forgotten.

"Yes."

He took out the envelope in his pocket and counted the notes. Tibi came over, his eyes wide.

"Two hundred pengő," Zeno whispered. "That's more than I earn in a month."

"Everything comes to you so easily," Tibi said.

"I wouldn't say that."

"Life's kind to you. But you owe me some money."

Playfully, he pulled a 20-pengő note free. Zeno didn't even mind. He still had the unimaginable sum of 180 pengő for himself.

"Sándor Steiner just arrived," Zeno said. "He wasn't anything like I thought he'd be."

"What did you expect?"

"He's older than her. Aloof."

"They're all aloof," Tibi said. "They're worn down by the weight of all their money."

He tousled Zeno's hair.

"With this," Zeno said, "I'll be able to come to Budapest at least a month earlier."

"That's great...great."

"You'll be able to help me, won't you?"

"Yeah, yeah. Of course."

Tibi saluted and closed the chalet door behind him.

Zeno stripped off his clothes, letting them fall to the floor. The day was still hot. He'd do as Tibi did and lie naked on his single bed until the night cool arrived. He placed the envelope and the money under his pillow. They had so much money, how could anything be of value to them? The crucifix had been given to her by her husband. Perhaps that explained its additional worth: sentiment. But her husband didn't seem the sentimental type. Zeno closed his eyes. What did a man like Sándor Steiner appreciate?

Despite his exhaustion and the heat, his mind fluttered over half-dreamed images of Catherine's bare breast, her slender waist, her hands, the intense heat he'd felt. He changed position in the bed, arranging and rearranging his limbs and torso until, lying on his belly, he ground his member against the soft flesh of his palms, his thumbs catching and releasing his foreskin. The glistening image of Catherine's bare buttocks pressing back against his thighs was all he needed.

CHAPTER FOUR

Zeno woke with a start, the room filled with sunlight. Tibi's bed was made. He'd either not come home or Zeno had slept so soundly that Tibi had slept, awakened, and gone again. He looked at his watch. It was ten past ten. He'd slept much longer than he'd expected and was really late for work. He jumped out of bed, then remembered it was Saturday and he wasn't due to work until the evening in the restaurant.

He sat back down on the bed, slid his hand under the pillow, and pulled out the envelope. He could afford to have the day off. Who was he kidding? He needed all the money he could get his hands on. But before work, he needed a glimpse of Catherine Steiner.

With his camera case over his shoulder, he spent what little remained of the morning hanging around the hotel grounds. She wasn't on the terrace with the other women, nor had she been in the coffee bar. Before lunch he saw Mr. Steiner playing tennis, men's doubles, but no sign of Catherine despite the three other wives in attentive audience. He filmed them for a while, a static shot where the players bounced in an out of his field.

Well, that was it. He wasn't going to see her. He'd not eaten anything and would go to the kitchen and see what he could sponge for lunch. As he walked around the rear of the hotel, something bright green moved against the dark building. It was Catherine, in a bland brown suit whose jacket had a bold emerald lapel. She walked towards a large black car, the driver holding open the rear door, and slid inside. The car began to move around the rear edge of the building, out towards the driveway. Why was she leaving by the rear of the building?

He ran towards the employee's chalets, bursting in to Ferenc's.

"Can I borrow your motorbike?" he said, slightly out of breath.

"Just have it back by six." Ferenc raised his eyebrows and smiled. "I've a date."

By the time Zeno had reached the main road he couldn't see the car. He pushed the bike to a hard whine, aware they couldn't get away from him as there were no major turns off the road before the village of Aszófő. He saw them, and when he was close enough, he relaxed the throttle. He wanted to observe, not interfere, and especially not to be observed. As they entered the village he encroached a little further. The car stopped. He pulled onto the curb. The driver rounded the car, opened her door, and she alighted. Now off the bike, he pressed back against a wall. With an remote expression, she surveyed those around her, then walked towards a smaller lane.

Zeno walked to the lane but she'd disappeared. He'd lost her so easily. She must have entered one of the smaller shops. With stealth, he walked. She wasn't in the barbers, not in the sweetshop -- but there she was in the florist. She admired a striking arrangement of pink and blue hydrangeas. She looked up at the shop window, directly at him. He froze. The florist called her. She moved quickly towards the attendant and Zeno took fright, turned, and walked further down the lane to wait for her. He took his camera from its case. He filmed the lane, the people passing.

She emerged, walked into his frame, and stepped quickly towards the car. She held a small flower arrangement in front of her. He began to follow, filming her from behind, trying to hold the long tracking shot still as if the camera ran along a fixed track.

Once back on the street, he ran to the bike. The car moved far ahead of him but he slipped in front of another car to be behind it. They traveled to the other side of the village and stopped outside a church, Saint László. Catherine hurried from the car to the building. Zeno waited a minute or two. The driver sat back in the car. He seemed unaware of Zeno's presence.

The cool air inside the church relieved the heat of the day, but the scent of years of burning incense hung heavy in the air. From the high windows the light formed rays, and each sound echoed in the vast cavern. He walked down one side of the central nave, scanning the empty pews. Perhaps she'd entered a confessional booth, but these doors hung open. A door closed at the rear of the building. He rushed towards it, his shoes tapping on the stone floor.

Outside, sunlight flooded a west-facing courtyard, smarting his eyes. It was a graveyard with stone pathways and low hedgerows. She was on the far side, seated on a stone bench. She hadn't noticed him. He eased the door closed. She'd laid the flowers next to her as if preparing to leave them at a grave. He took out his camera, the mechanical whirl ringing loud in the hush of the courtyard. She took off the crucifix. He changed the focus, tunneling into her. She wound the chain around the cross, looked at it, and placed it in her bag. She stood, leaving the flowers, and walked to another door at the rear wall of the cemetery. She disappeared.

Camera still in hand, he pushed the door open onto a lane. He could see her walking away and began to film and follow. People crowded the lane, a thoroughfare, buildings bald-faced to the street. She walked only a hundred meters, then stopped at a doorway. She looked left and right and mounted the two entrance steps. He slipped into the semi-shade. She raised her left hand and touched the side of the doorjamb. After a few moments, she lowered her hand and pressed her fingers to her lips. The door opened, the space inside so dark it yielded nothing of the person within. She slipped in and the door closed.

He ran the few remaining steps to the buildings. He ceased filming. He waited. He moved out of the direct line of sight from the building and waited longer. When she'd not emerged for over half an hour and no one else had come or gone from the building, he walked over to the door. There was a small plaque – Panzió Katy. It was a cheap hotel. Why would she leave one of the most luxurious hotels in the area and come here?

Without really thinking, he knocked on the door. After some time a man answered.

"I'm sorry," he said, without looking at Zeno. "We have no rooms vacant."

He closed the door.

Zeno walked back to his vantage on the other side of the street. Still no one emerged. People passed. No one else went into the hotel. He looked at his watch. It was now after five. He had to be back to work at six. And Ferenc wanted the bike. He walked back through the church courtyard. The posy of flowers, a sprig of hollyhocks, had wilted on the stone seat. Outside the church, her car was gone.

Zeno delivered the bike on time but arrived late for work, the restaurant already filled with patrons. He took a position near the chiffonier and hoped no one had noticed. He glanced around the room. Catherine wasn't there, but the young woman who'd arrived last evening was seated at a small window table. She gazed out the window at the few lights twinkling from the lake's far shore. She looked down at her nails, turned her hand over and looked at her palm. She smoked, sucking the fumes deep into her lungs.

Zeno took a clean ashtray to her. She looked up as he approached. She'd smoked four cigarettes. He held the clean ashtray over the old as he removed it, but the two sheared against one another midflight. His hand wavered. He steadied himself. She looked up.

"Better watch yourself, buddy."

Her lower class speech made the warning harsh. She smiled. He placed the clean ashtray on her table.

"You were working as a bellboy yesterday." She looked around. "What kind of crummy place is this?"

Zeno, taken aback, said nothing.

"Do you walk the dogs too?" she said.

He smiled with a closed mouth and nodded his head.

"I see," she said. "You aren't supposed to talk to me."

He nodded again and moved away to the chiffonier and Tibi.

"I nearly dropped an ashtray on that woman's table."

"Where?"

"Over by the window. On her own."

Tibi looked through the restaurant.

"Beauty," Tibi said. "Who is she?"

"How would I know? But Ferenc has his eye on her."

"Ferenc?" Tibi looked at Zeno. "No competition."

Sándor Steiner arrived at the restaurant and was greeted by the maître'd. He moved quickly to a table where they'd already ordered. He seemed calm, his movements considered and practiced, the type of man who was unflappable. Kovács motioned that plates were ready for Mr. Steiner's table.

As he set down the first plate Zeno took in Mr. Steiner, his fingernails cut neatly, polished, a cigarette comfortably held in his hand. His hair was thick, oiled back close to his skull. Although his face was full of planes and sharp angles, they threw the roundness of his lips into greater relief, giving him an air of generosity.

"And where's your lovely wife tonight?" a man seated opposite him said.

Zeno tightened.

"She'll not be joining us. She wasn't feeling well."

Zeno lowered the plate to the table.

"What a pity." The man smiled. "And you've just returned."

Zeno moved back from the table and the waiters walked Indian file to the servery. How could she be indisposed so quickly? She'd seemed well that afternoon. Perhaps she'd not returned to the hotel. Who the hell had she met at the Panzió Katy?

"Sorry to interrupt your precious thoughts," Kovács said. "But there's work to be done. Single main course for table twenty-five."

Zeno carried the plate through the restaurant to the young woman's table, but she wasn't there. He glanced around the restaurant and saw no trace of her. Perhaps she'd gone to relieve herself. But she'd left nothing at the table, not even a pack of cigarettes. He returned to the servery with the plate of food.

"She's not there," he said into the kitchen. "Keep it warm."

The plate disappeared back into the kitchen. He helped serve another large table and when he returned again to the kitchen, the woman's table was still vacant. As it remained for the rest of the evening.

On Sunday morning, he set out to find Catherine. After searching all through the hotel, he took the risk of going back to the forest. Despite the fact that it was reserved for guests, hardly any of them used it, and there was no sign of her along the trails. From the bluff he looked out onto the lake. He held the camera to his eye and panned across the expanse where they'd swum, committing it to film.

As brazenly as he dared, he walked back towards the hotel. With the remaining film, he took a distance shot, looking back at the tree from where he'd seen her, a revealing change of perspective. He returned to the tree and shot again the vacant spot where she'd stood. Then he ran as he'd done that day, camera still running too, towards the bluff until the film ran out. He'd splice all these pieces together into a story.

Back at the hotel, he walked around the whole building, through the restaurant and bars, but there was no sign of her. He sought out the chambermaid who serviced the Steiner apartment.

"Is Catherine Steiner ill?"

"Ill? Is that what you call it? No. She's just not left her room."

"Why? If she's not ill."

"She's embarrassed."

"By what?"

The chambermaid scowled at him. "You're still wet behind the ears, aren't you?"

Zeno felt behind his left ear. The chambermaid laughed and brought her mouth close to this ear.

"Her husband brought that little starlet, Anikó Páva, to the lake."

"She's in film?"

She rolled her eyes. "She's his mistress. They all know. So Catherine won't come out of her room."

The maid ran her dust cloth behind his ear.

Early on Monday morning, Zeno knocked on the door of room 505, a small suite of rooms at the rear of the building, facing away from the lake. After some silence, the door slowly opened.

"My God. It's you again," Anikó Páva said. "I swear this place doesn't hire anybody else."

He smiled as discreetly as he could. She stepped aside for him to enter.

"I owe you an apology," she said. Zeno remained professionally mute. "You just aren't gonna talk, are you? The other night, I left the restaurant without tipping you."

"You left without eating your meal."

"He does speak! Yeah, well… I had to. I decided I like my own company better."

Her bags stood near the door. The double bed's sheets were turned down on both sides, two ruts in the mattress. She looked at Zeno.

"You bill your tip to his account?"

"No!"

THE SKIN OF WATER

"Pity. He made me leave, y'know. Said it wasn't proper I was there."

She scowled. He picked up her two large bags. He hoped she wouldn't accompany him.

"Go on," she said. "You go first."

She followed him to the elevator, an excruciating silence hanging between them. He looked ahead with the blankest expression he could conjure. He called the elevator. She looked at him, up and down. He could see her from the corner of his eye. The bell rang. She stood back for him to enter the carriage with the luggage before she did.

"D'you live around here?" she asked, once they were moving.

He looked at her. "Just outside of Keszthely. Further south of the lake."

"That's quite a way from here." She leant closer. "You should move to Budapest. Pickings a lot better."

"That's where I want to go." He had no time to consider what was appropriate and what was not. "I want to work in film."

"Don't." She raised her eyebrows. "It's an impossible life."

Once out of the elevator, he moved as quickly as possible across the foyer towards the main entrance. He could see the Adler Limousine. Mr. Steiner stood near the car, a large amount of luggage being packed into the trunk. Parked behind this car was a taxi, organized in advance for Miss Pava. She stopped walking. She looked from the taxi to the car and to the taxi. Zeno stood still.

"I've been cooped up in that little room all weekend." She turned and looked at Zeno. "And as if nobody knows I'm here. I'm going in the big car." She pushed a card into Zeno's hand. "You wanna work in movies, you'll need a rich broad to support you. Call me when you get to Budapest. I'll match you up with someone."

With that pronouncement, she slid inside. Zeno looked at the other porter, still standing at the taxi's trunk, and raised his eyebrows. The two of them looked to Mr. Steiner. Without any noticeable hesitation he nodded his head. Zeno pushed the trolley over to the car and placed her pieces of luggage in the trunk. Mr. Steiner inspected the trunk.

"Damn it," he said. "I've left my briefcase upstairs in the office."

"I'll get it," Zeno said. "It'll only take a moment."

"Quickly," Mr. Steiner said. "The train will leave and I must be on it."

Zeno strode towards the lift shaft. Would it be quicker to take the stairs? The doors parted. At least half a dozen people involved in one conversation slowly alighted.

"Top floor," he said to the lift operator. "And wait for me."

The Steiner's chambermaid answered the door.

"Our ingénue," she said, smiling.

"Mr. Steiner's left a briefcase in the office." The chambermaid observed him. "It's urgent. Ring down to the concierge if you don't believe me. The train will leave soon."

She stepped aside, pointing to the office door just off the entrance foyer. The briefcase sat on the desk.

"I guess that's it," he said.

He picked up the flat leather case. The chambermaid stood at the door watching him. Once he moved out of the office, she closed the door again.

"I assume you know your way out."

He nodded. She walked deeper into the apartment. Standing on his own in the entrance hall, he couldn't help looking again at the magnificent room and view. Although the drapes were only partially drawn, the day's light muted and limited, it was still grand. What could he do in a lifetime to inhabit such rooms?

One last time, he breathed in the room and as he sighed again, something rustled. Catherine Steiner stood at the far window dressed only in a bathrobe, barely visible in the curtains in the dim morning light.

"What do you want?"

His mouth ran dry.

"Mr. Steiner…" He swung the briefcase in front of him. "He asked me to come for it."

She said nothing, returning to looking out the window. Should he just leave? The train would soon depart.

"Thank you for the money," he said.

What was he waiting for? This wasn't a normal interaction. Never could be. He looked at her, so small and fey, framed just off center by the curtains and the high window casing. He should leave. He moved towards the door.

"Is she with him?"

"I'm sorry?" Zeno turned back.

"Is his mistress in the car with him?"

Zeno shuffled from foot to foot. What could he possibly say?

"Of course she is," she said. "Poor little Anikó. Do you suppose she knows of all the others?"

"I'd better get this down to the car." He lifted the briefcase, though she wasn't looking. "They're waiting for it."

"I hate this lake."

"You hate the lake?" He took two steps towards her. "How can you?" She turned sharply towards him. "I'm sorry, I shouldn't have -- "

"Tell me why you like it."

He fought for breath, almost drowning. "I can't tell you…"

"You can't or you won't?"

"The lake isn't words." He tried to think, all but impossible with the intensity of her gaze. "I could show you."

"What on earth do you mean?"

"Could…"

He faltered, well over permissible boundaries. What the hell. She'd already seen his ass.

"Could you meet me after work tonight? Around six?"

Her whole body stiffened. "Do you know who I am?"

"I just want to show you something."

Her shoulders relaxed but she said nothing.

"If you like," he said, "we can meet away from the hotel. No one will see you." She looked back towards the window and out at the lake.

"What should I wear?"

"Someone just licked a bowl of cream," a passing maid said to him in the elevator.

He kept on smiling all the way across the hotel foyer. Catherine Steiner amused him. Something in her demanded she remain aloof and distant, and she so wanted to do that, but something kept drawing her in.

From the elevator, he ran through the foyer towards the main doors of the building. Mr. Steiner stood outside the car. He looked worried and all but snatched the bag. He pressed a tip into Zeno's hand.

"Thank you," he said.

As the car pulled away Zeno looked at his hand. Twenty pengő. Sándor Steiner too paid well.

CHAPTER FIVE

The side of the lake that lay opposite The Hotel Hungary was shallow, the shoreline peppered with low wooden jetties. Zeno heard her footfall.

"I thought you mightn't come," he said.

He stood in a clinker-built sail boat just three meters long, open like a dingy, with a mast in the forward sternum. Without rocking the boat at all, he stepped onto the network of jetties.

"I wouldn't go back on my word," she said.

They looked at one another. Why would she be interested in anything he had to say or do? This was madness. What could he say to her? But she'd come. He smiled broadly.

"Well, here we are," he said.

"Is that what I'm to see?"

He looked at the sailboat, tied to the jetty by a rope. He laughed.

"Well… yes and no."

"Are we sailing?"

"Yes, but it's not the boat. I'm sorry I couldn't borrow something better." He felt his cheeks warming. "It's a mild evening. We'll be safe."

"Where are we going?"

"That's a surprise, but we'd best get started."

He pulled the small boat nearer the jetty and stepped onto the craft, his body accommodating the shift of the vessel in the water. He turned to face her. She hesitated and looked down at the jetty. He offered his hand.

"It's all right," he said. "I'll guide you."

She placed her hand on his lightly, no grip at all, just warmth, and stepped onto the craft's center bench. When her weight bore down, the boat rocked. Her hand contracted, gripping his tightly.

"Oh," she said.

"It's all right. I have you."

Now that he had a firm grip, he placed his arm around her waist and pulled her forward. She swung down--into him, into the boat, which rocked about. He caught her perfume and felt himself weaken. Her free hand groped around in the air for something to steady herself, eventually finding a stay. She stepped from the seat down onto the deck. He pointed to the center seat.

"If you want to sit here, I'll raise the sail and we can go."

She looked at him for a moment. She wasn't used to being spoken to directly. But if they were to advance this evening, she'd have to accept that he was captain and to some extent she was his crew.

She sat down on the bench.

He smiled and moved to the front of the boat, flipping the rope from the jetty's piling and stowing it beneath the bow seat. They began to drift. He pulled at the halyard and the white canvas unfurled from the boom. Immediately, the sail took a little of the light evening breeze. He stepped to the stern and in one fluid motion swung around to sit on the aft bench, take the tiller in hand, and tighten the main sheet. They moved forward.

Once in fuller water, he pulled the mainsail tighter and pointed the bow into the wind. The boat began to heel. Catherine had placed herself on the port side of the boat. As the sail gathered wind and tension, the craft leaned further to that side and the lake water lapped at her.

"Shift to the other side," he said.

Gingerly, one hand on the mast, she shuffled along the bench, under the boom. With this small change of ballast, Zeno reined the boom tighter, picking up speed. And so they moved through the water, he at the stern, her in the transom, single sail taut against the breeze. She looked back at the shore, not at all at him.

"It's all right," he said, his tone trying to soothe. "The worst is we'll capsize."

Her eyes flared, that same violet color he'd seen in the restaurant.

"You're a good swimmer. No harm will come."

She slackened her shoulders and loosened her white knuckles from the seat. And they moved further over the lake in silence, save for the lapping water and the occasional rattle of the rigging. On the same stream of air, gulls hovered above them, suspended in lazy flight except for the occasional correcting tilt of a wing.

The silence became comfortable. He felt himself relax. She looked towards the sun, lost in the solitude, unaware of him. Her face was like nothing he'd ever seen, the skin so white, the hair so dark. Like hunger, some sensation nibbled at him, forced his sight to visit and revisit the curve of her back, the line of her breast, the shape of her hip covered in cloth. Before he'd felt muddled but now the rill of this sensation was clear.

He felt no embarrassment, likened himself to a scientist noting color and form and texture.

"How did you learn to sail?" she said, still intent on the view.

"My father taught me."

"But you told me he left you."

"I was eight. He taught me before he left."

"Fathers," she said, but the thought trailed off, and she looked again towards the deeper reaches of the lake.

"Look at that," she said. Even at this distance, they could see the small village of Tihany, nestled on the peninsular that divided the lake into two basins. A white baroque abbey thrust itself up between the mounds of low-lying buildings. Perhaps she already knew the aim of their travel and was just humoring him.

"We must change tack," Zeno said. "When I say, you need to duck down under the boom to the other side of the boat."

She looked at him, her eyes round and large.

"The worst that will happen is we'll—"

"I know," she said, now smiling. "Capsize."

It was the first time she'd smiled in front of him.

He steadied himself. He didn't want to swim, not now. As they readied themselves to tack, he heard a low mechanical drone. He looked around for a larger boat but they were nowhere near the ferry routes. They both looked towards the sky. A plane. It was flying low, close to the horizon, coming in from the northernmost rim, down the length of the lake. As it drew closer, so low, the under-wing swastikas were clearly visible, and the noise grew louder and louder.

"It's a Stuka!" Zeno yelled. "Let's go about."

He pulled hard on the tiller and the boat turned to starboard. The boom, at the mercy of the wind, moved over, the untethered sail flapping loudly. The plane seemed to change its intent and bore down on them, the noise of its engines deafening. As Zeno hauled in the sail, the craft caught the breeze again, motion picked up, and they continued parallel to the shore.

Still the noise of the plane increased. Catherine put her hands over her ears.

"What do they want?" she yelled.

"I don't know. Stay seated. They'll pass."

Zeno pulled his camera from beneath the seat. With practiced certainty he released the mechanism, raised it to his eye, and began to film. At just a few meters directly overhead, the noise peaked. They craned their necks, turning their heads to watch the underbelly. The noise finally began to abate as the plane flew on.

"Perhaps it's just training," he said, lowering the camera. "I don't know."

"I think it's just harassment. The sooner this country stands up to them the better we'll all be."

"But they're our allies."

"Are you so sure about that?"

They watched as the plane carried its roar away with it. The smell of the engine fumes enveloped them.

"Let's sail on," Catherine said.

By degrees, the evening's tranquility resumed. With the off-shore breeze they moved swiftly. Catherine looked up at the abbey, the white wall high and impressive. Zeno's eyes darted between points on the land.

"What are you looking at?"

He hadn't realized she was scrutinizing him.

"There are three points...."

"Three points?" She looked back at the shore.

"Sorry. I was concentrating." His eyes moved about between the on-shore points. "When they're aligned, we'll be there."

"What's this? A treasure map?"

He slackened off the sail, which caused the boat to nose dive slightly as it lost momentum.

"We're here," Zeno said. "Yes, a treasure map of sorts."

There were no other craft around. In the evening's amber light, they could see a few people moving around the base of the church.

"What's here?" she asked.

"I want to show you something. Nature working with the hand of man. No matter what happens, stay quiet."

She looked doubtful but shrugged her shoulders and nodded. He stood up in the center of the sailboat. The lightest of breezes came from the shore. He drew in his breath, fully, and held it. Then he sang, a single note, midrange, held on the Italian vowel *A*. He drew the note out, loud, full, a sapling baritone, resonating in his chest and sinuses.

And then, while she looked around to see what this note would summon from the sea, abruptly he stopped. But as he did, as he closed his mouth, as if by some magic, the note started again, just as it had been, perhaps more mellow, as if there were a gramophone player on board the small craft mimicking him.

She looked at him, her eyes marveling, and went to speak but he raised his hand to silence her. The note continued and then stopped, just as it had some seconds before.

He started again, sang the same note, full and rich and velvet. He stopped, he breathed in, and as if some invisible choirmaster had called, in exact time with the return of the first note, he took a second note, a third higher. Now he sang with himself, the repeating first note lower, the second note higher, the building block of a chord.

He stopped, in time with the first note. He breathed again. And sang again, now a fifth to his original first, but joined, in correct time and pitch, by his second note which had arrived back unimpeded. The unearthed chord rang, held, the two notes waving vibratos almost resonating a third note.

For his fourth note, he cut back down under the fifth, a major arpeggio to the original tonic. This thrilled her even more. She looked from him to the shore and back. Now he rested, the solo arpeggio returning from the shore.

"How are you doing that," she cried, her voice charged with excitement.

He held his hand up to her to stay quiet.

"How are you doing that," bounced back at them.

She was shocked to hear her own voice but then the two of them burst out laughing. He held his hand up again. Out of the quiet came their distant but soft laughter.

"The sounds echo back from the wall of the abbey."

She turned and looked at the high wall and then back at him.

"Do it again." Her eyes were shining and smiling, open in a way he'd never seen before.

He felt himself rise. He filled his lungs but as he began to produce the note, the drone of the flying plane began again, returning from the south, the echo of his pure note lost in the rubble of sound.

"Sod them," she said, her eyes now turned to the sky and defiant.

As the plane approached, the drone louder and louder, it began to strafe towards them.

"They're attacking!" Zeno yelled.

He'd no time to think of what the hell was happening, only what he could do to protect them. There was nowhere to hide in the open boat. Perhaps if they dived in the water and hid under the boat's flanks? But it was wood, bullets would rip it apart like flesh. There was nowhere to go. Defenseless, he stood, defying any challenge. Catherine came next to him, steadying herself with the craft's mast.

They flew as low as possible, the sound like a lifetime of mosquitoes in the ear, the sound echoing back from the cliff. They made one pass, turned, repeated it, repeating it again until they perhaps grew tired of the game and disappeared into the northern distance from where they'd originally come.

"Little boys," Catherine said.

"We must go," he said. "If we're going to return."

Catherine looked again at the wall of the abbey. He sat down in the stern of the craft and pulled in the boom. His heart still beat hard but he felt he could not show any effect to Catherine. Now moving without instruction, she, also showing no ill effect, jibed to the correct side of the boat. Once they were on course, the light off-shore breeze directly behind them, Zeno hoisted a foresail, splayed to the portside, the mainsail to the starboard. And so the craft steered itself, Catherine sitting with her feet on the bow and her back against the mast, Zeno in the stern, the day now fading. The gulls above them cried, hungry, perhaps misreading them as a fishing boat instead of a collector of echoes.

They stood together on the jetty. She looked back towards Tihany, the sunlight almost gone.

"How will you get back to the hotel," he asked.

"A boat's waiting for me." She motioned towards a boat at a nearby jetty. "Where do you live?" she said. "Do you live at the hotel?"

"I stay there while I work."

"I don't think it would be appropriate to offer you a lift."

"That's okay. I wasn't going back straight away." He paused, and she looked at him with some degree of expectation.

"I'm meeting some friends at a taverna." He swallowed. "Would you like to come?"

"Come now, I'm not a schoolgirl. I don't think that would be appropriate either."

"No." He felt himself blush. "Of course it wouldn't."

"Well," she said. "Thank you. I hate the lake less." He screwed up his face. "I was joking. Thank you for a lovely experience."

She held out her hand and he shook it.

"I'll see you again," he said.

"I don't think so. It's not possible. At the hotel, you mustn't acknowledge me in any way. I'll ignore you. My husband and I, when he returns at the weekend, will leave."

She turned and began to walk away from him. He watched her. She stopped walking and turned back towards him, looking beyond him, out at the lake.

"Perhaps it's just the view of the lake from my hotel room I don't like."

When Zeno arrived at the taverna, he could see his group of friends already outside, preparing to leave.

"You're late," Tibi called out.

"He's always late," Magda said. "He must have a new girlfriend."

The whole group turned towards him.

"I don't," Zeno said. "I went sailing. It's such a beautiful evening."

The others nodded and went back to their conversations.

"We're going to the Little Savoy," Ferenc said.

Suddenly Zeno regretted meeting them here. The dance club was on the other side of the village and he wasn't dressed for such an outing and he didn't feel like going there. He should have followed Catherine. Watching her at a distance, small as it was, would have been better than nothing.

"I won't come," he said.

"Come on," Magda said. "You're the only one who can do without your beauty sleep.

"I have to work in the morning. At six."

As the group trailed off, Tibi waved goodbye, that same laconic response he had to most things.

"I'm not going to come either," Magda yelled out to them. "You all go."

Magda and Zeno watched them disappear into the evening's dark.

"How are you getting back to the hotel?" Magda said.

"I'll sail back. Do you want to come with me?"

"Is that safe?"

"Of course it is. I've been sailing all my life. As natural as walking."

"That wasn't quite what I meant. Yeah, I'll come with you."

Magda sat down in the transom and he cast off. To his surprise, once they were free of the small jetty, she stood and hoisted the mainsail.

"Why are you looking at me like that?" she said.

"Nothing--"

"You're surprised I know how to sail." He said nothing. "Doesn't your girlfriend know how?"

"There's no girlfriend."

She glared at him for a moment. "Is that so?"

They set off into the dark, out onto the lake under the full moon. Zeno pulled in the sail and they accelerated as much as the night air's constant breeze would allow.

"Do you want me to blow at the sail?" Magda asked.

"A good sailor needs very little wind."

Magda looked out at the lake. "How are you going to tell where to go?"

"Look up at the stars."

She threw her head back to the stars, brilliant and bold in the sky.

"Stars my arse."

He laughed. Even without the stars, he knew the lake. With one glance at the distant shore, he could recognize a light, the shadow of a solid form or hill, no lighthouse needed.

"The night is velvet," Magda said, stretching her arms high in the warm air, the little movement rocking the boat forward, fluttering the sails. "I know you didn't find that crucifix," she said.

He tensed but didn't respond. After some moments, she turned around to look at him.

"It wasn't there. I'd looked exactly in that spot."

"I *did* find it there."

"Don't lie." She rolled her eyes. "I won't tell. I would've taken it too. Did you panic?"

"I didn't take it. I wasn't lying--"

"Well, where did you find it?" She turned and sat facing him, leaning in towards him. "Did you steal it from her room?"

"That's not what happened. I found it in that bush but the day before. I just forgot to hand it in."

Magda nodded her head slowly.

"She's so fortunate."

"Who?"

"Catherine Steiner."

He felt drawn to her name like a moth. "Why do you say that?"

"She loses something and someone finds it."

"That was just lucky."

"She's blessed. And she's pretty."

Magda turned her face away, back to face the night's dark. He shivered, remembering Catherine's presence earlier that evening. He almost caught her scent.

"She's filthy rich," Magda said. "And to cap it all off, she doesn't even have to make believe she cares for children."

"I'm sure she loves her children."

"She doesn't have any." Madga turned back towards him. She cleared the hair from her eyes. "I don't know why these wealthy people bother having them. I suppose they need heirs for all that lovely money. Do you know what? One of those little bastards bit me the other day. Drew blood. Heathen."

"Did he get into trouble?"

"What do you think? They were some family from Germany. Not a word was said."

Zeno pulled the sail in harder against the light breeze. He wanted to be home.

"Do you dream of getting away?" Magda said.

"From the lake?"

"Even further."

"I love the lake, but if I can get the money, I'm going to Budapest."

"That's right. You told me that. You want to be an actor."

"I don't want to be that. I'm not handsome enough."

"Well… I don't know about that--"

"Last summer I bought myself a camera." He pulled the camera case from under the seat. "Since I started using it, it's like I see the world through it."

She moved to his seat, sitting close to him.

"Careful," he said. "What're you doing?"

"Move over. I'm getting warm."

She took his free arm, draped it around her shoulder, turned her face to meet his. As she lifted her chin for a kiss, he pulled back.

"What're you doing?"

"I thought you'd know."

"Sorry, I know what you're doing. Why are you doing it?"

"Come on."

Why didn't he want her? She'd more than a certain charm, a charm she wanted him to explore. He closed his eyes. Magda's lips, warm and fleshy, felt close enough to how he imagined Catherine Steiner's would feel to ignite all arousal. Her breath was hot. She slid her hand down over his crotch, pulling at the trousers' button, which popped free of its threads and catapulted into the lake. Despite his attempt to wriggle away from her, she maneuvered him down onto the slatted floor of the boat, rocking with the unexpected shifts of ballast. He lay on his back and she hitched her dress, drew off her panties.

He felt helpless, pinned by her straddling weight and by the threatening reactions of the boat. She eased herself onto him, a wave shimmering through her abdomen as she flicked her hips. But this was not enough. With both her hands she took the floor slats of the boat, pulling herself down onto him, his cock higher and higher in her. She stared into his eyes. He closed his, imagined black, concentrated on the precursors of his own pleasure, alive and strengthening. He heard the wooden slats under them groan under the stress. Her waves increased, as did the boat's changes in direction. Catherine's scent, still alive on the boards, came to him. He was unaware of Magda. He could imagine what he liked. He tightened. He ran his tongue over his lips, chilled by his panting. He felt the final stages come. He should pull free of her but she renewed her force on the boat's slats. As he came, strong and intense but almost painful, an almighty cracking sound rang in his ears. She'd ripped the slat free from the floor, bowed it clean in two.

Over the next few days, he moved about his work as quietly as possible, trying to avoid Magda. Despite the thrill of their encounter (she really had been quite adroit) his sights were focused elsewhere. He did everything in his power to encounter Catherine. In that he failed, but Magda appeared at every turn in the hotel.

"It's okay," she said one afternoon as they passed one another on the service stairs. "I know you've somebody else."

"I don't."

"Don't lie. I could tell. All the time you were thinking of someone else." She raised her eyebrows high on her forehead. The truth was hard to deny. "So was I."

She turned and descended the stair.

He checked the guest register to see if Catherine had left the hotel but she hadn't. He couldn't imagine how he could ask any of the other hotel staff about her without giving himself away. Perhaps she returned each day to the cheap hotel. He didn't see her leave the building and he'd no way of knowing. Perhaps he should've made love to Catherine's chambermaid instead—at least then he could get some information. So he remained quiet, alert at all times, scanning the closest and most distant horizon for even the slightest glimpse of her but seeing nothing.

"Zeno," the concierge said. "Stop daydreaming. I asked you to collect the bags from room 705. The guests are already waiting in the foyer."

"Sorry. I'll get them at once."

As he turned, Catherine walked towards him across the foyer. She was dressed for dinner, a long slim gown that shimmered as she moved. Her face bore no hint of recognition, no recognition of anything at all.

As she passed him, at the very last moment, she thrust her hand slightly out towards him. He remained paralyzed.

"Zeno," the concierge said again with a volume only just below a yell.

"Take it," Catherine hissed.

He put up his hand to hers. He felt a piece of paper, small and folded. She continued walking, her gait uninterrupted and unnoticed. He felt unable to move, rooted to the spot.

"Zeno!" the concierge's voice boomed. "Will you please get those bags?"

He hurried towards the elevator. Once enclosed in the carriage, he opened the note.

> *On Friday morning, I'll go to the health spa in Hévíz.*
> *Meet me there.*

CHAPTER SIX

From the boardwalk of the pavilion, suspended above lake Hévíz, Zeno looked at the crowds of bathers. Generation after generation claimed that the warm water, pungent with deep-earth sulfur and oxygen, had healing properties for all movement disorders, nervous afflictions, even women's problems. Some bathers moved about on their own, some in pairs, some floated on their backs, faces and corpulent tummies and breasts protruding from the murky water, some suspended in wooden flotation rings, languishing for their health in the lush waters.

He picked her out immediately, floating in a wooden ring. For more than twenty minutes he watched. Her arms, slender and muscular like a ballet dancer's, lay along the rim of the wooden device, circling in a parted embrace. She progressed through the water, her propulsion slow and relaxed. At times she'd stop, raise her head, her eyes darting here and there. Yet she'd not noticed him, which surprised him. She passed directly under him but was looking the other way.

And why had she asked him here? What did she want? He'd asked himself these questions a thousand times and each time arrived at an answer he couldn't believe. She desired him. But then, as she looked about her, each of her nervous glances answered his questions. He fought off the desire to join her and remained above her, looking down at her, savoring the anticipation. In such repeated phases of agitation and relaxation, she circled the entire lake. A fine mist rose from the warmed water.

He could stand it no more. In the public change room he removed all his clothes. In a mirror he caught a glimpse of his naked body, clenched his biceps, tightened his thighs, turned to see the concave curve of his lower back turn into the convex round of his buttocks. He ran his hand over his still-hairless belly. Nothing but peach fuzz. Magda had teased that his skin was as soft as a woman's. Whilst there was rounding to his biceps, striation to the muscles in his thighs, a thin layer of baby fat spread over his body, layered on his paunch, occluding the knots of his stomach muscles. He turned away from the mirror. He knew he should dress himself and leave this folly. But he put on his bathing costume and tied it up with his mother's secure knot.

He entered the warm water away from her, far from her slow circle. He put off approaching her. Circled counterclockwise. She came, back turned towards him. She lay in the ring, her eyes closed, unaware of his advance. He touched the outer surface and spun her slowly. She made no recognition, no resistance. He closed his arms around the outer edge, completing her embrace. This was no time for hesitation. They were clearly, already, past the point of return.

"What ailment do you seek to cure?" he said.

Her gaze remained impervious, but as if she proposed to take the lead, she gently waved her arms in the water until the two of them were hidden in the forest of the pavilion's thick pylons. She leaned to him and kissed his mouth. How could lips, mere flesh and blood, inspire such feelings? Was it the thought of their cherry color? Their plump softness? Her tongue flicked his teeth, toyed with his tongue until, under the murky water in the shadow of the pavilion, he cupped each of her breasts in his hands. Her lack of resistance forced another wave of pleasure to surge through him. He was overheated, sweat washed away by the warm water.

"This isn't the place," he said, whispering in her ear. She pulled back and looked at him. "I've hired a room."

She raised an eyebrow. "Was I so predictable?"

"There's no place for pretense."

Separately, they left the secrecy of the pylons and the water. He dressed quickly in the changing room, ran a comb through his hair. Outside the spa, she followed him at a distance through the streets. Even his newly fleshed purse would run to nothing elaborate, but the room was clean and the sun poured in through the high open windows over the bed's ornate carved head.

By the window, he sat at a small wooden table facing the room, facing the door left ajar. He tensed when he heard her footfall on the stairs. He took a deep breath and smelled the slight tang of the lake's sulfur. He wished he could film every nuance of this surge of anticipation, the way the light came in through the window, the door ajar, this still life that refused to remain still but beat relentlessly forward.

She pushed open the door and stepped into the room, closing it firmly behind her. For a moment, she stood and watched him but despite his urgent need to touch her, he remained seated, legs apart, his gaze not moving from hers. She took the few steps between them. Then she knelt in front of him as if to pray. She lowered her head to his groin, running her hands around his waist to the small of his back, forcing her face into the folds of fabric. She exhaled fully, her breath as warm and healing as the water of Lake Hévíz.

"You can be discreet," she said.

The words woke him. Her head rested on his chest, his arm encircled her. He felt her warmth, her breath.

"I've spoken with no one. Said nothing about you going to the Panzió Katy in the village."

She raised herself on her elbow. "How did you know about that?"

"I was walking and I saw you go in."

A wave of concern passed over her face. He touched her cheek, gently.

"What were you doing there?"

"Nothing," she said.

"Was it… another lover?"

She looked hard at him, then relaxed back into the crook of his arm.

"It's over now." She was quiet for a moment. "I thought you were a virgin."

He laughed. "Because of my age?"

"Yes."

"How do you know I wasn't?"

Now she laughed. "You had no fear. You took your pleasure."

After some silence, he thought she was asleep until she sighed and got out of the bed. He remained there, watching her draw on her petticoat, her brassiere. She pulled her stockings on and fastened them to her garter belt. In the bathroom mirror he could see her fixing her hair.

"This can't happen again," she said, standing dressed at the side of the bed. "It's too dangerous."

"We can--"

"My husband returns this evening from Berlin. Over the weekend, we'll leave for Budapest. The summer's over. You mustn't say anything to anyone."

"I'm moving to Budapest--"

"That's another reason this can't continue." She turned and took two steps towards the door.

"No one need know."

She turned back towards him.

"I'm twice your age. As you get older," she said, "you'll realize this world isn't a bowl full of pleasure. It's filled with responsibility. Rarely do the two coincide. Today was all pleasure and no responsibility." She looked deeply into his eyes. "Please, remember me well."

Before he could summon any words, for his mind was grappling and blank, she left the room, closing the door lightly.

He lay back in the bed. Was she right? Was that all there could be? For hours he lay in the bed, resting on what he imagined to be her warmth, inhaling what he knew to be her scent, until his bladder forced him to rise and relieve himself. It was after four in the afternoon and he had to be back at the hotel by six to give Ferenc his bike and start the shift that ushered in the Bull Train. As it stood now, he was going to be late.

He dressed himself in no haste. He wondered how she could be so hard. She'd had another lover just a few days before. Had he just been another thrill? Most likely. But God, those breasts. He wanted more. How he envied her light freedom, the grace of her step. Magda was right. Catherine was blessed. Even now he could feel her leg resting between his thighs. He wished he never had to leave this room.

Outside the hotel, the day's last bustle jammed the streets. He walked quickly back towards the lake where he'd left Ferenc's bike. His only hope was to see her again in the next few days. She'd instigated this encounter. How could she just withdraw? How could she not want more of what had passed between them? No woman had responded to his touch like Catherine. No woman had given him such pleasure.

"Zeno!" a voice cried out from the other side of the street.

As he turned, he saw his mother crossing the street towards him. Jesus. She lived in the next village. What could he say to her?

"What are you doing here?" she said, embracing him and kissing his cheek. She held him by the shoulders and pushed him away so she could study his face. Despite all the unrest of her life, she was still an attractive woman, beautiful eyes and hair with a single swath of gray hair from one temple

"I had to come see someone."

"Who?"

"Just a friend."

"And you're not coming to see me?"

"I'm sorry, mama. I have to get back to work tonight."

"You've lost weight."

"No, I haven't."

"Something is different." She let go of his shoulder and stepped back and looked him over, his hair, his clothes.

"Nothing's changed," he said.

"Come and have coffee with me and tell me about this friend you've visited."

He smiled at her. "I wish I could, but I'm late, have to go."

She sighed and nodded her head. "When will you come to visit? Ottilia asks after you."

"Soon. The summer's nearly over. The hotel will be quiet again. I have to go."

He kissed her cheek. As he walked away, she called to him. He stopped and looked back at her.

"That feeling you're feeling," she said. "It's as old as forever. Be careful of it."

At the sound of Zeno approaching the chalet village on the motorbike, Ferenc appeared on the doorstep.

"Where have you been?"

"I'm sorry. I'm late."

"Oh, I hadn't noticed. And now I'm very late."

"Time got away from me."

Ferenc swung his leg over the bike. Once seated, he looked hard at Zeno.

"You're not the only one with a girlfriend."

"I told you," Zeno said. "I don't have a girlfriend. I had to visit my mother."

"The concierge is going to take your balls off. You promised the bike would be back."

"I know. I'm sorry, it's back now. It won't happen again."

"No, it won't. Because there won't be another time."

Zeno raced to his chalet and stripped off his clothes. He smelled of Catherine and sex and sweat but there was no time to wash. Once he had his shirt and work pants on, he grabbed his bowtie and jacket and made for the hotel. Magda was walking towards him.

"If I were you," she said. "I'd just run off now."

"Don't be silly. I'm just late."

"Yeah. A good two hours. You were meant to start at four."

"Shit."

He'd forgotten he'd agreed to an early start—the afternoon had made him punch-drunk. He couldn't afford to lose this job.

"Where have you been?" The concierge raised both his hands in front of his red face. "Never mind, I don't want to hear a word, we'll discuss this later. Get out there. "

Zeno made his way across the foyer to the main entrance. All his plans were now at risk. The Bull Train arrivals were at their height, bags and vehicles and men in all directions.

"Nice of you to show up," one of the other bellboys said.

Zeno applied himself to the task at hand, packing away his own concerns. By 7:30, the Bull Train intake was over and Zeno returned to the foyer for the last time.

"You're wanted in the Steiner suite," the concierge said.

"What?" Zeno's heart pounded in his chest. "But I didn't take anything up there."

"Then it's not to do with that. They want to see you."

"Who?"

The concierge glared at him. "I just said. The Steiners."

Catherine had changed her mind. She wanted to see him. He hurried to the top level of the hotel.

The housemaid showed him into the lounge room. He stood before the windows of the lake. He paced up and down. He heard someone coming to the room. He couldn't keep the smile off his face.

Mr. Steiner walked into the room. Zeno stood, sullied his smile, held his breath as Mr. Steiner marched towards him. This was something to do with Catherine. Everything in him wanted to walk out the door, away from this room, away from the hotel.

"Thank you for coming up," Mr. Steiner said, his voice light and sincere. "I won't take up your time. This week in Budapest, my personal valet quit. Volunteered for the army, damn him. He's been with me for years. I feel like my right arm's been cut off. Would you like the job?"

It took a few seconds for Zeno to believe what he'd heard. Mr. Steiner stood before him, his eyes expectant.

"But… I've no experience."

"I'm a good judge of character. Last week, you responded quickly to the situation with my briefcase."

"It was just a briefcase and an elevator ride, the obvious thing to do."

"There you go, good intuition." He smiled. "I'll wager you could do anything you put your mind to."

"But a valet, sir? You're always dressed so immaculately."

Again he smiled. "Who ironed your shirt?"

Zeno looked down at his shirt. "I did."

"Then you know your job. You must keep my wardrobe ready at all times, for all things, wherever I am."

"But--"

"And I'd pay you… what would be tempting, four hundred pengő a month and provide you with free accommodation in Budapest."

"I--"

He'd be in Budapest. Living in the same house as Catherine. While he worked for Sándor Steiner he'd surely be able to explore the possibility of work in the film studios. And this pay was more than generous. In fact, to someone new to even the idea of a valet, it was unbelievable.

"I'll be frank with you," Mr. Steiner said. "There are few young men left in Budapest. This damn war has bled the best dry. I'll make a wager with you. I'll arrange time for you to learn the job, if you'll take the job. How does that sound?"

"All right. I will."

"Good," Mr. Steiner said. "I'm pleased. How does sometime in October sound?"

Zeno thought for a moment. "Yes."

"You see? I know you better than you know yourself. You act quickly. Decisively. You *will* succeed."

CHAPTER SEVEN

Zeno stepped onto the platform of Déli Station in Budapest. His first impression was of a beat, strong and regular, surging with life, something more than his racing pulse and heart--he recognized the clang and thump and drive of the city as if it had always been his. The large vault of the station roof hung above him like another sky, gray and corrugated, intricate iron lace suspended in flight. The light flowed in defined rays. He'd entered another world within the world.

On the platform, people pressed, a thousand voices echoed and bumped together, whistles and horns, naturally amplified again and again like overlapping waves. He carried two pieces of baggage, a portmanteau and a case containing a small Pathé projector he'd bought with Catherine's reward money. The crowd consumed him and carried him along the platform towards the station's vast antechambers, past the waiting rooms, past the piles of luggage, past the poor and the mighty, into Budapest.

He pulled off to the center of the platform. On his tiptoes he looked around for Tibi, who was to meet him. Perhaps he was here, mixed up in the crowd. How would he know? In the play of hats and heads he couldn't see him. A small wave of disappointment washed over him. He'd been looking forward to seeing Tibi. He sank back down onto his heels. It was okay. Budapest was busy.

Outside the station, cars moaned, parked and double parked at the curb, waited on by boys with trolleys. The smell of people perfumed blended with the unwashed. It was a fine day, the air cold but warmed by a clear sun.

What direction was he to go?

Was the Steiner apartment right or left? He laid his change-of-clothes portmanteau on the pavement, sprang the locks, took out his camera and raised it to his eye. He panned up and down the street. He positioned his shot slightly in front of a passing trolley and used that as his guide. The lens orientated him. The apartment was that way, following the trolley car, on the same side of the Danube. He put the camera back in his bag, looked around for Tibi one last time, then started off in that direction, swinging the two cases in anticipation.

The Steiner building had a bold exterior, a bald-face wall rising three stories from the footpath. The window cases were made of large stones set one into the other and held high above the street level. Zeno breathed in deeply and walked along the castle-like wall. How could people afford such a building? He laughed to himself. This was wealth, this was power.

He came to the entrance of a central courtyard, large wooden doors held open. Directly opposite the street entrance was the portico of what he assumed to be the main entrance. The building ran completely around an entire block.

A large car came from the street. He stepped aside and watched it glide around the courtyard. The driver opened the passenger's door just as Mr. Steiner emerged from the portico and marched to the car. The driver returned to his seat and the car pulled away. Mr. Steiner sat in the rear, encapsulated, his substantial frame somehow made small by the car's vast interior.

If Mr. Steiner had come from this entrance, something told Zeno he shouldn't enter here. He'd walk around the exterior and see what he could find. In the rear lane, a group of five or six men congregated about a door midway along the wall. They were dressed in house uniforms, all smoking. A round of laughter burst out of the group.

"You wouldn't say that," one of the men said, "if he was here."

"Excuse me," Zeno said. The laughter stopped and as one body they turned towards him. "I'm looking for..." He had to think of the name. "...Ottó Técsy."

The one who'd spoken before looked at him.

"Are you the new valet?" He looked Zeno up and down. "God! Why would Steiner hire a boy to do a man's job?"

"Why would he employ a boy to do the job *you* wanted?" another man said. "That's what you mean."

This second man had a head of red curly hair and was about twenty-five years old. He too scrutinized Zeno, who said nothing. What was he to do--apologize for his age or for accepting a good job?

"Follow me," the man with red hair said. "He's been waiting all morning. I'm Hans."

"Zeno."

"I know."

Zeno followed through a doorway and down three or four stairs to a long dark passageway with a low ceiling. He heard laughter behind him in response to something the first man said.

"Don't mind him," the redhead said. "Gazsi's just pissed off because he wanted the promotion. He works for József

Steiner. That's Sándor's uncle. They live in the front wing of the house."

Something in his expression made Zeno ask, "What's wrong with that?"

"Second tier of the family. Besides, József Steiner's a tyrant. Sándor is far easier to work for."

"Who do you work for?"

"Peter. Sándor's brother-in-law. Sándor is never here. And he's predictable."

"So the whole family lives here?"

"No. Just those involved in running the business."

The passage opened up into a kind of windowless antechamber at the center of the building. Although a little light seeped in from the extremities, low-wattage bulbs still burned. But there was noise, the noise of many voices engaged in many conversations, the sounds of heels clattering on stone floors, boots thudding on distant stairs, cutlery and crockery tinkling. They'd come from the rear, roughly the west. Another wider corridor led to the east and the front of the building, two smaller ones to the north and south. People crossed the antechamber, blinded with purpose, and disappeared into another corridor as abruptly as they'd appeared.

"Ottó's in his office," Hans said, "down that corridor. Name's on the door."

Zeno thanked Hans and walked down the dim corridor, reading off the names of the cook, the various valets, the chauffeurs.

"Ottó Técsy," Zeno said to himself quietly. "Valet."

He knocked on the door.

"Come in."

The bass baritone voice sounded stern. Zeno opened the door and stood, smiling boldly and holding out his hand.

"You're late."

Ottó's voice fell like a guillotine. He had piercing blue eyes that didn't just stare at Zeno, they drilled. Zeno looked at his watch. It was only midday and he'd written last week saying he'd arrive on that particular train.

"But I--"

"You were to start first thing this morning, not first thing this afternoon. Not a good start."

Zeno swallowed. He'd not read anything like that in the letter. Ottó looked him over.

"Leave your bags here. Follow me."

Ottó stood from his desk, much taller than Zeno had expected and as firm in his presence as if he'd already joined the army. He walked from the room and turned back towards the building's central antechamber. Zeno stepped in behind him.

"As there's no one in the house today I'll take you to the apartment by the main stair, just to orientate you, but you're never to walk through the main stair unless you're accompanied by Mr. Steiner."

From the eastern corridor, Ottó took a small spiral stair that made Zeno think of a lighthouse. He opened a door and stood back and waited for Zeno to pass through it first. Zeno saw an incredible amount of light that made it hard to see after the dark of the stairs. If the ceiling of the railway station was another sky, this was heaven. The floor was marble and a large staircase revolved up to a mezzanine, the whole antechamber capped by a circular dome. To one side of the entrance hall was a spacious sitting room. He felt as if he was suffocating, then realized he'd simply forgotten to breathe.

"Quickly," Otto said, closing the door they'd come through which on this side formed part of the entrance hall's wood paneling.

"It's—"

"What?"

"So...grand."

Ottó took the main staircase to the mezzanine, where he saw that a wide corridor transected the whole building, north to south. From the mezzanine balcony he could see the main entrance hall windows, out into the courtyard, and to the other wing on the street side of the courtyard.

"Mr. Steiner's apartment is this way."

As they walked, maids dusted and a man carried a bronze coal shuttle. The door to Mr. Steiner's apartment was made of a heavy wood, the handles shining bronze. The apartment had its own entrance hall.

"You can walk through the apartment to familiarize yourself." Ottó looked him up and down. "Exactly what experience do you have?"

Under this heavy gaze, Zeno shifted his weight.

"As a valet? Absolutely none."

Ottó sighed. Zeno walked from the entrance hall through the lounge room to the small library. Ceiling to floor bookcases lined the walls, a dark wooden desk inlaid with dark green leather stood opposite the door. At the rear right-hand edge of the desk was a framed photo of Catherine and Sándor. He bent down to examine it. It was their wedding day. She was young, almost Zeno's age, but not so beautiful as now, the cheekbones and mouth less sculpted, the eyes holding less. She wore a white veil pushed back from her face. Although she smiled, it seemed forced, tired.

He walked to the bedroom. A double bed stood to one side, a large separate dressing room led off to the other. Once through this, there was an even larger bathroom, the white tiles rounded in the room's corners.

Ottó called out to him. He back-tracked through the rooms until he arrived at the lounge. Ottó called again, his voice appearing to come from the wall's wood paneling. Zeno pushed the panel and it sprang back.

"Mr. Steiner said you were smart," Ottó said. He was seated at a desk in a small room. Natural light came from a window at the far end. "This will be your office. There's a kitchenette you can use to make tea, breakfast if Mr. Steiner is in a hurry. Always make sure there's fresh milk. This is Mr. Steiner's appointment diary. You must liaise every day with his secretary to update it, cancellations, new appointments, sometimes months in advance. This…" Ottó picked up the book and shook it in front of Zeno's face. "…is the blood that runs in your veins. Without it, with errors, you'll never survive."

Zeno collapsed onto his bed. He'd been given his own room, high up—he lost count of the number of floors—in the rear of the building. It had two single beds and a small attic window that looked out over the rooftops towards the hills of Buda. He opened the window and hung out to view. Three in the afternoon and his head swam with facts: let Mr. Steiner choose cufflinks, shine all shoes, bed turned down by nine in the evening. He'd met so many people he couldn't remember any of their names, let alone their jobs. He had half an hour to change into his new uniform and meet Ottó in the apartment, if he could remember his way. He unpacked his few changes of shirts and underwear, some new socks his mother had bought him, put them in the small set of drawers between the beds and a hanging cupboard. He placed the case with the projector at the foot of his bed and arranged the rolls of film he'd developed on a small shelf. He took off his civilian shoes and put them at the foot of the bed.

Catherine, evidently, wasn't in Budapest. Ottó said she was in the country for some reason or other. And she lived in another part of the building, a separate apartment, nowhere near Mr. Steiner.

"You'll never even see her," Ottó had said.

Perhaps it was best, at least for a few days, until he'd trained with Ottó and had some confidence about him. But he longed to see her. He took off his trousers and picked up the black uniform pants. Ottó had found them in a storeroom and said "they'd do" until the tailor could come and cut his clothes.

"There's not a bloody decent tailor left in Budapest," he said.

"Why not?"

It was another question Ottó ignored. Zeno pulled on the matching black jacket. The fit was tight across his chest. He'd have to ask Ottó for a larger size. He made his way back through a warren of stairs and corridors to Mr. Steiner's apartment.

"There you are," Ottó said. "I thought you'd got lost in the building."

"I came straight here."

"Ottó," a voice boomed from the apartment's entrance hall.

"It's Mr. Steiner," Ottó said. "He's back early."

Mr. Steiner entered the room, followed by another man.

"Ottó," he boomed. "Oh… there you are. Has the new dinner suit arrived?"

"This morning."

"Good. Can you have it ready by seven?"

Ottó bowed his head slightly and motioned for Zeno to follow him into the dressing room. Once there, he pulled a jacket from the hanging cupboard, whisked it off the hanger, and hung it over a coat rack. He took a clothes brush and handed it to Zeno.

"Don't hang around like that," Ottó said.

"What do you mean?"

"Like you want to be introduced to Mr. Steiner. He knew you were there. He'd never acknowledge you and you must never expect it."

"I see."

At the lake, Mr. Steiner had been so friendly but this was Budapest and a different set of rules. Ottó demonstrated how to brush the lint from the shoulders of the jacket, always in one direction. Mr. Steiner came into the bedroom.

"I can't do that tonight," Mr. Steiner said. "You'll just have to apologize."

"Who is the other man?" Zeno asked, sotto voce.

"It's his secretary."

"Ernő Dohnányi gives few recitals…." Mr. Steiner left the bedroom.

"Sir, this meeting has taken weeks to organize," the secretary said, following him back to the lounge room. "The German officer will only be in Budapest tonight."

"I will not be dictated to by the bloody German army."

"That explains it," Ottó said.

"What?"

"Ernő Dohnányi is a concert pianist."

"Will you stop this?" Mr. Steiner roared. "It's rumored he will preview a new work."

Ottó brushed the jacket. "He'd cancel anything for a piano recital. Everything for Dohnányi."

CHAPTER EIGHT

Each week Zeno wrote to his mother and sister, Ottilia, high-lighting a few of his many new experiences. He'd not yet seen a lot of the city, but the number of people in any given place was unbelievable. You could never be on your own. With his work, he was trying as hard as he could. After four weeks of careful instruction from Ottó, the many new tasks were becoming second nature. He could iron a shirt to a knife-like crease, catalogue and file pairs of shoes so they were easily available under any conditions. Each morning he made sure Mr. Steiner's coffee arrived on time and hot, the moment he stepped from the bathroom.

Ottó had given him long talks on the need to be dutiful and responsible and on time. He'd made it painfully clear that on Sundays, Zeno's day off, if Mr. Steiner needed him, Zeno was expected to work. They'd worked all four Sundays since Zeno had arrived and he'd given up the idea of a day off. But with the amount of money he was being paid, he didn't really mind.

> *Despite all the changes, and it's taken some time, I now have some confidence. I like this work. I think Mr. Steiner likes me but most of the time it's as if I'm not there at all.*

Ottó says I'm good at my work. It must be true, or he'd be yelling at me. Still.

Preparations are already underway for Christmas and I've had to get travel documents organized which means at some stage I might have to travel with the Steiners to another country. Imagine that!

He sealed each letter with his love and a promise that he took confession each Sunday. The Steiner family had their own priest, Father István, who came to the house, but even when he was able to go to confession he chose to work. It was a white lie and it would make his mother happy. He didn't like the look of the priest who fussed over everything. And he included in each weekly letter half his week's pay. But even with this, his pay still stretched well beyond his desire to spend it. He hid the extra money in a book then one afternoon bought himself a warm overcoat. Budapest was cold, but the fox fur collar and lining were an indulgence. The overcoat resembled one of Mr. Steiner's.

"You've done really well," Ottó said one morning. "I didn't think you'd get it all so easily."

He liked Ottó, who was preparing to leave for the army. He'd miss him.

"It's like Mr. Steiner said. I just have to look after him the way I look after myself."

"I'm not so sure about that," Ottó said. "There's one thing you lack completely."

"And what's that?"

Zeno's voice contained an air of confidence that surprised even him.

"In a personal valet, you need a sixth sense, a kind of combination of all the others. Prescience. Anticipate in advance, before Mr. Steiner even thinks he needs something."

"How the hell do you do that?" Zeno face screwed up in wonder. "I can't do that for myself."

"It will come to you over time. Just learn to trust the instinct. Then you'll look after yourself."

Zeno nodded slowly. "There's something I've been meaning to ask you."

"What's that?"

"Life in this house is easy. Mr. Steiner is hardly ever here. The pay's good. Why are you joining the army?"

"There's a war."

"I know there's a war, but it's not *in* Hungary."

"Each day the Soviets push back the Germans. If we don't fight, we'll be run over by the Bolshevik menace. Do you want that?"

Zeno had never considered the war in such terms. "No…"

"You do understand that, don't you?"

He had only a sketchy idea of the war. It had been going on for so long. It wasn't clear to him who exactly wanted what.

"My God," Ottó said. "You've no idea, do you?"

"Of course I do."

"Why is Budapest called Budapest?"

Zeno tried to see the trick in the question but could only shrug.

"Because it was two cities, Buda and Pest, divided by the Danube, joined in to one city in 1873. Who's the Regent of Hungary?"

"I'm not that stupid. Admiral Horthy."

"And who's the Prime Minister?"

This, Zeno didn't know. He thought of some names he'd heard bandied around.

"How blissful a provincial life must be," Ottó said. "Miklós Kállay ring a bell?

"Yes," he said, which was a lie but he'd make damn sure he remembered it now.

The following morning the whole household gathered in the downstairs central antechamber to bid Ottó farewell. All the servants and even members of the family came, the first time Zeno had seen any of them below stairs. Of course Mr. Steiner was there, with his father, Karl Steiner, a large man but far older than his photo in the apartment had suggested. The matriarch, Ella, looked just as old but still had a mane of chestnut red hair. Erzsébet, their daughter, bore a striking resemblance to her older brother but was much smaller than Sándor, his features in her face smaller and softer. The Steiner's younger son, Zoltán, was away from Budapest, living in New York City and working in stocks.

József Steiner, Karl's brother, was accompanied by a woman Zeno presumed to be his wife, Terézia. Zeno hadn't seen much of this side of the family as they lived in the street-side wing of the house. Hans had also come to farewell Ottó. He'd not seen much of him, either. Ottó had kept him working so hard he'd not seen much of anything.

"Let's wait a moment," the father said. "Peter will come."

Erzsébet's husband, Peter Kresz, worked in the family's business. House gossip had it that he'd worked there for years, finally elevating himself to high management when he married the Steiner's daughter. But he worked with a zeal Sándor Steiner lacked, and some of the staff maintained he was the "better son" despite the lack of a blood tie. Erzsébet and he lived together in an apartment on the top floor of the building with their three children, Katalin, Flóra, and Ema, who now appeared with their nanny, but no sign of their father.

Father István arrived, a stout man. Not only did he spend a considerable amount of time at the house but he was related to the family, a cousin, although Zeno was unsure from which side of the family.

"Ottó," Father István said, coming towards him with hands extended. "You're far too sweet a boy to join the army."

Ottó colored. He shook Father István's hand. One of the maids had tears in her eyes and clearly kept a place for Ottó in her heart that he chose to ignore. The men remained stiff and shook his hand, looking uncomfortable. Were they afraid they'd be asked why they'd not joined the army?

More calls were sent out for Peter but after fifteen minutes of stilted conversation, word arrived that he was unable to attend, caught up in work at the manufacturing plant.

"Catherine?" Sándor said.

Zeno looked down at the floor. It was the first time she'd been mentioned.

"What about her?" Ella said.

"She returned last night," Sándor said. "I'm sure she'd like to farewell Ottó."

"We can't wait all morning," Ella said. "Ottó's no doubt in a hurry." She turned to her husband. "You should begin."

Karl Steiner smiled at Ottó.

"You've been with us a long time," he said.

"I was only fifteen."

"Just a boy," Ella said.

"Well…" the father said. "I'm sorry. Peter never stops working. He'd want me to wish you the best of luck. It's a brave thing you're doing, for yourself and for your country. We can only wish you all success and God willing there will always be a place for you here under our roof."

The first few days without Ottó passed without major incident, but Zeno missed him. They'd spent so much time together. Despite reports amongst the servants that Catherine had indeed returned to Budapest, there was no sign of her. Mr. Steiner made no mention of her at all.

"You're starting to become Ottó," Steiner said one evening in front of the dressing mirror as Zeno brushed the lint from the dinner jacket's shoulders and lapel.

Zeno was surprised. It was the first time he'd made any comment on his work, the first time their conversation had strayed anywhere near the personal.

"Thank you, sir."

"You do things before I say."

"Ottó told me to think ahead." Something bold took Zeno over. "Will your wife be joining you this evening?"

Zeno looked at him in the mirror as he adjusted the cufflinks of his left sleeve. No emotion passed over his face except vexation that the cufflink wouldn't sit properly.

"My wife never *joins* me, as you put it."

Zeno put down the brush, took Mr. Steiner's wrist, and correctly adjusted the cufflink.

On Sunday Zeno rose early, dressed in his uniform, and went to Mr. Steiner's apartment. To Zeno's surprise he was standing in the middle of the lounge room wearing only a robe. His hair hung this way and that. He focused and refocused on Zeno, screwed up his face.

"Why are you here?" Mr. Steiner said.

"I…" Zeno rested a moment. He could smell alcohol on his breath. "I thought you'd need me."

"It's Sunday."

Zeno stood firm. He heard the bedcovers rustle.

"Go," Mr. Steiner shouted. From the bedroom, a woman laughed. Zeno's face flushed. The woman sounded young and silly. Mr. Steiner remained impassive.

"You're a good worker, but enjoy your day off."

He held up both hands in front of his face and flicked Zeno away.

As he walked back down the hall his feet swung with a light gait at the thought of all the secret pleasure Budapest would finally reveal to him. He'd not even seen the Danube, let alone crossed over from Buda into Pest. He'd hurry back to his room, change, grab his camera, and head out. As he approached the servants' stair near the centre stair, Catherine was walking down. He stopped. His heart pounded and his face flushed again. She'd not noticed him. She looked down at the steps. He could just step aside and she'd pass. But why would he do that?

He maintained his ground, directly in front of her. She looked up from the stair and froze, caught between two steps. She was dressed in a strawberry red suit, the skirt cut tightly to her thighs. The crucifix hung on her chest, tucked inside the suit's jacket. Her face was impassive. Neither of them moved.

"Catherine--"

And then her face contorted, her violet eyes bulged, and her expression froze.

"What are you doing here?" she said, hissing sotto-voce.

"I work here. For Mr. Steiner--"

She reeled. Zeno thought she may faint.

"What?"

"He asked me--"

Her steel gaze left him cold and silent. Far off down the hall a door closed. Catherine looked towards the sound then back at Zeno.

"We must talk," Zeno said.

"No."

She descended two or three steps closer to him. The noise of someone higher on the stair caused them both to look up. Erzsébet's chambermaid slowed as she approached them, suspended two steps apart.

"I'll speak with Sándor," Catherine said to Zeno, her voice thin. "If Sándor wants that..."

The chambermaid continued past them but looked back before going on.

"Good," Zeno said. "I'll tell him to expect you."

Until the chambermaid was out of sight, he looked at Catherine, his face imploring.

"We have to speak," he said.

"Not here." She looked about her. "Go to Váci Street," she said, in a softer voice. "There's an old bookshop. At the back amongst the history books there's a door. Come this morning. I'll leave it unlocked."

Catherine moved quickly down towards him and he stepped aside to let her pass. He watched her walk through the entrance hall and out into the courtyard to a waiting car.

Only then did he notice she was thinner than she'd been at the lake, just two months ago. Much thinner.

Váci Street was busy, even though it was just past midmorning. Despite the war, people in Budapest went on with business much as they always had. He looked left to right along the rows of shops and cafes but couldn't find a bookshop until he asked an old woman, who pointed in the direction he'd come. He retraced his steps to a small poorly lit shop.

"Can I help you?"

The voice surprised him. A woman with a wrinkled face was looking at him from behind a counter and the few neat piles of books.

"I'm just looking," he said. "Where's the history section?"

"At the back of the shop."

An elderly man stood just to the side of the door. Damn him. He couldn't just walk up to the door and disappear inside. Zeno picked up a book. The man browsed the titles, pulled one out and opened it. Zeno looked at the door. The man snapped the book shut and returned it to the shelf. He crooked his head sideways to read the spines and Zeno's heart pounded harder with anticipation. Finally the man moved away, back towards the front of the store.

Zeno grasped the handle, cold in his palm, turned it and pushed. The door stayed shut. He pushed harder and at the same time pressed his foot against the bottom of the door. With some resistance, it opened. He turned and looked back into the bookshop. The man was talking to the woman up front. He walked through the door.

A splash of light slipped in from the shop. A narrow stair ascended to a dim electric light. Somewhere in the far recess of the building he could hear a piano, scales played with precision and fury through three full octaves. The air was musty and unused. He pulled the metal bolt across the door and started to climb.

"Hello," he called, a muted shout. "Is anyone there?"

The scales continued, from the major to the melodic to the harmonic minor. The wooden stairs groaned and creaked, leading him two, maybe three stories above the shop. When he reached the upper landing, the piano stopped. There was another door. He pushed on it—this too was unlocked. He smelled her perfume. There was a short corridor with a single door at the end. He pushed on the door and entered a room filled with glorious light.

Catherine sat in a large armchair, directly opposite the door. The sun came from the south through long casement windows that looked out over the city. The room was furnished with a small table with a single chair, bare floorboards, no rug, no curtains, a small kitchenette on the far side, the single armchair that Catherine sat in. Away from the direct sunlight was the piano, a small baby grand, the lid shut to mute its sound. On top was the room's only clutter, a jostle of printed music, single slips, small folders, books. The crucifix lay on the piano's top. A door, left ajar, led to another room. A metronome ticked in perfect time.

She was wearing the same red suit except she'd removed the jacket to reveal a cream silk shirt. He made no move towards her.

"Why are you here?" she said, her voice tight.

"You told me to come."

"You fool. Why are you in Budapest?"

"Mr. Steiner offered me a job."

"How stupid do you think I am?"

He recoiled. "I helped him at the hotel and he offered me a job."

"And you accepted it."

"How could I refuse?"

"Easily."

"There's a war going on. I've no skill, I'm lucky to get such a job."

The directness of his statement surprised him.

"You knew this would put me in a difficult position," she said.

"You hardly see your husband. I don't think I've put you in any position at all."

She stood from the chair and marched the few steps towards him. Standing less than a metre away, he returned the intensity of her stare without flinching. So close to her, it was impossible not to kiss her—

His cheek stung. His left foot stepped back to steady himself.

"Why did you do that?"

"You bastard!" she yelled. "How could you do this to me?"

She raised her hand to slap him again but let it remain suspended. The anticipation aroused him. She flung herself back into the armchair.

"I'll go," he said. His cheek seared. "I intend to look for a job in a film studio."

He held his breath, waiting for her to confirm his plan. She glared at the floor, said nothing. He turned towards the door. Behind his back he sensed movement. He turned back and at first he didn't understand. Her knees, which had been held together tightly, she snapped apart, violently, until each knee rested against the edges of the armchair. With lessening uncertainty, he took the steps towards her, their eyes locked.

Directly in front of her, he drew in his breath, smelled her again, the complexity of body odors and perfume. He knelt down in front of her, feverish, too close to heat but chilled. He wanted to start everything again, erase the time between their meetings, start as they'd been in the small hotel in Hévíz. He leaned forward, pushed his head into the folds of fabric around her crotch, breathed in and pressed in harder, exhaling fully. The metronome ticked perfect time.

"The light's so strong here."

Catherine turned her head on the pillow towards the windows, then back towards Zeno.

"Is it?" she said. "I've never noticed." She looked at the room. "I've never had need of curtains. Perhaps you're right, but the sun will be gone soon. Winter's around the corner."

"You can't tell me you'll never see me again."

For a moment, she glared at him with that impossible-to-penetrate expression.

"You've made this a difficult situation," she said. "Impossible."

"I've made nothing."

She rose from the bed and walked naked to a robe tossed over a chair. He felt a sense of regret as her breasts vanished from his sight. She paced the room.

"You may be right—we can live in that cold building and never see one another, but this can't continue. You're just a boy." She spun to look at him. "It's illegal."

"I'll be eighteen in March. Younger men have died in this war. I wasn't a virgin. What does it matter?"

"People will condemn me."

"People won't know."

"There!" She flung a hand out at him. "You've shown how damn naïve you are. Everybody knows of every affair in this city. Do you think I don't know the long list of women Sándor sees? Only they don't know of each other. The whole of Budapest society knows of them all. And people just *have* to talk. How do you propose to keep quiet?"

"Why do you keep this apartment?"

She stopped her pacing. "Why do you ask me that?"

"How long have you had it?"

"Years. Many years--"

"And you bring other lovers here?"

"How dare you! This is for myself. I need privacy."

"Then let it be for us." He continued to stare at her, aroused again by the fall of the garment from its gathering at her waist. "Would you tell me the truth, if I asked you something?"

She looked at him. "It would depend on what the question is."

"Haven't you dreamed of that day in Hévíz? Haven't you awakened in the middle of the night thinking I was with you? I have. Every night since then."

"I…"

"Yes?"

"I can't deny I've thought of you," she said. Zeno raised an eyebrow. "All right, I've often thought of you."

"I know you have. I might be naïve but we have these two rooms. No one need know."

At that moment, as she stood at the foot of the bed, as she raised her hands to her forehead in exasperation, the tie of her robe unfastened and the two front panels of the garment parted like the curtains in a theatre to reveal her cream thighs and dark patch. Zeno pulled back the covers of the bed to reveal himself.

"You want me just as I want you."

In the late afternoon when he returned to the apartment's other room, he smelled fresh coffee. Catherine placed a single espresso cup on the small table.

"I've only one chair. One of anything. One cup."

"I'll buy us two cups."

"No. We'll share."

"And one piano." She looked over at it. "I come here to practice."

"Why here?"

"I don't want to play at the house."

"Why on earth not?"

"I thought that would've been obvious."

Zeno thought for a moment. "Not at all."

"Because of Sándor. He'd enjoy it." She turned away from him, towards the windows and the last of the day's light. "We'll meet next Sunday."

"Sometimes I have to work."

"I'll wait for you here. If you can't come it doesn't matter, but you must never speak with me in the house. Even my maid doesn't know about these rooms. Leave now by the bookshop. There's another entrance I'll take to another street."

CHAPTER NINE

Zeno pulled his jacket tight and wrapped his arms around his middle. Fewer people wandered the streets, the sun low, the main illumination dim electric street lights. This light made a completely different mood, the street's shadows casting a dark promise over the scene. As he started to walk, a smile, bold as polished gold, spread across his face. He rubbed his hand over his mouth, tried to smooth it away, but it renewed itself. He was having an affair. His first. He'd had a few fumbling sexual encounters before Catherine, but this was an affair. That it was with someone as sophisticated and beautiful as Catherine Steiner made him feel like a man, a grown-up, infinitely desirable man. And it was their secret, which made it all the more piquant and precious.

A band of German soldiers marched towards him--off-duty, making too much noise. As they passed him, Zeno looked to the other side of the street. Tibi was sitting at an outdoor café with a young woman seated close, his arm draped over her shoulder.

Zeno called out.

Tibi turned a lazy eye towards the street.

"Good God," Tibi said. "You got here."

"I've been here over a month."

"I don't believe it."

Tibi stood up and hugged him. The young woman looked at them, delight on her pretty face.

"I've been meaning to contact you," Zeno said.

"Then why didn't you?"

"Today's the first day I've had off."

"Sit down." Tibi pulled another chair towards the table. "Zeno, this is…"

Tibi looked at the woman. She looked back and waited for him to say her name. When he didn't, she scowled and sat back hard in her seat.

"I'm Zeno," he said, stepping into the breach. She was blond and in her early twenties, just Tibi's type.

"*Enchante.*" She took Zeno's hand in hers. "I'm Gertrúd."

"Are you French?" He rushed at this thought, as if he'd found some small connection to Catherine.

"Heavens, no." She blushed. "But I'm very pleased to meet a gentleman." Still holding Zeno's hand, she stood.

"Where are you going?" Tibi said.

"Thank you, Tibor, for a lovely afternoon, but after everything we've done, if you can't remember my name I should leave."

"I'm sorry. Please, stay."

"It was lovely to meet you, Zeno." She was still holding his hand. "I hope we'll meet again."

With that, she turned on her heels and was gone.

"What do they expect?" Tibi said. "She's nicely put together, but she's got no brains."

"She seemed to have you worked out completely."

Tibi's expression turned to one of genuine offense. But then, as if he'd let something go as useless, he smiled and laughed. He flicked his hand, took a cigarette, and offered the packet to Zeno. He'd never smoked but it was a day for new things. He drew back on the cigarette, just a little, expecting it to make him cough. But he felt nothing save the warmth and a slightly acrid taste. Not unpleasant.

"How's the job?" Tibi asked.

"Busy."

"I didn't think Sándor Steiner would be so demanding."

"It's not that so much…just a lot to learn. But I tell you, he never stops."

"You don't get all that money without working for it."

"But that's the thing. He doesn't seem to work so much. It's social. He's always out. He drinks so much. Sleeps most days until ten or eleven."

"Does his father still run most of the business?"

"I don't know. I've only seen him once or twice. He's much older than I thought. He can't be doing that much."

"Isn't there a younger brother?"

"Zoltán. He's in America."

"Then who runs it?"

"Peter. Erzsébet's husband. I've never seen him. He's always working."

"Well, there's your answer. And how's the delightful Catherine Steiner?"

Over Tibi's right shoulder, Catherine's strawberry red suit caught Zeno's eye. She was walking away from them, back towards the Steiner building on the other side of the Danube.

"What do you mean?" Zeno said.

"Well, you asked a lot of questions about her."

"I didn't." He said this very quietly and looked behind Tibi's shoulder, but Catherine was lost in the crowded sea. "I never see her." He finally looked back at Tibi's eyes. "They live separately."

"Why are you surprised by that?"

"I wasn't. You seem to know a lot about them."

Tibi looked out at the people passing by on the street. "One hears things."

"Where are you working?" Zeno said.

"I'm not. Taking time to enjoy myself."

"Magda stayed at the hotel, working all winter."

"She'll be bored. There's no one there."

"Did Ferenc come to Budapest?" Zeno said.

"How the hell would I know? Have you got something better to wear?"

Zeno looked down at his clothes. "What's wrong with these?"

"You must have." There was a new animation in Tibi's voice.

"Not really. Why?"

"Come on." Abruptly Tibi stood and pinned some money to the table with the ashtray. "I've got a suit at home. It should fit you. You're bigger than you were."

"Why do I need a suit?"

"Trust me. You need a suit."

Zeno looked at Tibi, at the people in the street, then back at Tibi. He longed to run after Catherine. If he could find her, maybe they could go to a café for a drink. He looked again into the crowd. She was lost. Completely gone.

"Okay," he said.

Zeno's feet slipped about in his slightly large shiny shoes as he walked towards Arizona, a popular nightclub on the Pest side of the Danube. The suit fit perfectly. A long queue of well-dressed people stretched from the door of the nightclub. When he joined the queue Tibi tapped his shoulder.

"Come on," he said.

Tibi strutted down the line towards the door. People around him glared at his gall, waltzing towards the door. Entranced by the arrogance, Zeno double-stepped to catch up with his friend.

"There's a queue," he said.

"It's okay." He leaned in towards Zeno's ear. "Some things talk louder than money."

At the front of the queue, a great hulk of a man stepped back and allowed both Zeno and Tibi to enter. Tibi continued with confidence and Zeno scampered after him.

"How'd you do that?"

"I know the doorman." He winked at Zeno. "You can't buy that."

As they climbed the entrance stairs, small bells began to ring. Zeno stopped climbing and the bells stopped. At the apex of the stairs, Tibi turned back towards him.

"What's the matter?"

"I heard bells," Zeno said.

"Take another step."

Zeno moved up another step. A small bell rang.

"It's a trick," Tibi said. "In the step. Come on."

Zeno stood intrigued by the artifice. Tibi rolled his eyes and danced between them, creating something of a melody.

"The music starts before you're inside." Zeno smiled broadly. "This city is so bam-bam-boom."

"You haven't seen anything yet."

A waiter appeared and guided them to a free table near the dance floor. As they walked, the waiter stepped back to allow a party of five or six people to pass in the other direction. Zeno couldn't believe the finery of the women's garments, the amount of glittering jewelry. One of the men looked back at him and smiled. Suddenly he recognized the face. It was Pál Jávor, a famous movie star. Zeno swung back to speak with him but he'd headed into the crowd, and the waiter and Tibi were moving in the opposite direction. Zeno caught up to Tibi.

"That was Pál Jávor."

"Yeah, that was Pál Jávor. There's greater than him here."

The waiter pulled back a chair for Tibi to sit down.

"There're quite a few spare tables," Zeno said. "Why do they make people queue?"

"Supply and demand."

"I don't get it.'

"Got to keep the customers hungry."

Tibi offered him another cigarette and he took it. A big band, a full brass section, stabbed syncopated chords against the rhythm of the bass and drums. At center stage, a microphone stood at attention with no sign of a singer. The dance floor was circular and packed with people, German officers dotting the floor with young Hungarian women.

"There are so many Germans," Zeno said.

"They come here a lot.'

"It's like they've invaded."

"The sooner the better."

"The floor's moving," Zeno said, his voice high-pitched with wonder.

"You've been drinking?"

"No." Zeno dragged on the cigarette, blinked, and looked back at the floor. "It *is* moving."

"Relax. It rotates."

Zeno looked again. "How?"

Tibi shrugged his shoulders. "Watch it."

A waiter appeared with an ice bucket, a bottle of champagne, and glasses.

"Did we order that?" Zeno said.

"They know what I want. Look at the dance floor."

At that moment, the syncopation and volume of the band's brass section surged to a double march.

"What's the song?"

"Benny Goodman," Tibi said. "*Sing Sing Sing*. Perfect for jitterbugging."

The tune translated to dance-dance-dance—with as much flash and energy as possible. Men jumped and twisted in impossible positions, women were hurled in the air, each action and reaction heightening the momentum and fueling the dancers with yet more energy and speed. When the whole had reached what was surely a level where it must rattle and shake and fall apart, a couple rose from the center of the dance floor. The woman and man, both ecstatic, danced for the applauding crowd.

"How did they do that?"

"Stop saying that! You sound like a peasant. The center piece rises."

"Amazing."

Tibi looked around the crowd. "Good God! Will you look at that?"

He flicked his eyes at the other side of the dance floor. Zeno followed his gaze. As the dancers jitterbugged apart and rejoined, he tried to focus. The low light and frenetic movement made it hard to make anything out clearly. But for an instant, he saw Sándor Steiner seated at a table with a young woman.

"Christ," Zeno said, turning his face away. "I have to get out of here."

He started to stand but Tibi anchored his forearm to the table.

"Sit still. He'll never see you."

Zeno looked back again. Mr. Steiner was distracted. The young woman could only have been Zeno's age or younger. He seemed engrossed in her, and she responded to his attention with balmy smiles. Was she the woman who'd been in the apartment that morning? Mr. Steiner raised her hand to his lips and she demurely lowered her eyes.

"What a fool," Tibi said.

Zeno looked back at them. Why was he a fool? Was it the woman's age? How judgmental people were, even Tibi, whose behavior was rarely exemplary.

"Perhaps they're in love."

Tibi smirked. "You can't be serious, he has a different woman every night." He picked up the phone receiver on the table. "Let's see."

"What are you doing?"

He dialed a number and Zeno looked back and forth between Mr. Steiner's table and Tibi. Every table on the floor had a phone. The green light flashed at Mr. Steiner's table. For a few seconds Mr. Steiner ignored the light, his attention still on the girl. Then he lifted the receiver. Zeno turned so that the back of his head was to the table.

"Sándor," Tibi said, "my friend wishes to know if you're in love." Then he hung up. "He's not looking this way, you can turn around. She's a taxi-dancer."

"Why did you do that? Never mind, what's a taxi-dancer?"

"You're so naïve. You pay her to dance with you. The place is full of them. Look around."

There were a lot of young women. Some were with younger men but most danced with men double their age. When Zeno looked back at Mr. Steiner's table, it was empty. He and the young woman had left.

Tibi was laughing. "A woman will grind you up."

"We shouldn't have come here."

"What do you mean?"

"We have no right to be here."

"No right?" Tibi held his open hands out in front of him. "What are you talking about? We can go anywhere."

"I'm a servant."

"Those rules are over."

Without fare welling Tibi, Zeno rose from the table, tucked his chin down, and made his way to the door. There was no sign of Mr. Steiner or the woman. The bells chimed as he descended the stairs to the street.

Mr. Steiner's car pulled up to the curb. Zeno stepped back into the only shadow he could find. Before the driver had time to walk around to the rear door, Mr. Steiner opened the door himself and chaperoned the young woman to the car. As he collapsed into the seat, his eyes met Zeno's. Zeno remained in the shadows, caught, unable to move. No recognition passed over Mr. Steiner's face. He pulled the door shut. The car tore off into the dark.

CHAPTER TEN

The electric lights in Mr. Steiner's apartment already burned, even though it was just after six on Monday morning. Odd, as he usually didn't rise until ten. Zeno moved as quietly as possible from the hall into the main room. His head ached from too much to drink and his throat felt raw from the cigarettes. No one was there. Perhaps Mr. Steiner hadn't returned. Or perhaps he was still asleep. That would be more usual. He'd just left the light on. Zeno should start preparing the bathroom as he did every morning. He opened the bathroom door.

"Good morning," Mr. Steiner said.

He stood naked at the vanity, his back turned to Zeno.

"I'm sorry." Zeno turned to leave the room.

"Come now," he said. "We're both men. No need for embarrassment."

Mr. Steiner remained in front of the mirror, his face covered in shaving cream. Zeno stood still, unsure where to go. Mr. Steiner continued to shave. As hard as Zeno tried, he couldn't not look. The square breadth of his shoulders, the trapezium of muscles, the constriction of his waist denied not only his age but his sedentary lifestyle. Some are blessed, Zeno's mother said.

"Now you're here," Mr. Steiner said, "you can prepare my bath." Zeno snapped to attention. As he turned on the taps, Mr. Steiner took a towel from the rail and wrapped it around his waist. Once the water was flowing at the right temperature, Zeno turned to leave the room.

"Have my dinner suit ready for this evening. There's a concert."

"Yes, sir. What time will you be leaving?"

"Six."

"Yes, sir."

Zeno moved again to leave the room.

"Are you happy in Budapest?"

Zeno turned back. Mr. Steiner *had* seen him in the night-club. His breath came shallow. His throat stung.

"I'm not sure what you mean, sir."

Mr. Steiner looked at him in the mirror. "It's such an exciting city. I don't suppose you've had a lot of time to see it."

Mr. Steiner suspected he'd made the phone call. He'd be sacked. Mr. Steiner turned and faced him, raised a brow.

"Perhaps we could arrange some more free time for you. You're young. You should taste the... carnal delights of the city."

Zeno felt confused. After a pause, Mr. Steiner winked at him and turned back to the mirror.

"Very good, sir."

"You see, I was right about you. You're doing very well. Now don't you run off and leave me."

"No, sir."

Zeno prepared Mr. Steiner's small breakfast: black coffee, a cigarette, and a small hard roll. Once he was free of the bathroom, he sat at the table. Just as he opened the morning paper, the apartment's doorbell buzzed. Zeno made his way to the door.

It was Peter, Mr. Steiner's brother-in-law. Zeno recognized him from photographs.

"Is Mr. Steiner here?"

"He's having breakfast."

Peter began to make his way through the apartment, Zeno following.

"I was just coming to see you," Mr. Steiner said.

As Zeno entered the room, Peter stood over Mr. Steiner, still seated at the table. Both men looked at Zeno, who retreated to his office area.

"Where did you go last night?" Peter said.

"After the meeting, I took the officer to the Arizona. He wanted a woman."

"I'll not have you dealing with these people. They *are* the German army."

"They're also offering huge manufacturing contracts--"

"For munitions!"

"Machinery, not munitions."

A long, tense silence.

"This is suicide," Peter finally said. "You can't support Germany."

"It's nothing but business."

"The Allied forces will bomb the factories. Then where will we be?"

"I think that's being overly dramatic--"

"Germany is nearly bankrupt, Sándor. They have no money to pay. Each day Russia pushes them back. Did you agree on anything?"

More silence. Zeno strained and caught a snicker from Mr. Steiner.

"Only that he should take the lovely brunette onto the dance floor. I lost them after that. You know how it is at Arizona when the floor spins."

Still more silence.

"You won't win on this," Peter said.

"I think you might find I will. These contracts are worth a fortune. You've had your way too long."

"This has to be discussed. Try and make it to the ten o'clock meeting, will you?"

Zeno heard Peter's firm tread as he left. He remained where he was while Mr. Steiner finished his breakfast, walked around the apartment, then left.

Zeno made his way to the bedroom. He pushed the door ajar. The bed was still made. Mr. Steiner had not returned home last night.

From the dressing room he took the dinner suits with the roomier jacket Mr. Steiner preferred for sitting in the theatre. In the lounge room he pulled back the drapes and placed the jacket over the back of a chair in the morning sunlight, his eye methodically scanning each panel for imperfections. The fabric was unspoiled. He returned to the dressing room, placed the jacket on the hoist, and brushed off the lint. It was only when he'd finished that he saw a small spot, a stain of something oily on the edge of the sleeve. He inspected it more closely.

"Damn."

He'd brushed out the whole jacket and didn't feel like doing that again to one of the half dozen others. Besides, Mr. Steiner preferred this one. Hans had some solution that would remove it. He looked at his watch. He'd probably be downstairs by now.

He knocked on Hans's office door. No reply. He walked back towards the kitchen. At that time of the morning the servants often gathered for tea and conversation in a small dining room. When he entered, a lone young woman sat at the large wooden table. She looked up from the magazine she was reading.

"*Bonjour*," she said.

"Gertrúd," Zeno said. "What are you doing here?"

She smiled. "You remember my name. I could swoon. I thought I recognized you. I work here. For Catherine."

"Catherine?"

"Catherine Steiner."

This explained Gertrúd's fascination with French.

"I know who she is. I work for Sándor Steiner."

"Really." An impish smile. "Then, we're kind of married."

"Tibi didn't mention it."

"He didn't remember my name. I don't think he ever asked me where I worked."

Gertrúd's droll manner made Zeno laugh, though he really didn't think he should.

"He's such a heel." She screwed up her face. "Good-looking but a heel."

"He has his moments."

She looked at him closely. "He's your friend. I shouldn't say things like that."

Zeno thought for a moment. "How long have you worked here?"

"Nearly two and a half years."

"If I tell you something," he said, sitting down at the table. "Will you not repeat it?"

She wrinkled up her face. "I doubt there's much I don't know...."

"Last night, Tibi and I saw Sándor Steiner with a young woman at a nightclub."

Gertrúd laughed. "And what does that tell you?"

"I know what it means, but does he really see such a lot of women?"

"So I'm told." She moved slightly closer to Zeno. "He's not exactly the son the family wanted."

"How do you mean?"

"He's incredibly lazy. He just goes out to nightclubs and bars and concerts, all the time."

"True enough."

She moved still closer. "Rumor has it he's always been like that. It's why they let Erzsébet marry Peter. He has a fire in his belly. They say when the old man retires, he'll be put in charge."

"They just had an argument."

"Who?"

"Peter and Sándor."

"Really?" Gertrúd's eyes snapped. "Where?"

"In the apartment."

"What about?"

"Something to do with the factory."

"*Mon dieu!* That *is* something new." She paused for a moment. "Would you like to go for a walk on Sunday?"

"I can't," he said, pulling back a little from the table. "Not on Sunday."

"Why not?"

"Often I have to work and when I don't... I like to go out with my camera. Shoot some film."

"I'll come with you."

"No. Sorry." He fumbled for the words. "I like to be on my own."

"I could carry your equipment. And I know heaps of places in the city you should film."

"I like to find them on my own. It's…part of my process."

She scrutinized him. "Have it your way."

"Perhaps during the week?"

"You've free time during the week?"

He stood up. "Perhaps we could make time. I have to go now. Problem with a suit for this evening."

"Major drama, then."

"I'll talk to you soon."

As he climbed towards the apartment, he chastised himself for not having a better excuse. If he was going to see Catherine on Sundays, and he *was* going to see Catherine on Sundays, it was going to be hard enough to dodge Mr. Steiner, to prepare in advance all the possible outcomes on a Sunday, iron a range of shirts and clean a range of shoes. He didn't need all that preparation spoiled by another invitation.

So Gertrúd worked for Catherine. Budapest was only a small town, after all. Part of him envied her. She'd see Catherine wake in the morning, share the first parts of the day with her as he did with Mr. Steiner. Gertrúd was pretty. And very nice. And she wanted him, he was sure of it. She didn't want to go for a walk. If he weren't preoccupied with Catherine, he'd be happy to pleasure Gertrúd. Why was life always one thing or the other? Couldn't there be just an *and*?

And so the first week between Sundays dragged, cluttered by small events from emergencies with suits to creases in shirts to the demand for a certain pair of shoes that needed attention. In the late evening, he walked out onto the streets around the building and looked up at what he supposed to be the lights of her apartment until they were extinguished. If he woke during the night, when he woke in the morning, she was the first thought. There weren't fifteen seconds in the day when she didn't cross his mind. And despite all his attempts, waiting for sometimes an hour at a time on the central stair, standing in the window looking at the main entrance, he didn't see Catherine.

This lack of even a glimpse stirred up anger with her, frustration, feelings he'd never felt with anything like this intensity. If it hadn't been for his more and more enjoyable encounters with Gertrúd, he'd have suspected Catherine had left Budapest.

On Saturday evening as he left for dinner, Mr. Steiner told Zeno he wouldn't be needed on Sunday.

"I've a little…dalliance," he said. Evidently this was to be in the open between them. "I hope you've the same."

The following morning Zeno scuttled from the house as early as he could, crossing the Danube by the Chain Bridge and running to the bookshop in Vaci Street. He was so early he had to wait for the shop to open. But once it had, the rear door was unlocked and he slipped through and mounted the stairs two at a time, unconcerned by any noise he made.

"Catherine!" he called out at the head of the stairs. He flung open the door but the room was empty. The lid of the piano was closed, the metronome silent. He ran to the other room. And there she was, lying on the bed, her arm fully extended with the line of her body, wrapped only in a sheet and turned away from him, a cello silhouette.

The morning passed into afternoon. They made love yet again as the sun was descending. She moaned in a way she'd not before, the gasps for air intense like gusts of steam from an engine. He slowed his rhythm until she pressed her fingernails into his buttocks, pulling him harder into her. He felt himself change. She moved with him. Her fingers now played on his spine. This was new, this sizzling rush along his flanks, searing around his head, this lightness. The intensity caught him off guard and now he slowed for himself but she again dug in her nails in an unspoken command. He burned, for second after second after second. At times he caught her gasps but mostly he was away until all energy was spent, all shields shattered, the body given over and laid bare to pleasure.

He lowered his torso back onto her, her face turned away from him. He laid his head on her opposite shoulder, resting the line of his jaw along her clavicle.

"You've so much energy," she said.

He moved, still inside her and still hard. She let out a gasp, a little one. Quiet.

"I can do it again," he said. "If you like?"

For some moments she was silent. "If you like."

In the other room, Catherine turned on the radio.

"Bruckner," she said, almost immediately, returning to the bed.

"How do you know that?"

She looked at him. "You can hear the modern influences... I don't know. I just know."

As the string section rose in a wave, he thought with great pleasure of a long line of such Sundays stretching out into the future. This deceit could be maintained. The situation was perfect. No one knew they were there. They could do it again and again and again.

"Maybe we could go for a walk next Sunday."

"No," Catherine said. "That was a condition. It's far too dangerous."

"We could meet in a different part of the city."

"The city has eyes and those eyes are everywhere, every hour of every day. I can't. I won't run the risk of being seen."

"Then let's run away for a weekend."

For a long while Catherine said nothing. "I guess youth allows you such illusions."

"What's it to do with youth? What's there to stop us?"

"This room is our affair."

Zeno smiled.

"What have I said that makes you smile?" she said.

"Our affair. You said our affair."

Zeno rolled away from her. There they lay, separated, the cold air of the evening seeping down between their backs. She was right. He had to concede that. He'd met Gertrúd on the street. He'd seen Mr. Steiner in a club, though he didn't seem to care. The age difference between Catherine and him and between Mr. Steiner and the taxi-dancer were probably the same. But a man's reputation was more durable than a woman's.

"What if we met somewhere in the dark?" he said, still facing away from her, talking to the other side of the room. "So no one could see us?"

Zeno sat in the rear row of the stalls, behind and to the side of the central entrance ramp from the foyer. A line of flickering light emerged from the whirring projection booth, the rows of seats cast in the changing light and shadows of a spring day. The aisle lights peppered the cinema's dark. Catherine might not have been able to come. When he asked Mr. Steiner for the Wednesday night off, he'd checked his diary.

"Carousing?"

Zeno didn't answer.

"The young are polecats," Mr. Steiner said.

Zeno had come to enjoy his teasing.

"I'll dine with my wife," Mr. Steiner said, "so I'll have no need of you."

Zeno watched the movie, Buster Keaton's *Our Hospitality*. The war had forced economy--there was no orchestra to play the film's score, not even a piano or organ. Catherine might be sitting down to dinner with Mr. Steiner. He'd have to just wait and hope she could think of a good reason to get out of it. Risky. And she was nervous, no matter how dark it was, no matter how far removed they were from her normal society.

Someone came up from the entrance, a woman, disorientated by the dark, silhouetted against the screen. She wore a large brimmed hat, a coat pulled tight around her. She walked to the row of seats they'd agreed on, but he'd chosen a different row. She looked around the cinema, checked the row. She fretted.

He made his way down the aisle and touched Catherine's shoulder. She startled but he brushed his mouth across her lips, cold from the evening air. He ushered her into the seats.

"Don't do that to me again," she said.

"What?"

"Be late." He couldn't admit to his schoolboy stunt. "I didn't know what to do."

"I got held up," he said a little defensively. "Don't let it spoil our time together."

He slipped his left hand into her right, surprised by the cool of her leather gloves.

"Take the glove off."

She looked sideways at him, then pulled her hand from his and took off the glove, the skin of her hand soft and warm.

The first film came to an end. For a moment, the cinema was completely dark. A few threads of conversation trilled behind them.

"This is the film I want you to see."

Buster Keaton's *Sherlock Jr.* came to life on the screen, white type on black.

There is an old proverb
which says:
*Don't try to do two things
at once and expect to do
justice to both.*

"I've wanted to see this for so long," Zeno whispered. "Thank you for coming."

Catherine squeezed his hand lightly. The film opened with a person reading a book in the back row of a cinema. The point of view cut closer, to reveal the title, *How to be a Detective*.

"Why's he reading in a theatre?" Catherine said.

'That's what we'll find out."

As Keaton manipulated a broom and a pile of paper to great comic effect, she started to laugh and her grip on his hand relaxed.

"This is the scene I've heard of," he whispered.

Buster Keaton, the projectionist in a cinema, fell asleep by the machine and in a dream sequence left his projectionist booth and wandered through the rows of audience towards the screen. Infuriated by the on-screen antics, he jumped up above the orchestra and crossed over, becoming part of the on-screen action. Zeno slipped his hand from Catherine's and sat forward in his seat. And then Keaton was in a rose garden, then on a busy street, at a cliff precipice, and so on and so on. With each change, the audience swooned, gasped at how film could transport a man so easily from one place to the next. Keaton was completely disoriented. Zeno looked at Catherine. She was staring at the screen, unable to blink, mesmerized by every frame.

When the film ended, in the dark he turned to her and she to him. He kissed her.

"You enjoyed it," he said.

"I loved it. But how did they make him become part of the film?"

"They used incredibly accurate instruments to keep the angles and distances and proportions correct."

"But it was like someone clicked his fingers and he was somewhere else."

"It's the magic. That's what film can do. And this film was made twenty years ago. Imagine what they *will* do. It's only the beginning."

"I don't know what you're talking about. But I must go."

"No. Stay. There'll be another film."

"What will it be?"

"I don't know, but they haven't turned the lights on so there'll be another."

The screen came back to life. A crest, statues of two lions holding a Star of David with an eight candle menorah filled the screen. This film had sound, a tinny but loud orchestra belted forth major chords, resolving into a cantor's wails. The title, *Jew Suess*, filled the screen in that masculine calligraphy so popular with the fascists.

Zeno sat slightly forward. What film was this? As the cantor's singing subsided and the title credits flashed by, Catherine's hand in his tensed. The screen proclaimed: *The events in this film are based on historical fact.* He thought she moaned slightly, but the camera zoomed in on a map of Stuggart, 1733, resolving to the coronation of Karl Sándorander, Duke of Württemberg. There were grand scenes of celebrations in the streets, a huge throng of people moving in an orderly manner.

Zeno leaned back towards Catherine's ear and without taking his eyes from the screen said, "Imagine the coordination it took to film this."

She said nothing.

The Duke sent an official to borrow money from Jud Suess Oppenheimer. This scene opened with a plaque outside a building and writing Zeno didn't recognize, but Catherine winced. In a crowded lane, a man, a dwarf with a full beard, deep-set eyes, and a hook nose, dressed in a black frock-coat and skull cap, walked between the court official and his aide.

"I can't watch this," Catherine said.

"Why not?"

She pulled her hand free of his, got up and moved back along the aisle. Zeno scampered to keep up with her. By the time he'd exited the cinema, she was already through the foyer and out onto the street. He ran to her.

"Go away," she said. "We can't be seen."

"Catherine," he said. What's the matter?"

"Go away."

She struck out at him, her hand catching his shoulder. The slap, painless as it was, still hurt. He couldn't follow her. It was too risky. He let her go. He'd left his new overcoat in the cinema.

He watched the rest of the film. Jud Suess financed the Duke of Württemberg and corrupted and controlled the Duke and the kingdom until its people finally revolted against him. How would she know of such a film? And why did it disturb her so?

"Why did you leave like that?" he said the following Sunday.

"I couldn't watch."

"They were just actors telling a story."

She gazed intently at him. "How can you possibly say that?"

How *could* he say that? It reduced all the films he loved to some sleight of hand.

"When Keaton crossed over," he said, "stepped into the film? I recognized that. When I stepped onto the platform for the first time in Budapest, I entered a world that changes when I least expect it. The film is a window into one man's vision--"

"It's not just a stream of images flowing in one direction! Just as good intentions can move onto the screen, don't you think bad intentions can move out of it?"

He felt trapped. "If the director wanted…"

"Art can be beautiful, transcendent, inspiring. It can also be ugly, dirty, perverse, pornographic. So how can you dismiss the second film as just actors playing roles? Don't you see that others may recognize scenes from *that* film within themselves?"

"I didn't know of this other film--"

"And they'll take courage and strength from it. They'll not feel so isolated. The cinemas all over Budapest are showing it--"

"I didn't think you cared for film," he said. "How do you know about it?"

This caught her off guard and she took a moment to answer.

"Do you think I don't read newspapers? Listen to radios? Talk?"

"I didn't know--"

"It was made in Germany, by the Nazis. Don't you see what it is? It's propaganda to besmirch the Jews."

He let the images of the film flicker through his mind. The Jews were dressed in caftans, one a knotted dwarf. They controlled money. The Jews were like water that seeped slowly and imperceptibly deeper and deeper into the state of Württemberg until all the foundations rotted.

"You think art's just a lovely set of images," she said. "Some nice stories in your film, some nice sounds from the piano. Something we choose. Reverse the painting. Look at the space rather than the solid forms. Then see what you see."

"Why do you feel so strongly about this?"

She stopped for a moment. He was silent. Then she sighed heavily.

"I forgot you were so young," she said. "I can't expect you to understand."

His face grew hot. "You can't say that to me."

"What else can I say when you won't see this for what it is?"

Her argument had moved too swiftly. He felt battered.

"I should go."

She paused and looked at him intently. "I'm not sure what you're saying."

He walked towards the apartment's door. He wasn't sure either.

"Think of this," she said. "Does a picture tell a story? Or does a picture make a story?"

He glared at her and she raised the angle of her eyes towards him. She wouldn't turn away, so he did, towards the door.

"I'll be here next week," she said. "It would only be childish not to return."

CHAPTER ELEVEN

Gertrúd lay beneath Zeno, stiff as a board. Was she not going to be involved in this? Her body was there but her mind was somewhere else. What a difference. He felt no end in sight, no sign of her *petite mort*, as Catherine called it. His hip bones ground against hers. He felt no need to go on. He gasped a few times, thrust harder and harder and then slower, then rolled from her onto his back and stared up at the ceiling. She rolled on to her side, facing away from him. Did she believe he'd come?

This was a mistake. He'd done it because Gertrúd was there and seemed carefree and willing. And he was angry with Catherine. Somehow he'd thought sex with someone his own age would be fun, unimpeded by prickly questions. But it hadn't been fun, it had been a bore. Why was Gertrúd here? She seemed wholly absent, completing some preconceived notion of what she should do but not really caring for it. He rolled onto his side, away from her.

She'd pinned photographs of movie stars to the walls: Bette Davis, Greer Garson, Robert Taylor, Hungarian stars like Pál Jávor, and a still of Ella Gombaszögi from *Meseautó*. They'd talked all evening about films.

"Why do you like these movie stars?" he said.

"They're a window to a world I want."

"You want to be a movie star?"

"That would be lovely, but no." She sighed. "I want their freedom."

She loved films in a way completely different from him.

The moonlight made shadows on the bedroom wall. There were bits of a box and a circle, lines that more or less linked up if he squinted. He wondered what objects blocked the light to form the shadows. But then he thought, as Catherine had asked him to.

"The emotion, the truth," she'd said, "often lies not in the notes that are played but those that are left out."

So rather than concentrating on the blocks of dark, he wondered why the light was allowed to pass through on the other sections. He thought hard but couldn't come up with an answer. Her questions rattled his brain.

It was after four in the morning. He squinted again at the varying shapes of light and dark.

"What's Catherine like, first thing in the morning?" he said.

Gertrúd rolled from her side of the bed, propped herself up on an arm, and looked at him.

"Why do you want to know that?"

Damn. He felt himself blush but Gertrúd's small bed was in shadow.

"It's just that Mr. Steiner is such a mess in the morning. It takes me so long to wake him and make him look the way he does."

"You wouldn't think so," she said. "He always looks so well groomed."

"That's because I do my job so well."

She whacked him across the face with the edge of the sheet, then lit two cigarettes and handed him one.

"Well, if that's so, then Catherine looks twice as bad as Sándor."

"That's not possible."

Gertrúd sighed. "You're right. She has this natural beauty. Somehow it's still there, like that first touch of youth. She's like a movie star."

He knew it. He knew she must look like that first thing in the morning, and now he craved to see her. How he envied Gertrúd, how he wanted to take her place for just one morning.

"Some of the staff say she's vain," she said. "That she spends half the morning to look like that. Do you know Joan Crawford?"

"The actress?"

"She scrubs her face with a brush and plunges it into alcohol and ice to keep the skin taut."

"Really?"

"That's what the magazines say. One of the staff says that's what Catherine does."

"That can't be true."

"It's not. She just looks like that."

There was no artifice about Catherine. She just was what she was.

"I'd better go," he said. "I have to work in two hours."

Gertrúd watched him, didn't take her eyes off him as he pulled on his underwear and day clothes. He had no desire to see the morning light on Gertrud's face.

"When will I see you?" she said.

"What are you talking about? Probably in a few hours."

She rolled her eyes. "Not like that. When will we see one another alone?"

He raised his Sunday-protective hackles. "I've not got much time."

"Oh... that's right. Sunday is you and that bloody camera day."

She threw a pillow at him.

"I've got to go. I'll talk to you during the day."

As he walked in his socks with his shoes in hand through the cold corridors and stairs to his own room, he tried not to compare Gertrúd and Catherine. Despite all Gertrúd's physical temptations, the angular plans of her face, the plump lips, her full chest, she didn't actually like the physical. He'd no desire for a repeat with Gertrúd. He just shouldn't have done it. Catherine he wanted more each hour and with ever increasing urgency.

But in the coming days, Gertrúd waited for him in the servants' hall. She lingered on the stairs.

"I was hoping to see you," she said, as if this meeting just happened.

"Were you?"

She moved to kiss him.

"I'm sorry," he said pushing her advancing hands down and quickly glancing both up and down the stair. "I'm in a bit of a rush."

"Perhaps we could see a film this evening?"

"Not sure. I'll let you know."

Without thinking, he kissed her, quickly, just on the cheek. Before she had a chance to respond, he bounded off down the stairs, taking them two at a time, leaving her and her lingering glance alone. Damn. Why had he kissed her? He'd have to dampen her flame, but how?

Downstairs he checked his pigeon hole for any messages or letters. There was a letter from his mother and sister and a hand-delivered note. He recognized the handwriting. It was from Tibi. He wanted to discuss something important and suggested they could meet at the Café Parisette on Sunday morning at nine.

"Damn!"

He banged the letter against his thigh.

"Bad news," Hans said.

"Nothing. It's fine."

Sunday morning. Nothing, not even Tibi, could drag him away from what he intended to do on Sunday morning. Damn him. Zeno read the note again. He said it was important and he'd been meaning to catch up with Tibi. And the meeting would be early in the day. It was all right. He'd go and meet him, then go to the apartment and Catherine. Given their argument last time, something about being late for her appealed to him.

On the way to meet Tibi, Zeno decided to walk through Holy Trinity Square. It was a small detour but from the first time he'd been there he loved the center of medieval Budapest, as if another curtain had been raised on another scene, more of the city's infinite variety. At first he'd thought to find the eerie castles of *Nosferatu,* but instead he'd found the Fisherman's Bastion, a symmetrical group of seven castle towers, so pleasing in their design he thought they could only ever have been inhabited by princes and princesses, never vampires.

As he walked on, the morning broke into the most pleasant day, the air warm but not hot, with a light breeze. He increased his pace towards a small square but at the entrance a blaze of waxy red brought him to a halt. An old woman sat at a small table, surrounded by hundreds, no, thousands of waxed red peppers laid out over the cobblestones. With speed and accuracy she strung them and hung the long chains on poles held between stands at various heights. The cascades of peppers formed a background and framed the woman. If she'd been working without being framed, the image might not have drawn his eye. Not only did a frame delineate, it hurled the image at the viewer. He wished he'd brought his camera. And how he wished he had colored film. Color and film. These were unimaginable. Budapest demanded it. He breathed deeply and marveled again at the sight of the woman and her peppers. The curve, the plumpness, the color, reminded him of Catherine's lips.

When he arrived at the Café Parisette, Tibi was already seated, dressed in a woolen suit whose fine grade of fabric outstripped anything Zeno had previously seen on him. Tibi sat rigid in the chair, something firm and rod-like in his posture. They hadn't seen one another since the evening at the Arizona nightclub, but he looked different, his hair oiled down, his movements deliberate.

"Thank you for coming," Tibi said.

"Are you all right?"

"I'm fine." His lips smiled. "Yes, I'm fine. I realize your day off is precious so I've ordered breakfast."

Zeno had already eaten but couldn't refuse such hospitality. He sat opposite him.

"You look well," Zeno said.

"My position has changed."

"Where are you working?"

"I've joined the Arrow Cross Party. I have a position in their office."

"Who are they?"

Tibi smirked. He offered Zeno a cigarette.

"I forgot you've no interest in politics."

Tibi held his own cigarette in his mouth, drew in to ignite it, and leaned across the table so Zeno could light his.

"The Arrow Cross is a political party." Tibi exhaled the smoke. "Please don't speak of this with anyone. At the beginning of the war, Regent Horthy banned us."

"It's illegal?"

"For now, we operate underground. But we've forged strong affiliations with the Nazis."

For some seconds, Zeno was lost for words. Tibi had always avoided any political opinion except those necessary for the pursuit of pleasure.

"So you're a fascist," Zeno said.

"The word is hard. I believe in Hungary."

Zeno looked him over. "The suit fits you well."

"Thank you. How are you finding Budapest?"

"Great," he said. "I haven't had a lot of time to explore."

"I'm sorry. I promised to help you."

"I've found my feet."

"How are your inroads into the film industry going?"

"I've had no time." Zeno sighed. With everything going on, he hadn't made a single inquiry at a film studio. "I take my camera out with me." Today he hadn't brought it with him. "I film what I can. I've money to pay for the development and to buy more film. I've even bought an editing block."

"What on earth's that?"

"A device to cut the film cleanly so it can be joined to other pieces."

"Life cut to an illusion."

"It's amazing. You can't see some of the edits. It's like painting."

"What about work in the industry?"

"I need to settle in more, save some money, before I try to find work."

"If you don't risk things--"

"I have to send money home," he said. "I can't risk not being able to do that. If I can find the right job in the film industry, I'll take it, but until then..."

"Wise." Tibi lit another cigarette and dragged hard. He offered another to Zeno but he refused. "But you're out and about without your camera."

"I was coming to meet you."

Zeno changed his mind and took a cigarette.

"Do the Steiners treat you well?" Tibi asked.

"Mr. Steiner's very easy to work for. He's not home much and he's predictable."

"There're people I know in the film industry who could help you."

"Who?"

"Just people. But they'd require information."

Zeno frowned. "What information?"

"Information about Sándor Steiner." Tibi looked Zeno straight in the eye. "Any of the Steiners, for that matter."

"Like what?"

Tibi dragged on his cigarette. He held the smoke in his lungs and then shot a straight plume across the table to the side of Zeno's face.

"Does he do unusual things?" Tibi said.

Zeno recoiled from the question. "Tibi, what's this about? He has affairs. All of Budapest knows that."

"Is he unaccounted for at times?"

Zeno thought for a moment. "There's nothing I can think of."

"Think hard."

"What are you saying? What's this all about?"

Suddenly he felt overheated. Tibi stubbed his cigarette into the ashtray.

"There are those who think converted Jews are just hiding. That in secret they practice their religion."

"Why do you care about that?"

"They've suppressed us for too long."

"You speak like a…"

"I've joined the Arrow Cross Party. We'll lead Hungary back to her glory. Think hard. Have you ever found unusual items in the house?"

"Like what?"

"Prayer shawls, signs of kosher food or wine, books, skullcaps?"

"Nothing like that."

"Do they light candles on Friday evening?"

"No."

"Have you seen him naked?"

"What?" Zeno pushed his chair back. "What do you mean?"

Tibi smirked. "Does he have a foreskin?"

Zeno shuffled in his seat. "I'm not sure I've looked."

"Do I?"

"Yes."

"Then you've looked."

"You lay around the chalet naked. It was hard not to notice. Oddly, Mr. Steiner doesn't do that. Yes, I've seen him naked."

Zeno stopped himself. Why was he saying this? Why should he be pressured to betray the intimacies of Mr. Steiner's body? The state of his employer's penis had no interest for him. But more important, the whole conversation felt disloyal to his employer.

"They are Christians," Zeno said. "You saw the fuss Catherine made about that crucifix. She always wears it. His cousin, Father István, is a priest. He comes to the house to give confession. I've seen nothing like what you're talking about. Next you'll be suggesting they eat babies."

"Please, do *not* joke about it. What about other members of the household?"

"I don't really have much to do with them."

"The other staff, have they ever said anything?"

"No. Gertrúd…"

"Who's that?"

"Tibi." He could no longer hide the exasperation he felt. "You were with her when we met."

Tibi cast his mind back. "The blonde? Not so bright?"

"She's not so dumb."

"Does she work there?"

"Yes."

"Please, ask her to contact me."

Zeno wished he hadn't mentioned Gertrúd.

"I have to go," Zeno said.

Tibi took a small notebook and a ridiculously expensive gold pen from his pocket. He scribbled an address.

"You can contact me here, should you see or hear anything."

"Tibi, there's nothing to see or hear."

He bade Tibi farewell and left the café. He'd only walked a few steps towards Vaci Street when Tibi called out to him. Zeno waited.

"There's someone I know," Tibi said. "A movie producer. You should meet him."

"I won't spy on Sándor Steiner to meet a movie producer."

"I'm not suggesting that." Tibi smiled. Zeno turned and started to walk away. "He works at Hunnia Studios."

He turned back. "Hunnia…"

"I thought that might interest you. Viktor Bánky is directing."

Bánky was a giant in the Hungarian film industry, especially since his huge hit *Dr. Kovács István* in 1942. Just the thought of being in a room with him was--

"You look like you've seen a ghost," Tibi said. "I'll meet you at the front of the studio on Tuesday at four pm."

Tibi swung on a single heel with all the panache of a professional dancer and walked away. Zeno shook his head. What was all that about? He grew more irritated with every step. Those bizarre questions and the Arrow Cross Party— what on earth was Tibi thinking? Not that joining a party was necessarily a bad thing, he supposed, but *Tibi?* Not even money had ever really excited him. Nothing had, except the pursuit of women. And even that he'd never taken seriously.

When he arrived at the apartment, Catherine was actually playing the piano, not just practicing scales. It was the first time he'd heard her play, velvet sound spilling down the stairwell. He stood outside the door and listened. The piece, he'd no idea what it was, shifted from a clear oom-pah-pah of the waltz in the bass to a faster tempo, a million quick notes in the higher hand, then a third section. His spine tingled with each run as if he was being pulled and teased to his greatest height. He shivered. He felt confused, taken over, as if he'd never heard a single sound and now the whole aural landscape rushed in on him. How could something be so delicate? There it was again, that phrase, that spider rushing over the keys.

The piano fell silent. He opened the door. From the piano, she looked up at him. The sunlight caught the crucifix around her neck.

"You're here," she said, blushing as if she'd been caught in an act of self pleasure.

"What was that?"

"A waltz…"

"What was its name?"

"It's Chopin. Waltz Number Seven."

"What kind of name is that?"

"They're not folk songs. That's how they're named."

"How terribly unromantic. Would you play it again for me?" She hesitated.

"I'm sorry," he said. "Your music's only for your ears." He looked at the sky outside the window. "What's kosher food?"

When she made no response, he looked back. He couldn't read her expression.

"Why do you ask such a thing?"

"I heard someone mention it."

"It's food prepared according to the laws of Kashrut."

"What's that?"

She sighed. "I don't really know. They're Jewish laws. They have laws around the type of food they eat." She looked down at the piano's keys. "Let me play for you."

She straightened the music on the stand and began the waltz.

Again the sound, the complexity, rushed at him and left him breathless. Each turn of each section she varied, expressed differently, her fingers caressing, running, exalting over the keyboard.

"That last ascending run of notes…"

He felt embarrassed at the inadequacy of his expression and fell silent. She looked up from the keyboard.

"Go on."

"I don't have the words."

"If you've felt the music you'll find the words."

"They're so… light, so even, so rushing and yet slowing. Like they're never going to reach the end."

"They ascend to heaven."

"Exactly. But each time you played them, they were some-how different."

Her smile was radiant. "See, you've felt it. You've gone to the heart of Chopin."

"I have?"

"He wrote very simply, at least when you compare him to others, like Beethoven. This piece has three separate themes and he repeats them. But the magic, the inspiration, is that he wrote for the individual pianist. It's a matter of interpreting the notes."

"You mean another pianist would express them differently."

"I want them to rise to heaven. Another pianist could make the same notes in the same order descend to hell."

He winced. "I don't ever want to hear it played like that."

She got up from the piano and walked to the other room. After they'd made love and lain quiet together for some time, something clicked into place in his brain.

"It's both."

"Both what?" she said, her voice languid.

"A picture tells a story, but it also makes a story."

She moved closer to him. "It does. Art both represents and constructs its subject."

CHAPTER TWELVE

Budapest was a series of worlds within worlds, each of them discrete. This was Zeno's first thought when he saw the ceiling of Hunnia Studios' central sound stage high above him, like yet another sky. Black electrical cabling snaked across the floor in a seething mass, cleared only around the actual set stationed at the middle of the vast space. The set's back wall rose up into the airy flies far above.

Stagehands, an assistant director, electricians, a script girl rushed from place to place. Voices, so many echoing voices, the whole cavern held in half light. There were cameramen, at least three of them. Imagine that, not having to reshoot over and over from different angles just to bring a scene to life.

"Come on!" someone yelled from the darker recesses. "We have to get this done before dinner."

This stirred the anthill, and everyone's pace increased. Zeno noticed that the side walls of the set, an office, were splayed slightly outward, the opening for the missing forth wall much wider. The furniture was laid out around an imagined central point, leaving larger spaces for the actors. It wasn't a real office at all. If he were directing, the room would be more realistic, the walls square, the furniture arranged in a natural, cluttered way. And he'd add the fourth wall, find a way to light and move within this constrained space. That fourth wall gave it realism, authenticity. And why have the camera remain so static? Cinema demanded kinetics. He'd move the camera around the actors and the set. He'd film it as a director like István Szöts, more complicated but ultimately more satisfying.

"It's quite something," Tibi said. Zeno smiled at him and returned to the action.

The sound of the crew's voices waned. Viktor Bánky walked on stage, dressed simply in pants and a shirt and tie, his eye fixed on the heart of the stage--clearly he could see or hear nothing else. The actors resumed their places. The arc lights, held high on tall wooden towers, burned brighter than daylight.

"What are those large panels over the set?" Tibi asked.

Zeno looked where he pointed.

"They're sound buffers, used to dampen the echo so the sound comes through cleanly onto the film."

Tibi raised his eyebrows.

"There's a man…" Zeno looked about the crowd of people. "There. He moves the microphone to follow the action."

"How do you know that?"

Zeno smiled. "I've been reading about this since I can remember."

Tibi nodded. "There's my friend."

He pointed to the far side of the sound stage, away from the scene. The man was dressed in a shirt and suit, a golden cravat loose around his throat. He held a tape measure to a woman's shoulder and ran it down to her wrist.

"You said he was a producer," Zeno said.

Tibi frowned and shook his head. "He works in costumes. Come on."

Zeno wanted to stay and watch everything unfold around him. But he followed Tibi, something arrogant in the way he walked, as if he'd been to the studio before, as if he somehow owned the whole thing. He greeted his friend, shook his hand. He then turned to look at Zeno. György Hernády was in his early fifties, well groomed and maintained.

"You make a handsome pair." György licked his upper lip. "Let's go talk at the café."

He dismissed the young actress.

"I'd like to stay and watch the filming," Zeno said.

"You *are* an ingénue, but let me give you a first lesson in film production: nothing happens fast. This lot won't get started for at least another hour or two."

Tibi and György walked towards the exit but Zeno trailed as slowly as he could. He looked back at the set. Bánky was tête-à-tête with an actor, and he wished he could hear what they were saying. He looked from Bánky to the three-walled office. He thought of Catherine and her disbelief that someone could cross from the audience into a film. The irony was that for this transition to be realized, rather than tearing down the fourth wall, it had to be constructed. He yearned to introduce himself to Bánky, discuss his idea for the set. But what right did he have to say anything to such a great man?

The sun outside the sound stage now seemed muted. Tibi and György were already sitting, wedged between neighboring buildings. Actors and technicians from other productions wandered between them, a secretary in a gray woolen suit, a Dominican nun with a cigarette, and a man in a pinstripe suit with white spats who may or may not have been an actor.

"What acting experience do you have?" György asked Zeno.

"I don't really want to be an actor," he said.

"You don't?" György looked at Tibi.

"Zeno's more interested in production. He's very good with a camera."

"A camera man, then."

"That would be a place to start," Zeno said. "Then I'd like to try directing."

"My, my... directing. But with your looks, you'd do well to reconsider." György smiled at Zeno without revealing his teeth. "At any rate, you've chosen a most fortuitous time to enter this noble profession."

Zeno felt confused.

"Now Hungary has regained her territory lost in the last war, the audiences are much bigger. There'll be a renaissance of film. The best will get better, both artistically and commercially." György looked at Zeno, who didn't see the fortuitous connection. "Many more jobs."

"I see," Zeno said.

"At any rate," György said. "Now the purge is nearly over, Hungarian actors and directors will come into their own--"

"Purge?" Zeno was lost again.

György and Tibi looked at one another.

"Jews," György said. "Now they're gone—"

"But how can that be?" Zeno said. György and Tibi smiled at one another. "So much talent's been lost."

"Talent?" György sat forward and raise his bushy eyebrows. "I can't think of any."

The names of Hungarian directors and actors and technicians who'd self-exiled in the last decade ran through Zeno's mind. Many had fled into Northern Europe, then on to Hollywood. But he remained silent. It would be impolite to tax this man, this man who could be his benefactor.

"It's just hearsay," Tibi said, "that talented people have been lost. No one can name any."

György laughed.

"Manó Kertész Kaminer," Zeno said. "Surely *Casablanca* can only be seen as a success on any level, artistic or commercial."

György's face tightened. Tibi seemed genuinely horrified.

"He can change his name," György said, "but he's still a grubby Jew. With Jews in charge of the industry you wouldn't stand a chance."

"Zeno is young," Tibi said. "He doesn't realize the complexity of the situation."

"America can have him."

Zeno stood. He didn't understand all this hate. What did it matter who these people were? All that mattered was what they projected on to a screen.

"Can we go back to watch the filming?" he said.

Tibi and he left György to finish his coffee.

"Why were you so rude to him?" Tibi said as they approached the soundstage door.

"Rude?" Zeno glared at him. "Didn't you hear what he said?"

"He only said what everyone's thinking."

"And that makes it right? What's got into you?"

Tibi looked around to see if anyone was listening to them.

"I'm sorry," Tibi said, sotto voce. "György can be a little zealous. Artistic type." He pressed his mouth into a closed grin and raised his eyes. "But in essence, it's the truth."

"And what's that?"

Tibi sighed deeply. "György says...there's talk they'll re-make *Jud Suess*, here in Budapest."

"What?"

"It'll be more... effective, in Hungarian, set in Hungary."

"Effective?"

"I know, it's already a masterpiece, but there's talk--"

"It's filthy propaganda."

Tibi moved back. "It's the truth."

Zeno started to walk away.

"Don't be a fool," Tibi said. "He'd get you a job working on it."

"No."

"Yes."

Zeno turned back to Tibi. "But I don't want a job like that--"

"Grow up! Don't you realize what he said is to your advantage? Once the Jews are gone there'll be many more chances of work."

"I don't want a seat someone's been forced from."

"Don't be so proud."

"When did you become so... Dammit, Tibi, you never cared about politics before."

"I've always known Hungary has to return to the correct path."

"*What* path?"

György had finished his coffee and was walking towards them.

"You're speaking like a fool," Zeno said.

"*I'm* speaking like a fool?"

"I don't begin to understand you or György or your Arrow Cross Party but I know I don't want any part of it."

Despite his desire to return to the sound stage, Zeno turned away from Tibi and headed for the front gates of the film complex. He walked with no detours back to the Steiner's building, which now stood as some bastion of straight think-ing. What had got into Tibi? Why did he hate so much?

He went to Mr. Steiner's apartment, finished his chores for the day, and after dinner went to bed early. As he fell asleep he decided he no longer wanted to see Tibi.

He woke from heavy sleep with a start. He held his breath. The door of his room clicked shut.

"Who's there?"

No one answered. Did Catherine know where his room was?

"It's just me."

"Gertrúd?" He let out his breath and turned on the lamp. "What the hell are you doing here?" he whispered.

He squinted at her. She stood looking at him, dressed in her work clothes.

"I wasn't sure this was your room."

"So you thought you'd barge in and check."

She smirked and ran her eyes over his bare chest, the neat line of hair that ran to his belly.

"I might have known you'd sleep *au naturale.*"

"What're you doing here?" He looked at his watch. "It's two-thirty."

"I just left work." She walked the few remaining paces to his bed and sat.

"At this hour?" he said.

"Drama. You don't want to know."

She sat down on the bed.

"You can't be here."

She lay down next to him. "It's all right for you to come to my room…"

"That was different."

"Oh yeah? How?"

He rolled onto his side and she returned his gaze. He felt himself harden. How easy this would be. He'd not seen Catherine for days. And then he remembered how unpleasant sex with Gertrude had been, and how she couldn't accept it for what it was. He twisted his body, swung his legs to the floor, and dragged the sheet around himself. She remained lying on the bed.

"Don't be so coy. I've seen it all before. Once. Or maybe you've forgotten."

He tried to pull on some trousers but couldn't manage it until he let the sheet fall to the floor.

"What do you want?" he said.

"You've been avoiding me all week so I came to see you."

"Look… I don't think I feel the same as you."

"How do you know what I feel?"

She looked as if she was going to cry and rolled away from him.

"I'm sorry about what happened. We did too much too soon." She moved back to face him. "I think the Steiners would be really upset if they knew what happened. Can we just take things slower?"

The minute he said the silly words he wished he could take them back. Her gaze softened, her forehead smoothed out. She obviously hadn't gotten the subtext.

"You do like me, then?" she said.

He swallowed hard, turned away to pick up a jumper. "Why wouldn't I?" He pulled the jumper over his head.

"I really don't think Catherine would give two hoots if I told her I was seeing her husband's valet," she said.

He froze, the jumper covering his face.

"You can't."

"She'd think it's funny."

He pulled the jumper down. "Please don't."

She had the upper hand. "All right." She flashed that impish grin. "You're so old-fashioned."

"It's not that--"

"We'll take it slowly."

"Thanks."

He sat down next to her on the bed. He thought he should kiss her but realized he'd be digging a deeper hole.

"Something odd happened earlier this evening," she said.

"What?"

'I went out on an errand." She rose and sat on the edge of the bed, facing Zeno. "Tibi was walking down the lane at the rear of the building."

"Did he recognize you?"

She nodded. "That's not the odd part. He'd been trying to send me a message."

"Why didn't he just leave it?"

Gertrúd said nothing. Zeno felt irritated.

"I guess he couldn't remember your name."

Gertrúd blushed.

"He'd asked you to contact me." She glared at him. "Why didn't you?"

"I…"

"Were you jealous?"

Somehow she'd twisted this to suit her own point of view.

"I don't want to tell you how to run your life, but…"

"Then don't." She stood up. "I'm seeing him on Sunday."

"He's going to ask you questions about the Steiners. You need to be really careful about what you say."

"I'll say what I like."

She met his gaze, tilted her head up, down, to the side. The angles of her face changed her expressions, from defiance to anger to questioning. What a difference an angle could make. Each plane of her face made her something else entirely. She turned to leave the room.

"Could I film you some time?"

She faced him and her skin tightened. She lifted her head back, enough to glimpse the underside of her chin, the shadows from the lamp rising up into her face. How this expression froze him, Gothic anger yet yearning and brittle. She raised her eyebrows, another vector of heightened emotion he'd not even imagined.

"Speak to my agent. *Bonne nuit.*"

She closed the door far too loudly for that hour. He stood in the middle of the room until the cold set in and bit at his bare feet. With his clothes still on, he jumped back into bed. What else was he to say to her? He didn't want her to cry, didn't want to upset her anymore than he had. And if she confided in Catherine… Jesus! He'd bought some time. He'd find a way to let her down gently.

These thoughts carried him through the remainder of the night. He turned his alarm off before it rang and raised himself exhausted from the bed. Amongst all the conflicting arguments that ran through his mind he'd concluded there was nothing he could do. He just shouldn't have had sex with Gertrúd. It was unnecessary. And actions had consequences.

Mr. Steiner was already out of bed when he arrived at the apartment for work.

"Zeno?" he called out from the bedroom. "I'm glad you're early. This evening we're leaving for Berlin."

Zeno tensed. "Yes, sir."

This must have been why Gertrúd was up so late last night. She'd been preparing Catherine for the trip.

"I'm not exactly sure how long we'll be." Mr. Steiner came to the bedroom door with a smile for Zeno. "Pack for at least a week. Remember, it'll be a good deal colder there."

"Are there any particular events I should prepare for?"

"It's business. Meetings. The social will be meals only. Nothing else."

"Yes, sir."

His heart faltered. Catherine would be gone over the weekend. He wouldn't get to see her. But if it were a business trip, why would Mr. Steiner take Catherine?

"Sir, is your wife accompanying you?"

"Catherine?" Mr. Steiner sneered, screwing up his face. "Oh. When I said 'we' I meant you and I were traveling to Berlin. I can't be without you. You must pack for yourself as well. Your travel documents are in order, I presume."

"Ottó organized them."

"Good. We leave at five this evening."

"Very good, sir."

Mr. Steiner turned back into the bedroom. For a moment, Zeno just stood where he was, trying to gather his thoughts.

"I was just thinking...." Mr. Steiner returned at the doorway. "While we're there, I'll need you to act as my secretary. You'll accompany me to the meetings, arrange papers, take notes if need be."

"But sir..."

"You'll do fine. We can discuss the details on the train. Now get to work. There's plenty to be done."

Again Mr. Steiner turned to leave, then looked back.

"One last thing. Please don't mention our destination to anyone."

Once the packing was done he hung around for a little while in the servants' antechamber in case Gertrúd showed up—if she knew he were going, she might mention it to Catherine. But he didn't want to see her, didn't want to risk her misinterpreting an encounter, so he left after twenty minutes or so. Surely Catherine would know her husband was away for the week. Surely, when he didn't show up on Sunday, she'd conclude that Zeno had traveled with him.

Just two days later, Zeno and Mr. Steiner stood together in the largest office, possibly the largest room, Zeno had ever seen. The space was at least twenty meters by twenty, the ceiling two stories above the floor. A large wooden desk made of honey- colored wood faced the double doors they'd been ushered through. A chair with a high carved back stood behind the desk, two smaller matching chairs in front. A long thin flag, red with a swastika at its center, hung from the wood-paneled wall behind the desk. But for them, the room was empty. Light poured in through ceiling-to-floor windows and spilled across the parquet floor. As if in defiance of this natural illumination, a huge crystal chandelier hung in the center of the room.

Zeno shifted his weight from foot to foot. What was he to do? He looked to Mr. Steiner, but his employer walked to the windows, placed his hands on his hips, and looked out across the busy expanse of the Platz.

The door behind Zeno opened.

"The lieutenant colonel's delayed," a man said, coming into the room.

Mr. Steiner turned from the window and for a moment looked at the secretary, tall but full with cropped blond hair, only in his early twenties, his face long and hollow. His olive green uniform seemed tailored, perfectly cut to accommodate his perfect figure: broad shoulders, tight waist, fuller thighs. He radiated something, a pinnacle, supreme in form, a purity of design.

"He'll be a few minutes," the secretary said. Mr. Steiner continued to stare at him. The man turned to Zeno. "If you have papers, please arrange them on this table."

He pointed to a smaller table at the left side of the room. Mr. Steiner nodded to Zeno. He carried the portfolio to the table to arrange the documents in piles, as they'd discussed on the train, should they need to be accessed quickly.

"Is there something the matter?" the secretary asked.

Zeno turned back to Mr. Steiner, who shook his head as if to clear it.

"No." He raised his hand to his mouth, his forefinger resting like a mustache under his nose, his thumb vertical to his cheekbone.

"Have we met before?" The secretary stepped closer to Mr. Steiner.

"No...perhaps. Perhaps, the last time I was in Berlin."

"Dieter Bohm." He extended his hand towards Mr. Steiner. They shook hands and Bohm stepped back. "If there's anything you need, I'm just outside. Please, call out."

He turned and walked a few steps, then--as if he remembered something--spun back towards Mr. Steiner, stopped, clicked his heels, and raised his arm in the air, at the last moment snapping out his hand into an erect position.

"*Sieg Heil!*"

At first Sándor tensed, then he relaxed and nodded his head. With all the flourish of a dancer, Bohm spun and marched from the room, closing the heavy wooden door.

Sándor walked slowly towards Zeno and the papers. He looked over the various documents and nodded his approval.

"You suit your new role well," he said.

Zeno looked down at the papers. His stomach bubbled. If only he felt as confident as Mr. Steiner.

Some time passed before the room's doors opened again and an officer stood in the doorway, a large man in his early forties. Zeno recognized him. Just a few months ago, during the summer at Lake Balaton, this man had dined with Catherine at the hotel. Zeno stepped back slightly. Lieutenant colonel Müller surveyed the room, then strode across it with that unmistakable air of ownership.

"Herr Steiner, I am sorry I kept you waiting."

"Not at all."

"There's so much happening... So busy. If you don't mind we need to get down to business straight away."

"Certainly."

Müller walked to the other side of his desk and Mr. Steiner sat opposite him. Zeno stood at attention to the side.

"As you know," Müller said, "the German army has suffered losses. The Russian front's been a challenge. We've lost many of our manufacturing plants to the Allied bombing."

"Our plant could immediately start production of trucks."

"I'm sure."

"What quantity are you looking at?"

"An initial order of a thousand."

"A thousand…"

"Budapest hasn't been bombed. You're entirely operational?"

"Yes."

"Geographically, you're well placed. You're close to some of our major battle fronts, Poland, Yugoslavia, even Russia. It would appear we both have everything to gain."

"It would appear."

Müller studied Mr. Steiner intently. Mr. Steiner's returned the intensity.

"We can deal with the details," Müller said. After some moments of silent paper shuffling, he met Mr. Steiner's eyes. "These contracts would be quite advantageous for you."

Mr. Steiner remained still. Zeno admired his mettle.

"Herr Müller, my family is in business. I wouldn't travel this far if there wasn't a fair profit."

"Indeed. We're in dire need of trucks. That's no secret. An army may march but without transport of equipment and supplies it soon grinds to a halt."

"I see." Mr. Steiner paused. "Might I compliment you on your Hungarian? Your accent is perfect."

"I'm Austrian. My mother was from Budapest. She insisted I learn." He paused a moment and smiled. "The best is always passed from the mother."

"Indeed. We're linked, then."

"How so?"

"Our ancestors, on my mother's side, moved to Hungary from Austria during the Empire."

"Perhaps." He studied Mr. Steiner. "Returning to our discussion, you must admit that even the most swiftly managed factory will take months to produce its first vehicles."

Mr. Steiner sighed. "It's true. The war has depleted our staff. Some materials are short. It will take time to source things."

"Time is an opulence we don't have."

"Budapest has a thriving black market. A lot can be found, for the right price."

"We can only grant this contract on one condition."

"And what might that be?"

"We need trucks," Müller said. "Immediately. There are companies producing suitable models all over Europe, Switzerland, Portugal, but they won't sell them to us."

"So you need me to act as a go-between."

Müller smiled. "You're a quick man. I'm sure this comes from your mother." He laughed and Mr. Steiner smiled. "The Saurer and Berna company in Switzerland will sell the trucks to you." He raised his left hand in the air. "We'll provide you with the financing and pay you a commission." He raised his right hand in the air. "You'll receive these contracts." He raised both hands higher in the air and then joined them.

Mr. Steiner was silent for a moment. "This isn't something I'd considered. I'll need time to think."

Müller collapsed both his hands to the desk. "We don't have time."

"You're asking me to draw attention to myself and my family."

"I'm asking you to accept a most profitable contract."

Müller opened the drawer and slid a large envelope over the desk. Mr. Steiner stared at it.

"I don't need to be bribed."

"You'll receive a contract. That's more money than I could possibly bribe you." He gazed at Mr. Steiner. "We need someone skillful. Someone who can negotiate."

Mr. Steiner raised his hand to the desk. At first Zeno thought he was going to slide the envelope back over to the gloating Müller. But then slipped his hand over and took the envelope.

Zeno and Mr. Steiner stayed in a hotel a short walk from Müller's office. Zeno had his own small room and bathroom, which conjoined Mr. Steiner's suite. He wanted to film some of Berlin, but each day they walked to the office in the dark of morning and returned to the hotel in the evening. Some days they were joined at the office by Dieter Bohm, sometimes by a fleet of unknown men. Although they said very little to one another, Bohm seemed to want to compete with Zeno, striving to be more efficient, not losing track of anything Müller wanted, half the time anticipating Mr. Steiner's needs for tea or food or water.

Zeno didn't understand the length and breadth of the discussions, but he did understand that the Nazis were desperate. They pushed and pushed at this deal, wanting more and more for less and less. The discussions ran late into the night, when more food and wine was brought into the room.

As Zeno stood by his table organizing the growing piles of paper on Sunday, he detached, his thoughts lost completely to Catherine. Would she be at the apartment? Did she know where he was? Did she miss him half as much as he missed her?

"Zeno," Mr. Steiner said.

Zeno looked at him. Mr. Steiner was scowling, comically.

"Your secretary is just a boy," Müller said. "I bet I know what he was day-dreaming of." Both men laughed and Zeno felt himself color. "What's the maiden's name?"

"No name, sir."

The men laughed again.

Late on Sunday evening, the particulars of the deal were finalized. Mr. Steiner would go to Switzerland and negotiate to buy the trucks. At the successful conclusion of this deal, Müller would sign the contracts for the initial construction of a thousand trucks at the factory in Budapest. If all proceeded as planned, the Steiners would be offered more contracts with similar schedules of remuneration.

Zeno knew what this deal meant to the family's fortunes, but more important, it was a testament to Sándor Steiner's ability. With this he'd change the family's notion of him as a lothario.

Zeno made to clear the desk of their papers.

"Leave them," Mr. Steiner said. "I'll have Bohm tidy them up."

As if anticipated, Bohm brought cognac into the room. While he poured the cognac, Mr. Steiner took Zeno by the arm and led him away from the group.

"You've worked very hard. Thank you for your help. We'll leave in the morning—now go and see something of this great metropolis."

Outside the office building, Zeno suddenly felt tired. The last few days had exacted a toll. As for seeing some of the great metropolis, he didn't know where to start. Despite the fact that it was Sunday night, people in couples and pairs hurried past him. They all had places to go. The air was cold.

He started to walk towards the hotel. He didn't really want to see Berlin. He only wanted to see Catherine. Would she still be at the small apartment, practicing her scales? He looked up at the moon. If she looked at it now, would they feel one another?

By now he'd walked to the vast expanse of Pariser Platz. The Brandenburg Gate straddled the Unter den Linden like a colossus. If he had his camera... But it was too dark. How many arc lights of what massive strength would it take to illuminate the gate for filming? He stood and looked, examining the balance and intricacy of the design, swept again with melancholy for Catherine. He made his way back to the hotel to sleep.

Zeno rose at his usual hour of six and packed his few possessions. He looked onto the street but it was still too dark to film. He walked into Mr. Steiner's suite, tidied his brief case and coat, strewn over the sofa. The bedroom door was shut. He hesitated to open it, but they had a train to catch and it was now already after 7:00.

He pushed open the door. The room was close. The electric light from the lounge spilled into the bedroom. There were clothes all over the floor. There were two people in the bed, one spooned in behind the other. It was inevitable Mr. Steiner would bring a woman home to celebrate his win. As he turned to leave the room he glimpsed a crop of close-cut blond hair—Herr Bohm's. He was spooned in behind Mr. Steiner. Zeno gasped. Bohm opened his eyes.

"*Scheiße!*"

Zeno simply stepped back. Mr. Steiner woke, saw Zeno, and turned to see that Bohm was still in the bed. Bohm pulled back the covers and rose. He was naked. His erect cock slapped against his stomach as he made his way to the bathroom, grabbing up clothes on the way. Mr. Steiner was now sitting up in the bed, his chest naked, his expression sleepy yet faintly troubled.

"Wait in your room," he said.

Zeno walked back through the lounge to his room, closing the door behind him and leaning back against it. Mr. Steiner was married and had a thousand and one mistresses. How could this be? Why would he do this? Zeno's legs gave way and he sank slowly down to sit on the floor. He'd never thought about this, not really, never known anyone who.... What was he to do? Did Catherine know? Did anyone?

There was a light knock at the door. He jumped to his feet and opened it.

Mr. Steiner had on a robe. "I'll go to Switzerland to complete the transactions on my own. You'll return to Budapest. The hotel in Arbon will have adequate staff."

Zeno felt he should offer to accompany him. But beyond any sense of duty, he wanted to return to Budapest.

"Zeno, I know I can trust you to be discreet with everything that's happened here. At times, men like… this." He stopped, searched Zeno's face for a reaction. "Why would one only eat figs when there are meats?"

Zeno made sure his expression was neutral. Mr. Steiner sighed.

"When you return," Mr. Steiner said, "tell people I'm at Lake Balaton. Don't mention I've gone to Switzerland. Best kept amongst ourselves. And of course you know not to mention the purpose of the trip."

"Yes, sir."

"I'll only be two or three days."

Zeno nodded. Mr. Steiner went to his briefcase and handed Zeno his travel documents-- and 100 pengő.

"You don't need to pay me to say nothing, sir.'

"I'm not. I'm saying thank you for your efforts here."

Without meeting Mr. Steiner's eye, Zeno nodded and turned to leave the room.

"Zeno." He turned back to Mr. Steiner. "I don't look at you that way. You're staff. That's our relationship. Nothing need change."

CHAPTER THIRTEEN

As Zeno alighted from the train, he felt the air of Berlin in Budapest. Budapest was cold, colder than he remembered it just a few days ago. While he'd liked Berlin, the little he'd seen, the people seemed burdened and inhibited. There was some similarity to Hungarians but something huge was missing, a zest for life. Perhaps the war had worn them out and like the German army the German people had no way to carry their increasing load.

He was glad to be away from Mr. Steiner. With no amount of reflection could he understand what he'd seen, even though Mr. Steiner claimed men often did such things. He was married to one of the most beautiful women in Budapest and it wasn't enough. Why did he always want something more, something different? But as the train had crossed the border to Hungary, Zeno realized the most obvious thing in the world: life was, always had been, and always would be, entirely different for Mr. Steiner. In every respect they were different, so why not in this? Zeno smiled. He wouldn't think of this like a peasant. It was part of the infinite variety he was discovering. Not that he wanted to have sex with Herr Bohm, but he envied Mr. Steiner his freedom. He admired his frankness. Mr. Steiner was naughty and life was never dull with him. Zeno liked that.

The late-evening streetcar rattled and jarred to the Buda side of the Danube. No one in the building knew he was returning, and had he not been so starved for a glimpse of Catherine he might have stopped for a day or two along the way, as Mr. Steiner had suggested.

In the late evening when he entered the servants' antechamber, the ever-present rattle of crockery and utensils came from the kitchen, but not a voice could be heard. Perhaps it would be quiet for a few days. He heard quick footsteps from the east hall.

"Hey," Hans said. "You're back."

"Yes."

"Where have you been?"

"Mr. Steiner is visiting Lake Balaton. He's staying a few more days."

"What's he doing?"

Zeno thought for a few seconds. "I don't think I need to say."

Hans rolled his eyes. "It's good you're back, there's a lot to be done. People are arriving for Christmas."

"Christmas!"

"It's only ten days away. You won't know what's hit you, there's so much to do."

Disappointment spread over Zeno's face.

"No rest," Hans said and smiled.

He burned to see Catherine. Should he go to her apartment on some pretext? He could take a message or a gift from Mr. Steiner. No, too flimsy. She'd be upset if he showed up. But not if she was on her own.

"Is Gertrúd around?" he asked.

"Catherine's gone to stay in the country, so Gertrúd's with her, I think. They won't be back till just before Christmas. I've got to run, talk to you tomorrow."

Hans dashed off down the southern hall. Zeno tilted his head back towards the ceiling and breathed deeply. Catherine was away. *Unfair, unfair.* If only he'd been able to tell her where he was and when he'd be back. If only he'd known where she was, he might even have been able to go to her, or--what was he thinking? Gertrúd would be there. Damn her. Damn this situation. Damn all this silence and stealth and lies!

As he climbed to his room, he wondered if her absence was in some way linked to his. The last time they saw each other, she hadn't mentioned the trip. But their communication was always erratic, stretched across a week, so much information crammed into a few hours, no accommodation of change or spontaneity. He hadn't told her, either, hadn't known about the trip the last time he saw her. So why should he expect her to have known? The chill of the air of his room took his breath away.

Hans had made no understatement. In the few days he'd been away, guests, relatives, and friends of all the branches of the family had descended on the house. There was much to be prepared, bags to be transported, clothes to be unpacked. A huge tree, God knows where it came from, was brought into the main hall, so tall it passed up to the ceiling of the mezzanine floor. Tall ladders helped the staff dress it with candles. Zeno had never seen anything like it. The perfume of spruce reached every crevice of the house. All day, Christmas music, *Mennyből az angyal* and *Csendes éj*, rang out from a gramophone player. Each evening, roving bands of choristers sang carols on the street.

When not helping with the festivities, Zeno retreated to the silence of Mr. Steiner's apartment. There was work to do there, clothes and shoes that needed attention, repairs that needed to be ordered. One evening he took his projector to Mr. Steiner's apartment and set it up to project on a large blank off-white wall in the lounge room. He looked at the film he'd taken of Catherine, the first time he'd seen her. She seemed... preoccupied, concerned. Her face was set hard, an expression he'd never actually seen again. Perhaps he'd soothed whatever fed it away? It occurred to him he'd never asked her why she ran through the forest that day.

The film shot when he went back to the forest offered alternate points of view of the same event. He'd done a good job. The light was similar to the first day. You couldn't really tell the two sets of film apart. He made a list of the scenes from the various pieces of film, then cut the paper list into individual sections, laid them on the table, and tried to fit the pieces together to tell a story.

He played the film in his mind. Catherine came into the forest. The camera point of view changed to show what she saw, searching the empty woods. But there were limits to his imagination and he lost the thread. The only thing to do was cut the raw film into the sections he wanted and splice them back together. In such a fury, the scenes were severed and joined.

"Opening night," he said out loud when he'd finished.

The pieces came together, the sum of the parts much greater as a whole. There was a story, small and fleeting. A woman ran into a forest, looked around her and decided to run to the bluff to throw herself into the lake. But with the changes of scene and angle, the film suggested she was being observed. Just as she'd been, just as he'd wanted.

Zeno liked the feeling of action. As she ran, the scene switched to her point of view, the camera jostling and jerking to reveal her frenetic pace. But there was something wrong with the scene of her throwing herself in the lake. To suggest this, he'd used a shot looking down the face of the bluff towards the water. All the energy of her running dissipated to a still shot. At the point where the film needed to be most energetic, it was static. He looked over this section again and again. He wanted to make the viewers to feel that they were spiraling towards the water with the woman.

But how? How?

Maybe next time he was at the lake, he could film something else. But he'd no idea when he'd go back there. Or what he could film that would—

He stepped directly in front of the screen and pointed his camera. What if he reshot the existing film with the camera but at the same time moved the camera towards the screen? This movement would create the sensation of getting closer and closer to the water. If he also rotated the camera, that might create the sensation of twisting and turning. He knew it would look very different, but if he could overlook its strangeness--and the technique worked—the effect would be marvelous.

As quickly as he could, he set up the shot. He repeated it a few times, then ran out of fresh film. It would take days for the film to be developed.

Just as he'd finished, Mr. Steiner walked into the apartment with his father. He'd returned to Budapest without any warning. Zeno froze.

"I don't want to talk about this!" He sounded as angry as Zeno had ever heard him.

When the two of them walked into the lounge room, with cut-up bits of film and machinery all over the place, they stopped.

"What's all this?" Mr. Steiner said.

"I'm sorry, sir." Zeno looked at the mess. "I was using the wall to project a film."

"I see."

Karl Steiner was already at the door. He turned to his son just before he slipped out of the apartment.

"We'll speak of this further."

Mr. Steiner looked at the door, as if expecting his father to return any moment.

"How was your time in Switzerland?" Zeno said.

"It went well. But you must always travel with me. The staff in Arbon were fucking deplorable."

Zeno retreated to arrange his things.

"Will you leave that till the morning?" Mr. Steiner said. "You can go for the evening."

Zeno picked up the newly spiced reel of film and placed it in a case. He looked at the litter of frames of film about the table and the floor. He felt a wave of panic. They were frames of Catherine. His eyes bulged as he looked over the floor, on the chairs, over the table. As calmly as he could, he started to brush them to a pile.

"I said to leave all that till the morning. I want to be alone."

Zeno looked at the thousand discarded images of Catherine. What could he do?

"Very well, sir."

He picked up the tin containing the edited reel of film. At least that wouldn't be there. He left the apartment and ran to his room, closed the door and leaned against it, breathless. There was a good chance Mr. Steiner wouldn't look at the photos. He was tired and irritable and had argued with his father. Most likely he'd soon just go to bed. And if he did look? The images were small, he might not even see that it was Catherine. But if he recognized Catherine, how could he explain it? Mr. Steiner might accept that he thought her beautiful and thus film worthy, but Zeno had been watching and editing the film in his apartment. No, he'd lose his job. He'd have to leave Budapest. He wouldn't be able to see Catherine.

After a restless night, Zeno went back to the apartment as early as he could. Mr. Steiner wouldn't rise early. He could have the film cleared away before he was out of bed. But when he entered the apartment at 6.30, Mr. Steiner was already dressed and had cleared an end of the table and was sitting with a cup of coffee and a newspaper.

"Good morning, Zeno."

His voice was buoyant and cheery. He looked up from the newspaper. Zeno's eyes skirted around the room. The projector was still positioned where he'd left it. There were still pieces of film littering the floor, some still on the table.

"Good morning, sir."

"Don't look so surprised. I've an early meeting at the factory."

This was odd.

"Will you have my car brought round?"

Zeno was caught. He wanted to sweep away the remaining images but feared to draw any attention to them. He'd simply do as he was told. Mr. Steiner would soon be at his meeting. It was best to leave them. Later he'd sweep them into a tin.

In the coming days, Mr. Steiner said nothing of his time in Switzerland. Although Zeno kept his ear to the ground, there was no mention of German trucks, no evidence of a delivery, no mention of a new commission for the factory, but Mr. Steiner now commenced work at seven every morning. And nothing was said of the film. He hadn't looked at the images. He didn't care about Zeno's film. Why should he?

On the Sunday, Zeno wandered the streets looking at the Christmas displays in all the shop windows. Never had he seen so much on offer, the windows filled with brightly colored sweets and coats and toys. He brought his mother chocolate-colored leather gloves, just like Catherine's.

As the twenty-fifth approached, the city streets filled with settled snow and the house with guests and gifts. Confusion and business reigned in the lower rooms of the house as trunks were unloaded from cars and carted through the house to rooms that hadn't been used all year. The food that came out of the kitchen was enough to feed an army.

Despite all the opulence, Zeno perceived nowhere near the joy there was in his mother's house, where they had umpteen times less. He wished he were home.

On Christmas Eve before the feast was served, as he rushed through the servants' antechamber, Gertrúd walked out of the eastern corridor. She smiled at him.

"*Mon cher*," she said. "How are you?"

"You're back."

She kissed him on the cheek. He felt her breath on his ear. "This morning. How have you been?"

"The house has been busy."

She stared into his eyes. She rocked her hips back and forth slightly. He returned her gaze, tempted to ask her of Catherine. While their eyes remained so linked, he weighed what he could possibly say, how benign and yet exact he could make such a request. He couldn't. There was nothing he could ask and with all his might he suppressed any urge.

"After Christmas," he said. "Perhaps I can film you?"

Something flickered in her eyes, perhaps resignation?

"Perhaps," she said. "*Joyeux Noël.*"

"I don't know what that means."

"Merry Christmas."

She smiled and continued to the western corridor.

Catherine had finally returned. What mixed emotions it brought, an exhilaration that had to be tempered down and down to no discernable degree.

At six o'clock on Christmas Eve the servants amassed in the hall for the family to wish them their season's greetings.

"Why do they do this?" he asked Hans.

"Makes them feel better."

Upstairs, the smaller children ran through the house, wild and untethered, their footsteps tumbling and running. The family moved along the line, thanking each servant by name.

Despite all the generosity and gifts, the proceedings were obviously perfunctory.

Catherine was with Mr. Steiner. Zeno hadn't seen her for nearly three weeks and now he couldn't look at her. She smiled at the servants. Zeno watched her.

"Zeno."

Mr. Steiner was standing in front of him.

"Sir, Merry Christmas."

"Merry Christmas to you." Mr. Steiner held out his hand. The intimacy of the gesture took Zeno by surprise but he slipped his hand into Mr. Steiner's. Catherine stood by them. Zeno couldn't take his eyes from Mr. Steiner. She stood back slightly and remained distracted and cool. Mr. Steiner made no attempt to introduce her. Then, perhaps to alleviate their tension, Catherine walked a few paces to Gertrúd, who stood away from Zeno. Mr. Steiner presented Zeno with a gift, a small rectangular box.

"Thank you," Zeno said. "It's very kind of you."

"Not at all," Mr. Steiner said. "I didn't realize you were so interested in film."

Zeno seized. He fought to keep his expression open.

"I…"

"I'm sorry," Mr. Steiner said. "I looked at pieces of film on the table. It looked like you had shot the film at Lake Balaton."

"Yes, sir." His voiced croaked.

"It's such a beautiful forest. And a beautiful woman…"

"Sányi," a voice called from across the room. "I've not seen you since you got back."

The matriarch Ella moved towards them. She kissed her son's cheeks and whispered something in his ear that Zeno didn't catch. He laughed. Zeno felt he was being toyed with.

Was he? Mr. Steiner whispered something into his mother's ear and she moved away. Catherine came back from Gertrúd to join them. Mr. Steiner turned back to Zeno.

"I was correct when I chose you," he said.

"Thank you, sir."

"You've more than proven your loyalty." Mr. Steiner smiled at his own keen vision--or was he alluding to their shared secrets? "I don't expect you to be here this evening," he said. "It's Christmas evening. You've been in Budapest now for what, three months? You must have friends. Please, go and visit them."

Zeno kept his eyes fixed on Mr. Steiner's, unsure if Catherine was aware of what he'd said.

"If there's nothing else you require?" Zeno said.

"What else could there be?" He beamed. "You're always five steps in front of me."

"It will be wonderful to have the evening free." Although still unable to look at her, he felt Catherine's attention change. He paused a second to punctuate the importance of what he'd say next. "I'll go visit my friend."

"I hope the gift assists your hobby," he said.

As Mr. Steiner and Catherine moved forward, for the smallest fraction of a second, his eyes met Catherine's, luminescent and violet. In such an instant, how does one express a command? *Meet me!*

"Father István will offer communion," Karl Steiner announced. "Upstairs in the main drawing room. Everybody is welcome to join us."

Once the family entourage had cleared the lower levels of the building, the voices of the mass of servants erupted, comparing gifts, filled for the moment with no work and the joy of Christmas. Zeno left the antechamber without speaking to anyone and raced to Mr. Steiner's apartment. He opened the rectangular box. It was a Bolex light meter, a professional device that could be set to different shutter speeds. It was complex. It was expensive. He felt humbled.

He placed the meter back in its box and left it in his small office. Despite what Mr. Steiner had said, there were things to be readied, things he'd probably not notice until they weren't done. Once his bed was turned down and the lights organized, from the apartment's small pantry he took an unopened bottle of cognac and two whiskey glasses that would just have to serve as balloons. He walked as quickly as he could to his room to change from his work clothes but when he opened the door there was a note pushed under the door.

> *I too have the evening free. It would be nice to talk some more. We've not seen one another for a while. I'm ready for my close up.*
> *Gertrúd*

Gertrúd still wanted him. Despite all his tepid emotion, her hope still burned. He was a fool. He'd compounded it all by asking to film her. He'd have to be more remote, let this infatuation burn out for lack of air. Catherine had given Gertrúd the night free. This meant Catherine understood what had happened. She'd go to the apartment.

As he ran through the streets, fresh snow drifted down in the air. He laughed out loud and jumped and clicked his heels together. As the bookshop was closed, he walked to a side street and the front of the building to wait for Catherine. There was a kind of warm after the snow had come, especially this evening. He hummed a tune to himself. It was so very quiet. No one walked through the square. Perhaps she'd not been able to get away. Surely the dinner wouldn't drag on? Everyone seemed to want to be away from it. As his toes grew crisp, he stamped his feet to keep them warm, the snow so thick no footfall made a sound.

She appeared in the small square, a heavy sable thrown over her evening dress. She came to where he stood under a street light and kissed him deeply. Her mouth, so longed for, felt unfamiliar, all new again, something to be rediscovered.

"What a gift," she said.

"It's Christmas."

She held up a key.

"What's that?"

"It's a key to the apartment." She smiled. "So you don't have to wait in the snow anymore."

He took the key from her hand and kissed it, then her.

"Come," she said.

For the first time, they walked through the main door of the building and climbed the stairs together. Outside the apartment door she turned to him, her lips fluttering over his face. He opened the door with his freshly minted key. He surprised her, scooped her up and carried her into the apartment, then kicked the door shut. Onto the floor they tumbled, so desperate their shared need.

"My darling," she whispered.

The sable acted as a mattress. She pulled him into her.

Later, they lay on the floor facing each other. He'd placed both his hands under his cheek to form a pillow. She stroked the curve of his buttock, her palm cupping the roundness.

"They're perfect," she said.

"What?"

"Your buttocks. Michelangelo couldn't have shaped them better."

Blood surged to his head. "Who's he?"

"What?" She laughed at him. "One day you'll know."

She moved the same hand the entire length of his body, cupped her palm around his deltoid, ran it down to the bicep and them gently pushed him onto his back. She straddled him, her buttocks resting on his knees, and ran her open hands down his body, over his chest, on either side of his stomach muscles which in the last few months had lost all trace of baby fat, now rigid and defined. She placed her hands on both sides of his waist.

"A waist defined, so compact, so contained." The violet of her eyes flashed. "The teardrops." With the forefingers of each hand, she traced the pronounced muscles that sat on the obliques of his hip bones, the shape of two tears.

"They're from swimming," he said. "They're drops of water."

"But I don't have them."

She took his penis in her hand, pulled it up off his belly.

"This as it was, as it should be." She pulled back the hood. He smarted from the tenderness of the exposed glans. "But aroused it disappears." She let go of it, smiled at the slap as it hit against his belly.

"It's a mirror of your body," she said. "The shaft echoes the girth and strength of your body." She leaned forward, her hair falling over her head, lightly touching his stomach. "This is your stomach muscle." She ran her tongue from the base of his penis along the mound formed by the urethra, at the same time moving her hands, lightly and in time, touching each side of the knotted muscle of his stomach. He felt as if he was being tickled but felt no urge to resist or have her stop.

"This ridge is the line under your chest."

As the tip of her tongue ran along the edge, she moved the tips of her fingers below the plates of his chest, moving slowly, meeting at the sternum, her tongue flickering over the folds of membrane, her thumbs touching the tendons of the neck.

"And this triangle is your shoulders and head."

She ran her tongue over the outside of the glans, her hands moving from his shoulders towards his head, meeting at his mouth.

"This is what you fuck with."

The heat of her breath caused a new level of sensation. What else was there he could fuck with? For a moment he thought she knew of Mr. Steiner and the men he lay with. But he dismissed the thought, reached up and touched her shoulders. She forced his lips apart, put her forefingers into his mouth. He sucked on them. As he sucked he felt a kind of power come into him and then a massive shudder throughout his body, his tongue tingling, his flanks seared. He felt himself explode.

Later, as they still lay on the floor, he remembered the bottle of cognac.

"Look what I have." He pulled the bottle and glasses from the bag.

"How lovely."

He looked at the bottle. "I took it from Mr. Steiner. I'll buy another one to replace it."

"Don't. He won't ever notice."

"I don't want to be a thief."

He placed the two glasses on the floor and opened the bottle.

"Just pour one glass," she said.

"Why? I brought two."

"Here, we have only one of anything."

He smiled, filling one glass with the cognac. He handed it to her and lay down.

"Merry Christmas," he said. She raised the small glass and drank the entire contents.

"You're meant to warm it in your hand."

"It's meant to warm me."

"But I'm here for that."

She handed him the glass. He licked the remains and they slid down on the coat. He wound a lazy strand of her hair around his finger, her head pillowed on his breast.

"What do your family do for Christmas?" she said.

He looked sideways at her. She was staring at the ceiling. He shrugged his shoulders.

"Just the usual things."

"The usual things." She began to laugh. "What's your mother like?"

He thought for a moment. "What do you mean?"

She rolled over and faced him, her chin resting on his chest.

"Is she pretty?"

"I guess so."

"You're not going to tell me much, are you?" She waited for a response but he didn't offer one. "Of course she's pretty. She must be. How old is she?"

"She's ancient."

"Ancient?"

"She's thirty-seven." Catherine's smile faded and she looked away and then rolled onto her back. He realized the gravity of what he'd said. "Not that old."

"You just said it was ancient."

"How old are you?" He had no idea how old she was. It had never seemed important. She stood up and dragged the sable with her, leaving him naked on the floor. She wrapped herself and walked over to the kitchenette window and looked out at the sky.

"I'm thirty nine," she said. "Older than your mother."

He walked over and stood behind her without touching her.

"It's okay," she said and turned to him. "How about your father?"

"I don't know. I think he was a bit older than her."

"You've no contact with him?"

"No…"

"How old were you when he left?"

He felt cold. He walked back to the clothes on the floor and pulled on the various layers. She hadn't realized he was no longer behind her and turned to him.

"He didn't leave us." His mouth had run dry and he sucked for spit. "He died."

Her face clouded. "How?"

"He was a farmer. There was an accident with a tractor."

"How old was he?"

"It was just after my sister was born. That's… eight years ago. He was only twenty-nine."

Her eyes were moist, the violet color glistening. She came to him and rubbed her hand in a circle on his back.

"Why didn't you tell me this?"

"I don't usually tell people. I always say he left. People usually accept that and don't make a fuss about it."

"I see."

And he hoped she did see, see that he had no desire to talk about this. Then she took his hand and led him to the other room. With his spare hand he caught up the cognac and the glass. In one fluid motion she dropped the sable to the floor, pulled back the covers, and slipped into bed. Without stripping his clothes he joined her.

"Loss," she said. "It's such a thing to bear."

"I suppose. I don't remember not feeling this."

"It's been so awful not to see you," she said. "Why didn't you come that Sunday?"

"Mr. Steiner took me with him."

"Where did you go?"

"Don't you know?" She was silent. "To Berlin. Some business deal."

"So, Sándor has decided to deal with the Germans."

Now he was quiet. "Where did you go?"

"To Gödöllő."

"That's so close to Budapest."

"I had to be on my own."

"Wasn't Gertrúd with you?"

"No. I had a lot of time to think."

"What about?"

She rolled away from him. "I think I'm in love. For the first time."

The words left him confused only for a moment. They were words he'd not thought, but now the sensation was named it was visible. This, amidst all complexity, was love.

She was smiling at him.

"You're meant to say it too, you know?"

"I just hadn't thought…"

He felt himself flush. Love had only ever been a constant thing, the love of his mother, his sister, not something new, something that grew. What did it mean to fall in love? Was this urgency he felt for Catherine, this comfort in her arms, this excitement, was that it?

"Perhaps you're right," he said.

Her expression darkened. "I know my own mind."

Now it was his turn to smile at her. "Even though I've tasted sweet things a thousand times, how could I ever know the word *sweetness* until someone told me?"

A light came to her face.

"I do love you," he said. She rolled back into him, her chin tucked over his shoulder. "Yes. I guess that's what I feel. But you must have loved Mr. Steiner."

"I don't think I've ever loved Sándor."

"Why do you stay with him?"

It took her a long time to answer. She pulled away and rose on her elbow and poured another cognac, but this time sipped it.

"I thought that was obvious." She paused. "I'm married. I've no other place to go."

"But your family, in France?"

"Paris is occupied by Germany, is it not? I can't go back."

"How did you meet Mr. Steiner?"

She looked at him. "Don't tell me you haven't heard the staff gossip?"

He thought about the things said in the lower rooms of the house.

"No. Well, nothing to do with this."

"Perhaps it's old news." She rested a moment. "I was sent to marry him."

"Sent?"

"It was an arranged marriage, between his family and mine."

Zeno stared at her. "Why would you agree to that?"

"I'm afraid the life of a woman is very different to a man. I had no choice. The dowry my father received made it worth his while."

"But Mr. Steiner is…" He was going to say that Mr. Steiner was a good-looking rich man, in no need of an arrangement, but he stopped himself. "Why would he want that?"

"I don't think he did. There'd been a scandal of some sort. I think he'd wanted to marry a dancer, someone the family considered unsuitable. The family wanted someone without a past. I was very young. Coming from another country, I could be anything they wanted me to be."

"What do you mean?"

"My father is a lowly merchant. They told everyone he was a wealthy manufacturer with ties back to French aristocracy. The story sat well with the Budapest elite."

"But your father?"

"He had five daughters, only one son. It was after the Great War. I don't blame him."

"How can a marriage like that work?"

"Just like this." She sighed. "You're too young to understand."

"Don't patronize me."

"I'm sorry." She kissed him. "The more money people have the less likely they'll marry for love. I tried to make Sándor happy, and I believe he tried too. We weren't dissimilar. I did what he wanted. I played the piano for him. For a time I think he didn't see the unsuitable person—for a time I don't think he saw anyone. But I failed."

The image of Herr Bohm rushing to the bathroom flashed across Zeno's mind.

"I don't think *you* failed at all."

"I did, rather spectacularly. I bore no children."

"What do you mean?"

"I've never been pregnant. For years, Sándor and I tried. Then for even more years only I tried. Sándor was seeing others. I tried. I tried. But it was not meant to be. *Salut.*" She raised the glass of cognac to him and downed the remains. "The whole of Budapest knows. They tolerate his indiscretions because he can't be blamed. 'His wife is barren. Poor Sándor. How could he have known? It's no wonder he drinks and is such a philanderer.'"

Zeno knew how he would feel if he'd been married off in such a way. Just as she felt—desolate, betrayed, lost.

"That expression on your face," he said.

"What expression?"

"When I first saw you in the forest, I had my camera. I filmed you. Your expression was so tense, cold, trapped. I've never seen it since, until now."

"I wanted to run away. From all those women at the hotel, from Sándor, from even the memory of Sándor, from the whole Steiner family."

"We can run away. We must leave all this."

"What country would you have us flee to? Everything around us is torn apart."

"America."

"You're dreaming! What would we do for money? I don't want to shatter such a beautiful fantasy but we're both dependent on the Steiner family. I've no reserve, no income, and you've only just begun to work. You've no references. I've no skill. This is it." She waved her hands in little circles in the air. "These walls of this apartment are our dominion. You can rail against it as much as you want, but we're incarcerated."

"But what about after the war?"

"Zeno, if there's one thing I've learned as I've grown older, we must live only today. Forget the past and the future. This is all we have. I love you. Tomorrow everything could be different. We must act only for today."

CHAPTER FOURTEEN

The news arrived on Tuesday, caught between Christmas and the New Year. Zeno was passing through the servants' antechamber and the maid, Ottó's sweetheart, began to howl. The other women dragged her off to a room and closed the door.

"What the hell's happened?" Zeno said.

"Ottó Técsy's been killed."

For some moments he felt light, like he'd been lying on a canvas with six or seven men tossing him high into the air. How could Ottó be dead? And then he felt like stone, thousands and thousands and thousands of years' old stone. How could someone like Ottó be dead?

"How?"

"A truck he was traveling in—"

"A truck?"

"One of those transport trucks. It was hit by heavy Russian fire. A surprise attack. Everyone was killed. They didn't get to fire a shot."

The news dragged the whole house down. How could Ottó be dead? This thought remained with Zeno all day. Ottó had been so kind to him, just two months ago. He'd been looking forward to seeing him. The finality of his father's death flared in him. There was no going back. Once this had happened, there really was no going back.

Most of the Christmas house guests decamped, anxious to be home for the New Year. For days the staff picked their way along the lower antechambers, luggage trunks prone against the walls, jutting out into the corridors.

"When is this all going to stop?" he asked Hans.

"Not till they're all gone, I'm afraid. Have you seen those bloody children?"

"Which ones?"

"The Kresz children. Peter's brother's. They'll all miss their train." Hans started off down the cluttered hall as best he could. "And none of us want to see that."

"Try the library. It's one of their favorite hiding places."

"The library, of course."

Hans set off, tripping on the edge of a case.

In those disrupted days, he saw Gertrúd and managed to avoid her, but then she confronted him in his office.

"I heard what you said." She crossed her arms. "Christmas Eve? About visiting a friend?"

"I went for a walk along the Danube."

"I know you're seeing someone else."

"How?"

"See! You don't deny it."

"What?"

"You didn't deny that you're seeing someone."

"I'm not seeing anyone--"

"I've seen you leave the building on Sundays. It's always early. You don't have your precious camera with you half the time. And there's something awfully urgent in the way you walk."

Zeno breathed in deeply, partly to steady himself but mainly to buy time. She had him cornered.

"I just don't feel that way about you. I can't help that. I thought you'd change, go cold."

"I'm not *blancmange*."

"You're right, I'm seeing someone, but before you ask who it is I can't tell you. I'm sorry about what happened between us."

"How long has it been going on?"

"Quite a while."

"So, when you slept with me, you were sleeping with someone else?"

He rolled his eyes, having fallen into a carefully spun trap. "Yes."

"Odd that only women should be seen as whores--"

"I'm sorry. It shouldn't have happened."

"But it did." She moved away. "Cat's out of the bag." She thought for a moment, chewing her bottom lip. "It doesn't matter, anyway. I'm seeing someone."

"Good." He feared it was Tibi. "Who?"

"I'm not telling you either." She started to walk out. "And you can shove your camera."

On Friday night, to ring in the New Year, the staff organized a small celebration in the downstairs antechambers, but with the news of Ottó's death it was a half-hearted affair. They set up a small bar with bottles they'd purloined from unnamed sources. The Steiners turned a blind eye. From the corner, a radio played swing music. Long paper streamers colored the air and confetti sprinkled the floor and tables and chairs. The staff members came, stayed for a drink or two, and left when called away by their master's or mistress's bell.

Mr. Steiner hadn't given Zeno the night off but he'd gone out, and Zeno was sure he'd not be back till very late if at all. But despite a quantity of wine and whiskey, he felt anxious. He looked around for Gertrúd but she hadn't come down. Catherine hadn't given her the night off, which meant Catherine was in the building. So close. Could he make contact with her?

"Gertrúd's gone out with someone for the evening," Hans said.

"Why do you say that?" Zeno said.

"You were looking out for her."

"No."

"You like her, don't you?"

"No."

"She likes you."

If only she didn't. "She's seeing someone else."

"Then what's bothering you?"

"Nothing."

"Don't tell me that. You're so tense."

"It's nothing, really, just a few things on my mind."

"It's sad about Ottó."

"Yes." Zeno felt his throat catch and he turned away. "Very sad."

The frivolity of the party seemed forced and contrived. As he walked towards the makeshift bar, he plunged his hand into his pocket and felt the small apartment's key. Someone blew a whistle close to his ear. He heard Gazsi laughing. Without saying goodnight to anyone he left the party and ran through the streets, crowded with revelers, to the square onto which Catherine's small apartment faced. He walked straight through the main doors and climbed the stairs, two at a time, taking great pains to cushion the sound of his soles. He stood before the apartment's door. He breathed deeply and inserted the key. He heard the door to the other apartment on the landing close with great care. He'd been observed. The whiskey had a profound effect on him. He slammed the apartment's door behind him.

"Catherine?" he said.

He gazed into the dark, the air chilled. He made his way towards the bedroom. Calmly, tentatively, he reached out and touched the bed, his hand advancing, wanting to perceive but at a distance, employing some other kind of touch. The covers held no warmth. He collapsed onto the bed. On his elbows he pulled himself up, rolled his face into the single soft pillow, her pillow, their pillow, and inhaled the fragrance of their love, their most intimate trails entwined. Without volition, a cry, a mourning, escaped from him. He'd been wrong. She simply wasn't there. He'd have to wait.

The apartment's chill seeped in. He wouldn't go home tonight.

"Fuck Sándor Steiner. Fuck all of them."

He took off all his clothes, left them in a heap on the floor, and slipped in between the bitter covers. Even after an hour his cold feet wouldn't let him dream of Sunday. Echoing through the streets of the city, the rolling cheers for New Year 1944 resounded. He dressed again and walked back to the Steiner's building. There was no one left in the antechamber, and the torn streamers hung limply from the ceiling.

On Sunday morning, when he returned to the apartment, she wasn't there. He passed the whole day pacing the few square metres of floor. Reading a book. Playing chopsticks on the piano. When she still hadn't shown up by five in the evening, he left. Had something happened? When he returned to the house he asked and asked, but no one thought Catherine and Gertrud were away.

The week dragged without a glimpse of either of them. But when he entered the square early the next Sunday morning, a light burned in the apartment's window.

"Catherine?" he said before he'd even closed the door.

"I'm here, my love."

She smiled broadly when he entered the room, standing rather formally by the piano. She held out her arms to him. Their embrace, so firm, took him by surprise.

"Where were you last Sunday?" he said. She pulled away and looked at him. "I nearly lost my mind."

"I came," she said, "but it was very late. You'd left. Come. Sit. We must talk."

"I don't want to sit down."

"Please."

Her brows had knitted together.

"What's happened?"

"Don't look so scared."

She took his hand, led him to the armchair. The minute he sat down, she began pacing the room.

"The reason I couldn't come last Sunday? There was a meeting--just the family, while the servants weren't in the house."

"What's happened?"

"There's talk the war may end soon."

"The Russians are pushing the Germans back," he said.

"You mustn't repeat what I tell you." She glared at him. "The Hungarian government is holding secret talks with America and Britain."

"What would they talk to them about?"

"There are grave concerns the Allies will bomb Budapest. The government wants to stop this, at all costs."

"Bomb Budapest?" Zeno said. "Why?"

"We supply the German army."

"But Mr. Steiner has--"

"I know, he has courted contracts to manufacture trucks. Nothing has been signed. Peter and his father are completely against the idea."

"But he bought trucks on their behalf."

She stopped pacing. "*What?*"

He'd betrayed Mr. Steiner. To hell with it. He explained in detail the deal struck in Berlin.

"I didn't know any of that." She sighed.

"These contracts represent something else, don't they?"

"What do you mean?"

"It's not just the business. The Steiners are wealthy, successful. They don't need more business. In Berlin, Mr. Steiner worked with a fever. It's about Mr. Steiner winning."

She sighed. "You're right. Sándor has always been disinterested in the business. Inept. These contracts are a private victory. But Peter and his father are sure the factory will be bombed. They want Hungary to join the Allies. If this happens, there'll be no bombing."

"But Hungary has gained so much from the Germans," he said.

"What's land where there's so much life to lose? The Russian army is close--"

Müller was desperate, so desperate he'd resorted to a bribe. Perhaps Herr Bohm had been instructed to sweeten the deal?

"How can a country change sides?"

"Of course it can happen," she said. "Italy has done as much."

"Germany will be furious."

"But Hungary will be protected." She stopped for a moment. "Or so the story goes."

"From what I've seen of Germany, I don't think they'll take such a slight lying down."

CHAPTER FIFTEEN

Zeno tuned the radio dial, from stations in Berlin to Paris to Vienna to Budapest to London. He caught snippets of music fading in and out-- That was *Sing Sing Sing*. He wound back the dial. Since Mr. Steiner wouldn't be back until late, he turned up the volume and remembered the couples dancing on the Arizona Club's moving floor. He moved his limbs, spun around on his heel, but like so many other pleasurable sensations the dancing wasn't so enjoyable on his own.

How can you dance with yourself?

He collapsed into an armchair. What would Catherine think of such music and the Arizona Club? He doubted she'd like either of them but if he asked her to go, she'd go. And once she was there, she'd enjoy it, perhaps just a little, in her own quiet way.

He reached for a cigarette. Damn. He'd taken to smoking, but keeping an adequate supply was another thing. If he went out now he could buy some and be back before Mr. Steiner was home. Without his coat, he ran through the streets under the clear night sky. The cold air ripped through his uniform to his skin.

A German officer was at the bar's counter, buying cig- arettes, other things, paying for some food or a drink. He wasn't a large man but Zeno hated the way the German army seemed to take up so much space. The officer's Hungarian was bad but he doggedly persisted with text-book cordiality to pick out another item for purchase. Zeno looked back at the door. Perhaps he could go to another bar?

Finally the officer clicked his heels and turned to leave. The owner looked at the wad of money in his hand.

"You've given me too much," the owner said.

"Oh… *Dummkopf!* How much?"

The owner counted the money, looked again at his till, took what was due, and gave the remainder back.

"You're honest," the officer said. "Thank you."

"Of course."

Back in Mr. Steiner's apartment, Zeno lit a cigarette and dragged the smoke deep into his lungs. He turned the radio on again and swung through the dial, but there was no swing music. It was the BBC news, transmitting all the way from London in Hungarian. Mr. Steiner often listened. Its content varied widely from the local news but often, in the long run, its assessment of events proved to be more accurate.

The growing tension between the Hungarian Government and the Nazis the BBC reported hadn't been evident to Zeno that evening. It was suggested that Hungary had formally asked Germany to withdraw Hungarian troops from the Russian front to prepare to defend its own territory, especially Budapest, from the advancing Russian army.

Too late for Ottó.

Zeno dragged on his cigarette and shrugged his shoulders. Who knew what the truth was? The radio made no mention of Hungary meeting with the Allies. But Germany's position was changing, that was evident.

The following Sunday, he told Catherine what he'd heard.

"The meetings were a secret," she said.

"I haven't told anyone."

She glared at him. "I'd hope not. But if they're a secret, the BBC isn't going to report it."

"I just want the war to be over. I barely remember a time when it didn't hang over everything."

"You just want it over. Who do you want to win?"

"I..." He'd never really thought of anyone in the war except Germany. "Do you think the Allies will win?"

"It could only be better than Germany."

"Why do you say that?"

"The Germans have created havoc, in France, in Poland, even in Germany."

He felt himself prickle. When he'd been in Berlin, people on the street seemed no more intent on war than people in Budapest.

"It's a war, Catherine. Both sides create havoc."

"Don't you see, at the very least, Germany wants to reduce any opposition to rubble?" She looked away. "One day you may understand."

He banged his palm on the table. "Why do you do that?"

The flop of hair fell over his forehead. She glared at him.

"You can't go on dismissing me like that," he said.

"Then open your eyes and see what's going on."

He turned away from her, towards the window. He felt like he was being banged about the head.

"If my age bothers you so much, maybe we shouldn't have started this."

He walked towards the door.

"Don't go."

He stopped walking and slowly turned back towards her.

"I remember that sting," she said.

"What sting?"

"My father... he always dismissed me, saying I was too young to understand."

"If you know how it hurts, why do it to me?"

She glared at him for a moment. "Don't be cruel."

"*I'm* cruel?" He stopped himself.

"I'm sorry. I'll never say anything like that again."

He was unsure what to do. He thought he should kiss her but felt no desire.

"I'm going to go."

"It's still early. Don't leave when you're upset."

"It's okay." He felt his anger and didn't want to share it. "I want to walk back over the Margrit Bridge."

"That's a long way."

Her petulance had marred the afternoon. But their time together was always brief and precious.

"Why don't you come with me?"

"Don't be a fool."

He felt his anger sear again but tried to overpower it. "You can walk ahead of me. I want to film the Danube. It's famous and I want to film it."

"No." She shrugged her shoulders. "It's not possible."

The Danube was drab, not a hint of "beautiful blue." He filmed the water coming towards him from either side of Margrit Island, crossed to the other side of the bridge, and filmed the river traveling away. Perhaps the river was blue in Vienna and by the time it reached Budapest faded to sludge. He should tell Catherine this theory—he was certain she'd ridicule it. One day he'd be worldly like her. He would.

Once off the Margrit Bridge, he walked back in to Buda. Up ahead of him, the street was filled with people, but the people weren't walking, not smiling, no sense of happiness. A crowd had gathered to a halt, forming a circle around something or someone. As he got closer he could hear men yelling. At first the words were indistinct but then he heard.

"You're a Jew! How dare you!"

One man repeated this, over and over and over like an imbecile. His voice tore with rage and rang louder than the others. At a distance, Zeno skirted the edge of the group. A man in his fifties, fit and strong and very frightened, stood at the center. Zeno recognized him, the bar owner from whom he'd bought cigarettes the other evening.

"How dare you!"

It was the man with the loud voice again. He stepped into the clearing with the accused, his back to Zeno. As he made his way around the circle, his face came into view.

It was Tibi, backed by four young men.

His face was red from shouting, his jaw held tight.

"Since when can't I kiss a beautiful woman?" the man said. Like a vaudeville performer he raised his open palm to the crowd and drew down the corners of his mouth.

"The laws of 1941," Tibi shouted, "forbid all intimacy between a Jew and a Christian!"

"It was just a kiss."

The man looked again for support.

"I saw your hand under the table." Tibi raised his arm to point to the tables at the café. "You had your filthy Jew hand on her thigh."

The man shrugged his broad shoulders, his face muted but fearful. There was no woman in tears, the co-accused long since departed. In his day, this man would have been a match for any of these younger men. But a mob surrounded him. He continued to look for support. People either stared him down or looked away. Someone pushed his shoulder. Another knocked off his cap.

"Leave him alone!" someone in the crowd yelled.

Tibi spun around.

"Leave him alone? Leave him alone to grope another Hungarian and pollute her chastity?"

"I fought for Hungary in the First World War," the man said. "How can I now be an alien?"

Zeno lifted his camera to his eye and began to film. Tibi punched the older man in the face. He stumbled back but stayed on his feet, his hands clasped to protect his face. Blood poured from his nose. No one in the crowd said a thing, no murmurs, no protest, no offers of protection.

Another of the youths went to strike him in the stomach but he was quicker and his open hands flew from his face into a fist and caught the young man under the chin. This act of revolt enraged the other three and as their friend reeled back, the three began a flurry of punches and kicks, the older man soon bent over, failing, soon felled. Zeno brought down his camera. The youths went to work, kicks to the head, kicks to the stomach, kicks to the kidneys as his body convulsed on the pavement.

"NO!" Zeno yelled, with all the might he could muster.

He moved forward a few paces. The attackers were unaware of him. He suddenly had no idea what he could do. He yelled again. And that was all it took. The mob of people, women and men, old and young, gathered themselves and surged forth to protect their neighbor, their shopkeeper. Men grabbed the youths and pulled them away. The attackers attempted to flee but the mob blocked them.

Zeno lifted his camera and began to film. A few metres from the center of the fray he saw Tibi, his face bloodied, his clothes torn and pulled asunder, running directly towards the lens.

Zeno moved out of his way but as he ran past, Tibi punched the camera. It hit Zeno's face, the edge catching the arch of his right eye as it fell to the footpath and burst open, its roll of film exposed to the dying sun.

Zeno's sight went red. He blinked and blinked and held his hand to the sticky flow. With his free hand he herded together the parts of the camera and held it to his chest and moved as quickly as he could away from the few men who'd started to chase the youths. The band split in separate directions, some heading to the Danube, some to the hills of Buda.

His bits of camera and film still clutched to his chest, Zeno sank to the pavement. So suddenly things had changed. He steadied his breathing. Each time he took his hand from his eye the blood gushed. A few metres away, others helped the attacked man back to his feet, then to a chair someone had brought from the café. The man was covered in blood and full of apologies.

Zeno had never seen someone attacked. In the battles in movies, a crisp crack accompanied knuckles hitting flesh but this had been a dull thud accompanied by the rush of breath forced from the body. He wanted to be away from this. With one hand still clutching the ruined camera and the other to his eye, he left the square and struggled through the streets, blood running down his face.

"What the hell's happened?" Gertrúd said as he walked into the building's antechamber. "There's blood pouring out of your eye. Go sit in the tearoom."

She returned with a damp cloth. He took it from her and held it to his eye.

"What happened?"

Zeno explained the scene he'd confronted in the square, how it ended.

"Tibi pushed the camera into my face. He was the leader."

"Who was the other man?"

"What does it matter? It was disgraceful. Why would Tibi do such a thing?"

"Tibi is high up in the Arrow Cross Party. They have their plan."

He looked up at her with his one good eye. "Then you're seeing him."

Incredulity crept over her face. "You can't possibly be jealous. You're seeing someone else."

"I'm not jealous, I'm confused. Why would Tibi do that?"

Zeno felt tears swell inside him. He scrunched his eyes to stop them and the pain sent him reeling. The emotion lodged in his throat.

"The Tibi I know wouldn't hurt a fly," he said. "Why's he changed?"

"The Jew was obviously sleeping with a Christian," she said. "It's against the law. Why don't you understand that?"

The air about Gertrúd changed from concern to something he didn't quite recognize. Like the mob who'd surrounded the man, she too thought it was just that they'd attacked this man. But unlike the mob, she wasn't swayed in her conviction by the ferocity of the attack. He'd been wrong with Catherine.

War might create havoc on all sides, but this side pitted neighbor against neighbor. This was *Jud Seuss*. This was the creation of fascism. Suddenly he felt he was on trial, as if his response would color all future interactions with Gertrúd and Tibi.

"Of course." He stood up. "I see that. The man was a fool. He deserved it."

"Tibi will be pleased to hear you say that."

"You're serious with him?"

"We plan to marry in the spring."

"How nice."

"Yes."

He pulled the cloth from his head. "The bleeding seems to have stopped." His head ached mercilessly. "I'd better get to bed. I've an early start in the morning."

"We all do."

"Thanks for helping me. No hard feelings about what happened between us."

"No." She straightened the table's chairs, caught his eye and smiled. "It's all worked out for the best. No hard feelings."

On Sunday, Catherine moved about the small apartment tidying and dusting the few possessions while she listened to everything he had to say.

"Now you understand," she said, "why I was so appalled by that film."

"This is where these feelings start."

"We're all scared of people that aren't the same. We huddle together under the banner of… a city, a country, a religion, but we've always been scared of the person over the border."

Zeno took some time to consider what she said. "How do you know all this?"

"What do you mean?"

"You sound like a professor."

She blushed. "I'm no professor. I'm just older than you. Age brings a kind of wisdom with it, I guess."

"Don't say that."

"What? It's true."

"That you're older than me."

She smiled. "That, too, is true."

"But I never feel it. You do."

She considered her response. "For some time I've waited for the feeling to descend on me."

"You do feel it, don't you?"

"Well, occasionally, in some small way, but no."

"Nothing will ever come between us."

As he said this, he thought she'd remind him again of the impossible situation they were in, but she didn't. She smiled at him. Was she humoring him, allowing him this fantasy? Or had she too started to believe that one day they'd escape the constraints that crimped and clipped them?

She sat down at the piano and played, a piece Zeno hadn't heard. As the notes, low and constant, steady and without embellishment, came to him he closed his eyes and imagined there were no war. He'd been twelve when it started. He thought hard but really couldn't remember a time when it hadn't been. He thought of beauty. Of Catherine's touch. What would it be like to be able to flit across all borders, like her music did? Touch whenever they wanted. Would there ever be such a time?

Suddenly, mid-phrase, Catherine stopped playing.

"Next Sunday is your birthday," she said. "Isn't it?"

He nodded.

"We'd better do something about celebrating, don't you think?"

"Celebrating? How can we celebrate?"

"Don't be like that." She stood from the piano. "Why don't you ask Sándor for the Saturday night off and we can spend the whole weekend here."

"But that's not possible."

"We'll not leave," she said with a broad smile. "Not for anything. I shall cook."

"How will you explain your absence from the house?"

She thought for a few seconds. "I'll say I'm traveling to the country on my own for the weekend. I'll catch a train out of Budapest, then return on another. No one will know."

The plan was too simple. But he couldn't think of anything wrong with it.

"Come now," she said. "Don't fail me, now that I've become so daring!"

"It's just... the prospect's too delightful for words."

If he asked for the Saturday free, something he'd never done, there was a better than average chance Mr. Steiner would say yes.

"Even if he doesn't, I could come late on Saturday evening, when I've finished."

"Then it's agreed. Next weekend. All weekend."

As he left the apartment that evening he said, "How will I let you know if he agrees?"

She thought for a moment.

"Leave a vase of irises on the table on the main stair landing. Then I'll know."

CHAPTER SIXTEEN

Twice on the Monday morning, Zeno walked into the main room while Mr. Steiner was having breakfast. He opened his mouth to speak, then panicked and left the room-- easier to savor possibility than swallow reality. But damn it. He needed an answer. He'd just entered the room for a third attempt when Mr. Steiner preempted him.

"I'll be away from Budapest for the following weekend," he said.

"Yes, sir."

Damn. If Mr. Steiner was traveling, he couldn't be spared. He'd made that clear last time. All hope drained from him.

"For how long should I pack, sir?"

"Just for four... maybe five days."

He remained reading his paper.

"I beg your pardon, sir. I need some indication of where you're going."

"Berlin. I believe it's still cold."

"Will it be work or social?"

"Both, this time."

Both. Hadn't there been at least one social event last time? He left the room and returned to his small office. The opportunity to spend the whole weekend with Catherine, his birthday weekend, had slipped through his fingers. Now he'd spend the day on his own in a hotel room or an office in cold Berlin. When would they end all this deception? Why could it not end?

Zeno had to let Catherine know Sunday as well as Saturday was out. Perhaps he'd run into her in the building, but that was a rare event. If only they'd been able to take Gertrúd into their confidence. He decided to go to the small apartment and leave a message. At least she'd get this on Friday or Saturday when she arrived and know exactly what had happened. He dragged himself through the week and the necessary preparations. Early on Thursday evening, he traveled to the factory to collect Mr. Steiner.

He'd never been to the factory before, located along with other manufacturing plants on Csepel Island, a long strip of land in the Danube. The air tasted acrid. At the factory gates, a delicatessen and a bar served the employees. Beyond them he could see the factory's works, entrails of pipes suspended in the air between buildings, wires slung between concrete silos. Thin brick chimneys belched smoke.

Outside a single-story building which housed the executive offices, Zeno waited. He looked at his watch. They'd waited almost half an hour for Mr. Steiner. If he didn't soon emerge, they'd miss the train. He started to worry, mixed with a tinge of hope. But then Mr. Steiner swooped from the building, followed by a colleague. The driver started towards Nyugati Railway Station, slowed by the early evening press of traffic.

"So what's it you need to talk to me about," Mr. Steiner said to his colleague.

"The situation you're dealing with is more complex than you first thought. Hitler has expressed great dissatisfaction with Regent Horthy's suggestion that Hungary withdraw its troops from the Russian Front."

"One can imagine."

"Some have labeled it treason. The German army needs support."

"But this is what we'll provide. Transport. Everything will follow from that."

"You need to be aware that in these negotiations, Hungary is in a tenuous position--and you by association."

"I appreciate your warning but we have what they need."

"They may not negotiate. They may just take it."

"What on earth do you mean?"

"There are rumors Hitler is so incensed with Regent Horthy he may occupy Hungary."

"But Hungary's been compliant."

"They know of the talks with the Allies. The only viable Hungarian troops are on the Russian Front. And those few troops in Budapest are faithful to Germany."

Mr. Steiner sighed heavily. "The prospect is untenable."

"But realistic."

Mr. Steiner thought for some moments. "What's your advice?"

"You need to be cognizant that your position has weakened. Considerably. At the least, I wouldn't drive too hard a bargain."

The driver pulled into the railway station. Crowds of people massed everywhere. Zeno loaded their luggage onto a trolley. They made their way down the crowded platform to the first class carriage. Mr. Steiner looked at the luggage and turned to him.

"Oh dear," he said. "I'm not sure I told you. I'll be traveling alone."

"But sir, you said--"

"You may have the whole weekend free," Mr. Steiner said. "It's your birthday, I believe." He took his wallet and gave Zeno 100 pengő. "You must celebrate."

"Thank you, sir."

He took the money, lifted only Mr. Steiner's cases from the trolley, and took them to his cabin. When he returned to the platform, Mr. Steiner was still in discussion with his colleague, so Zeno nodded his farewell, took his own small bag, and walked back down the platform, smiling like an idiot. No doubt Mr. Steiner was meeting Herr Bohm and was willing to put up with poor hotel service for greater privacy. It didn't matter why. He had the whole weekend!

A young woman walked towards him--Anikó Páva, the one Mr. Steiner had brought to the hotel over the summer. Their eyes met and she smiled at him.

"So, you made it to Budapest."

"I work for Sándor Steiner."

The moment he said it, he felt foolish.

"Wow," she said, rolling her eyes. "I wonder how that happened?"

"Did you say something?"

"Of course I did."

There was no sign of a blush on Anikó's face. Zeno mulled the information.

"Thank you," he said and smiled.

"Don't mention it. How do you find yourself in Budapest?"

"I like it very much."

"And have you got yourself a rich broad?"

He hesitated.

"You have, haven't you?" she said. "Good for you. All your dreams will come true." She looked him up and down, then smiled again. "I've got to go. Got a train to catch."

Anikó turned and walked towards the carriage, that same walk she'd affected across the hotel foyer. Evidently, Herr Bohm was not on the menu for Berlin after all.

As Zeno passed through the vestibule, he stopped at the florist and bought the largest bunch of irises he could carry.

"They're the first this spring," the florist said.

When he arrived at the small apartment Friday evening, Catherine wasn't there. He hadn't expected her to be. It was unlikely she'd get away until Saturday morning, but he'd stay at the apartment and wait, just in case. With the money Mr. Steiner had given him, he'd bought a bottle of cognac. Catherine had been to the apartment. She'd brought bread, cheese, some onions and a bowl of eggs. She'd augmented the apartment's kitchen utensils with a new frying pan and a wooden spoon, a single dining plate, knife, fork and spoon. Two bottles of wine, a rare coupling for the apartment, stood behind a single long stem glass.

Suddenly he regretted not knowing what train she'd catch back to Budapest. He could've met her, followed her at a distance. Perhaps she'd arrive later that evening. He unpacked the few things he'd brought, then set his projector on the piano to play her the completed film he'd made in which she starred. He settled in the armchair. He took up a novel, read a page and then began to fidget. He went to the window and looked down to the square. He turned the radio on but there was no swing music to be found from any station. It would be a long evening.

Saturday morning arrived but Catherine didn't. He wasn't worried, just sorry she'd passed the evening without him, and he without her. She'd come today, as they planned. He was sure of it. Each set of feet on the stairs set his heart racing, and finally there was a key in the door.

"You're here," he said walking out to the corridor.

"And you are too," she said, her voice filled with delight, her smile set to explode. "I thought you might not come till this evening."

She carried a small travel bag and some bread rolled in paper. He took them from her and she followed him into the main room. He set the bag and bread in the kitchenette and turned towards her. He held her tight while they kissed. He inhaled her perfume. Her usual elegant suit was replaced with a raw fabric skirt and knitted cardigan. The only sign of another life was the crucifix, too heavy for her outfit. He lowered his face to her breast.

"The clothes suit you," he said.

She laughed. "I had to disguise myself."

"Mr. Steiner went to Berlin on Thursday…."

"I know. We must speak."

He screwed up his face. "We mustn't speak at all."

With one hand he covered her mouth and with the other guided her towards the bedroom.

When he woke in the early evening, he knew she was awake. He sighed. Was it a sign of intimacy that you could tell when someone lying beside you was awake? But he lay still and listened to the city below them, the heave of it, her breathing regular but for the occasional shallow sigh.

"You sound restless," he said.

"You once asked me," she said, "why I bathed in the water of Lake Hévíz, what ailment I hoped to cure."

He waited, suddenly worried.

"I think the waters have done their magic. For some time now I've suspected something."

"What?"

"I'm pregnant."

Suddenly it was as if the world had stopped, as if the film had jammed in the shutter.

"You..." He sat up.

"I'm going to have a baby. You're going to be a father."

Catherine was smiling, broader and fuller than he'd ever, ever seen before. His heart raced. He wasn't sure how he felt, what to say. He'd be a father.

"Please be happy," she said.

"I'm not unhappy," he said, almost defensively. He thought for a moment. "We should've been careful."

"Hang being careful." She threw her hands in the air and laughed. "I'm pregnant!"

"Are you sure?"

"The doctor in Gödöllő confirmed it yesterday. Don't you see what this means?"

"I don't know what you--"

"For years I've been blamed for this bloody barren marriage but it wasn't me. All along it was Sándor. Sándor can't have children. I'm not at fault. What a shock to him this will be."

"But he'll be upset, he'll know you—"

"No, no. Don't you see? This is perfect. There's nothing he can say about it. When he knows, he'll have to say the child is his. His pride won't allow it any other way. If he tells people it's not his, they'll draw the correct conclusion, that it's he who can't have children, not I. I'm blameless."

"But what'll happen?"

"Don't be anxious, I've thought of everything. Nothing can happen until after the war. Then, and only then, we can plan to escape."

"So we'll be together."

"Yes, but we can't do anything now. The baby will be born, the war needs to end. The world needs to settle. Then will be our time."

She kissed him in a way he'd never felt before, with a kind of desperate tenderness. She pulled him back in under the covers.

"But I don't understand," he said, breaking away from her. "There are lots of people who can't have children. Why was that such a problem? It's no one's fault."

She sighed and relaxed, pulled away from him. Her wave of excitement receded.

"You really don't know, do you?"

"Know what?"

She paused.

"You must promise never to repeat these things."

"What things? Catherine, I don't understand."

She was quiet for some time.

"I'd never betray you," he said. "Of course, I promise."

She breathed in deeply. "My name isn't Catherine. It's Eva."

"What?"

"Eva." She placed her hands on her belly. "It means life."

"Why would you change your Christian name?"

"I'm... an imported wife. I was brought here to marry Sándor."

"I know, I understand that. But why did you change your name?"

"I'm not a Catholic. I'm not even converted. None of the Steiner family are. We're Jews, hidden by a web of lies and covers."

He held his breath for a moment while incidents over the last few months raced through his mind. All the nonsense Tibi spouted was true.

"The crucifix…" he said.

"Why do you think I was so upset when it was lost? What do you think I was running from in the forest that day? I wanted to throw all this off, cleanse myself in the lake. But you interrupted me."

"My God," he said.

"And you followed me one day to the small village, Aszófő. I told you I went to that cheap hotel for a lover. That was a lie. There was no lover. It was a Jewish house. We made it do as a synagogue."

"But why did the Steiners bring you from France?"

"They needed someone they could rewrite. Marriage to a Catholic was the final act of Jewish assimilation into Hungarian society. I was to have children. *Mater semper certa est.* The children would be Jewish but safe in their Catholic identity."

"Racial purity."

She glared at him. The idea rocked unsteadily between them.

"I hadn't thought of that."

"But you're safe in Hungary," he said.

"Safe? Each day restrictions are tighter. Each day this façade is harder to maintain. Look what you witnessed the other week. Each day the armies advance and contract. And Sándor is dealing with the fucking Germans."

"He's with them now."

"There's little I've ever agreed on with Peter, but this is suicidal. Sándor thinks he can control them. He can't. They're vicious fanatics. They'll shoot him the first opportunity they get."

For some moments Catherine was quiet, her head turned away from him.

"In Hungary there are restrictions, but we've survived. Ella says over and over, 'It could never happen here.' I wish I were sure she's right."

In the new frying pan she cooked fish in butter. They ate from the single plate. After the meal, they made love. Aware of the child, he was cautious at first, merely a series of caresses but she took hold, straddling and drawing him in, using her fingers to extend her own pleasure, her own enthusiasm, which seeped into him like sleep.

Zeno woke. The curtain-less room was full of light. It couldn't have been so early in the morning. They'd spent a whole night together. They lay back to back. Their buttocks and shoulder blades touched. He could feel her warmth. He twisted and raised his head to look at her. Her shoulder was elevated, her face turned out of sight, her hair over her face, nothing visible save the line of her cheekbone. What had he expected to see? An angel? Catherine was, after all, exquisitely human. Perhaps that was all he'd wanted to confirm?

Despite wanting to, he wouldn't wake her. He nestled his shoulders and buttocks back to hers. The wine glass stood on the table beside the bed. It was half full, the wine a deep crimson, darker than it had looked last night. The morning light pierced the glass, a point from which it radiated like some painting of God's radiating commandments. He was a father. Such an odd thing, such an odd birthday present. Something he'd never considered. But how lovely to think he was growing inside Catherine.

The rays of light moved in the wine. Jiggled. He was sure of it. He blinked his sleepy eyes. They moved again, this time the wine disturbed, concentric waves moving from center to rim and back. Then the glass began to rattle, the broad base ticking as regularly as Catherine's metronome. Then he felt rather than heard something, felt it in his innards. The glass continued rattling, the rumbling grew more audible. It was happening. The rattle grew alarming. Something was happening. He rose from the bed and went naked to the window. He looked down into the streets below. Where normally people rushed to church, rushed home, there was no one. The noise grew louder, insistent. He ran to the windows in the other room. He looked down at the street, but there was no one.

"What's happening?" Catherine said, sitting up in the bed.

"I don't know." He walked back to the bedroom window. He looked out over the rooftops towards the Danube. "Good God."

"What?"

Catherine stood behind him, still naked. In the distance, a huge machine crossed the Erzsébet Bridge.

"It's a tank," Zeno said. He strained to see more. "It's a German Tiger tank."

The thing prowled with utter certainty, slowly, evenly, almost gliding. More tanks followed, moving through other parts of the city as if a colony of ants, stirred and irritated, had surfaced from underground.

"Where are they going?" Catherine said.

"I don't know."

Some shots rang out from the direction of the Royal Palace. Voices erupted in the apartment building.

"What's happening?' someone yelled.

Catherine and Zeno waited but no one replied.

Occasional voices shouted on the street, nothing they could understand. Zeno remembered what Mr. Steiner's colleague had said.

"It's an invasion," he said, unable to take his eyes from what was unfolding before them. "Germany is invading."

Catherine moved away from the window and sat on the edge of the bed. He was unable to avert his gaze. More shots rang out from the palace.

"We're done for," she said.

He turned to Catherine, her feet flat on the floor, her hands resting on her still naked belly.

"What do you mean?" he said, turning to sit near her.

"The Germans are here. These were our last days, our last hours are now."

Zeno slipped an arm around her and tried to comfort her, but she remained like a statue.

"Nothing will happen," he said, as much for her as for himself.

"They've marched in like they did to Paris."

"Nothing will change. Your secrets are guarded. Well guarded."

She glared at him. "Let's just hope you're right."

She flung her hand aside to silence the chattering wine glass. But in her haste, she slapped the half empty glass to the floor, where it splintered into a million sharp pieces in a pool of blood-red wine.

For a time, they sat silent. There seemed no point investigating what was going on, no point in cleaning up the split glass and spilt wine. Intermittent fire rang out but only from one point in the city--the same point, Zeno tried to convince himself. The German army had had an easy ride into the city, little resistance. The Hungarian army in Budapest was loyal to Germany. Nothing the palace guard could do would match their fire. Catherine started to shake. Zeno lay down on the bed, pulled her against him, covered them both, and held her close. Her skin was cold and clammy.

"You must calm yourself," he said but she made no reply. What was there to say? They lay so for a long time.

"My letters have been returned," Catherine said.

"Letters? What letters?"

"To my family. In Paris."

What on earth did she mean? "I'm sure the mail is disrupted."

"For over a year now, all my letters have been sent back. My family don't live in their apartment anymore. There's no trace of them."

"Perhaps they had to move."

"Then why wouldn't they write to me?"

They'd never really spoken of her family. In fact since she'd reproached him for being naïve about the dynamics that allowed her to be sent to Hungary, he'd avoided the topic. He smoothed her forehead. She closed her eyes. Outside the apartment, the noise of the invasion abated. At first the gunfire ceased, then the drone of the tanks. The city sounded clean, as if there'd just been a heavy storm.

"I'll go out," he said. "Find out what's happened."

"It's dangerous. We mustn't."

"We can't stay here."

She thought for a moment. "Turn the radio on."

He dressed himself, walked to the other room, and switched on the radio. The valves took forever to warm. Slowly, music came to them, melancholy strings, lyrical, no dissidence. Catherine came to the doorway and glared at the radio. Her left arm encircled her waist, her right hand held to her throat.

"How daring," she said.

"What?"

The music changed complexion, the lower string taking a steady march.

"It's Chopin's Funeral March."

He went to her, placed his hand on her shoulder. She didn't move. Together they listened to the final few moments, as this strings tried again, tried to rise above the dirge only to be over powered, forced down again to the lower march of the bass. The radio fell silent. There was no announcement. Everything had been said. Zeno went to the radio to find the BBC or some other foreign service, but in daylight the signals were weak, just a mass of static.

"I can't believe they've said nothing," Catherine said after they'd listened for twenty minutes or more.

"I'll go out and find out what's happening."

"I'll come with you."

"You must stay here."

"I'm not staying here on my own."

He had no time to protest. From her travel bag she dressed herself in a pale blue suit, much more her attire than the raw fabric. She picked up the crucifix, considered it. As he was about to say she should wear it, she drew the chain over her head and snuggled it into position. She was right, they were better together. And she must be filled with fear if she was prepared to be seen moving around the streets together. As they left the apartment, Zeno grabbed his camera.

Outside, they stood still for some moments. There was quiet, a type of quiet he'd never heard in the city before. A bird twittered on the branch of a tree in the square. They looked left and right. There were no trams running, no cars running, not even a sound of voices. No mechanical hum. A bird called again. Then they heard steps, quick steps. Catherine pulled back into the doorway.

"It's all right," he said. "It's just one person."

A man appeared in the square, overweight and moving in a half-run, half-walk. He kept looking left and right and back over his shoulders. When he was closer, Zeno made sure he'd seen them so as not to alarm him by calling out. The man halted, rigid with fear.

"You'd best be staying indoors," he said.

"What's happened?"

"I was having my breakfast at a café. The waiter told me the Germans were invading. They've taken control."

Catherine and Zeno looked at one another.

"Is it safe to move about?" Zeno said.

"There's no more fire but I wouldn't move unless you need to."

Without further salutation, the man moved off, starting his curious walk-run again.

"We must get back to the house," she said.

"I don't think we can." Zeno sighed. They'd be safer there. "Okay. But we're going to have to take a long way."

They started through the maze of little side streets. As they walked, he raised his lens to the upper floors of the buildings. The pavement shook like an earthquake. He reached out his hand to Catherine and they ran to a side street. He raised the camera again. The noise increased exponentially. A tank rolled past the mouth of the street and the rattling noise started to recede. Still filming, they walked towards the mouth of the alley. She walked in front of him, turned and looked directly into the lens, then crossed to the other side of the street. A half-dozen Tiger tanks were now in view, moving persistently forward. Some soldiers strolled alongside them, others alighted from the slow-moving tanks.

"I see people," Catherine said. She crossed to the other side of the street to get a better view. "It's all right," she called back to Zeno. Together they walked to the mouth of the lane in the square. The shops and cafes were open. People were already eating at tables outside the cafes, taking their breakfast, their morning coffee.

"It's as if nothing has happened," she said.

"People are just going about their business."

"Look."

She pointed to the upper floors of a building. A long Nazi flag already hung blood red down over the windows of the lower floor, the dark swastika at its centre.

"It's a celebration," she said.

"They had the flags ready to unfurl."

They crossed the Danube via the Chain Bridge. There were soldiers but no one stopped them. The Buda side of the city was just as busy with German soldiers but just as calm. When they reached the Steiner building, Zeno said he'd go to the rear entry but already Ella ran across the courtyard towards them.

"Where have you been?" Ella said to Catherine.

"I was away for the weekend--I just got back. I bumped into Zeno at the train station. He escorted me home."

Without saying more, Ella took Catherine's hand and led her towards the house. Zeno hesitated, but behind Ella's back she motioned him to follow. She ushered them into the main lounge.

"Peter and Sándor are missing."

"What?" Catherine said.

Zeno felt his panic rise.

"Why?" Catherine said.

"This morning, they came to the house."

"Who?"

"Who do you think? The Gestapo. They were looking for them."

"Where's Sándor?" Catherine said.

"We don't know."

"And Peter?"

"He went out early this morning and hasn't returned."

"What did the soldiers say?"

Ella looked at Zeno and realized he was listening.

"We're not sure," she said. "But they were specific. They wanted Peter and Sándor."

"Sándor?"

"Thankfully he's not here."

"He's in Berlin," Zeno said.

The two women turned and looked at him.

"Then he's safe," Catherine said.

"How safe can he be in Berlin?" Ella burst into tears.

CHAPTER SEVENTEEN

Zeno waited the rest of Sunday in Mr. Steiner's apartment. What else could he do? He'd told the family where he thought Mr. Steiner was. He couldn't tell them he was with a woman. How the hell did he get into this turmoil? There was nothing he could do except be present when Mr. Steiner got home.

Around two in the morning, he lay on the sofa. As he drifted in half sleep, he thought back over the day. Somehow in the momentous events, his birthday had been lost. Even his mother hadn't sent him a letter. Budapest was under German control. But what did that mean? Life in Berlin had seemed much the same. If only Catherine had told him her story before. Missed opportunities washed over him. He'd been blinkered, seen only what he wanted to see. They should have left Budapest weeks ago, if only he'd known.

Now that he was going to be a father, he felt vulnerable. More than that he felt responsible, not just for Catherine, but for someone else. Had his father felt such a thing? If only he could ask him. He breathed deeply to swell his chest. What would he provide a child?

At first light, he washed his face with bracing water. He darted up to his room to change into his uniform, then went down to the house kitchen for his morning supplies.

"Is there any word?" he asked Hans.

"Peter has returned."

"Where was he?"

"He took refuge in a hotel during the invasion. He waited till it died down."

"Hans, I'm not sure Mr. Steiner is in Berlin."

"Why?"

"He left Budapest with a woman. The train was going to Berlin but I'm not sure he went there."

"I see." Hans thought a moment.

"Should I tell them?"

"You can't tell them he was with another woman."

"No."

"Anyway, he's still missing. Whether he was in Berlin or not is irrelevant."

"But if he's arrested, maybe they know someone to help?"

"They've already contacted everyone they know. They'll survive."

As these were extraordinary circumstances, Zeno decided to go to Catherine. It wouldn't be considered so unusual. Gertrúd answered the door. Her jaw set tight when she saw Zeno.

"What do you want?" she said.

He looked beyond her into Catherine's apartment, which was smaller than he'd thought, a small entrance hall and a not-so-large lounge room. A door on the left hand side led, he presumed, to the bedroom.

"Is there any news of Mr. Steiner?" he said.

"None that I've heard."

"Is Mrs. Steiner here?"

"She's with Ella."

Zeno turned to leave.

"Why would you come to Mrs. Steiner?" Gertrúd said.

He faced her. He felt himself blush.

"I thought she might have heard something. I'm worried about Mr. Steiner. She *is* his wife."

"Is that right?"

"These times are hard enough. Don't play games."

From the windows of Mr. Steiner's apartment, Budapest stretched in front of him and he could see it felt no loss. This new power that had dismissed the government of Miklós Kállay might have been an uncle or a father they'd long been expecting. They'd made room at the table, shifted the chairs together so he could come to the head and eat. Perhaps all the fear Catherine had was unfounded and life would just continue on.

He set up a temporary bed in his small office in Mr. Steiner's apartment. He pressed shirts, polished shoes, in such a frenzy that two days later on Wednesday morning when he noticed a foul odor in the apartment, he didn't notice Mr. Steiner standing in the lounge room.

"Zeno."

"Sir."

Zeno stood dumbstruck. His hair hung slick about his face, his clothes were stained, and he literally smelled like shit. There seemed less of him, as if he'd been reduced.

"Where have you been, sir?"

"I was arrested."

"Why, sir?"

"Will you please draw me a bath?"

Zeno started towards the bathroom. "Sir?" Mr. Steiner, still standing at the center of the room, gazed into the middle distance. "Have you eaten?"

"Just water."

He swayed. Zeno ran to him and managed to break his fall, save his head from cracking on the hard floor.

"I'll get a doctor."

"Just water."

Zeno returned from the kitchenette, knelt, and raised Mr. Steiner's head to his knee. He drank from the glass, his eyes dulled and fixed, slowly swallowing the water.

"I'll get some food brought up."

"Some soup." The water had rallied him. "But first a bath."

With Zeno's help, he struggled to his feet. How could the substance have been knocked from a man in just a few days? In the bathroom, he sat him on a low wooden stool. While the water poured into the bath, he started to remove his clothes. He struggled with the jacket. Mr. Steiner was so weak he could barely lift an arm.

"They're ruined," Mr. Steiner said. "Just cut them off."

With scissors, Zeno cut away the remains of the shirt. At this range, stale excrement augmented the stale-milk stench of body odor. The breadth of Mr. Steiner's chest was gone. He cut the trousers down the outside of both legs. When he helped Mr. Steiner to his feet, they fell away. His bandy legs and arms belied the fullness he'd always maintained. It then occurred to Zeno that there was no blood. He hadn't been beaten, not badly at any rate. Given the stains on his skin it was hard to make out bruises, but no skin had been broken.

"I must sit."

Zeno helped Mr. Steiner back to the stool while the hot water was drawn. He turned the faucets as hard as they'd go. Steam swirled about the room. Zeno looked at Mr. Steiner's groin. There was no foreskin. He was circumcised. Mr. Steiner caught his gaze and despite his exhaustion pulled a towel over himself. Zeno plunged his hand into the water.

"That will do," he said.

He braced Mr. Steiner under his arms, lowered him into the bath. He bathed him with a wash cloth, gently cleaning off the stains.

"We were returning from Berlin. On Sunday evening. I was arrested at the station."

Zeno soaped his back, small soft circles.

"I know you'll not tell anyone I was accompanied."

"No, sir."

"You're faithful. I can trust you."

Zeno drained the water from the tub, refilled it, and repeated the process. He dressed Mr. Steiner in a gown and had soup brought up. It wasn't long before word spread through the house that he was home. Even before he'd dipped his spoon in the soup, the apartment was filled with his father, Karl, his sister, Erzsébet, and Peter. Even Catherine came, propping up Ella.

"Sányi, Sányi," Ella cried, rushing to hug him, kissing his forehead. "I thought you were dead."

Despite coming within a metre of Zeno to retrieve and placate Ella, Catherine didn't even glance at him. She looked unwell, tired and pale and drawn. Zeno hovered around Mr. Steiner, filling his glass to quench an insatiable thirst.

"Where were you arrested?" Peter asked.

"At Nyugati Railway station."

"Why were you in Berlin?" Peter said.

"Why do you think?"

Father Karl raised his hand to silence the escalating spat.

"Where were you held?" Karl asked.

"They'd rounded up a number of people, other industrialists, public figures, academics."

"Why you?" Karl said.

Sándor smiled ironically. "Why me? I'm not sure. They were arresting Jews for traveling without papers."

"When did this become a law?" Karl turned to the group.

"It hasn't been announced yet," Peter said.

"So people are now arrested for things they don't know are against the law?" Erzsébet said.

Concerned glances passed between the family.

"They just needed to strike hard to help establish order," Karl said.

"Where were you kept?" Ella said.

"I'm not sure. I was blindfolded and taken to a building. It wasn't removed until I was in a room. With three others."

"They've taken over every household," Erzsébet said. "Even Chorin's place on Andrássy Boulevard."

"Who were the others?" Peter said.

"I don't know them."

"Were they Jewish?" Karl said.

"No. One was a journalist, a... I'm sorry, I don't remember. We were taken, one at a time, to be interrogated. Over and over this happened."

"What did they ask about?" Peter said.

"They asked me what I knew about the economic affairs of Hungary."

"What?" Peter pressed his palm to his forehead. Erzsébet came to his side.

"They wanted to know the big players, how the country's economy works–"

"They've just occupied," Karl said. "To some degree they need to work within our existing structure."

"What did you say?" Peter asked.

"What could I say? These aren't state secrets. I told them what I knew."

"Why would they want this information?" Erzsébet said.

"Clearly they asked other things," Peter said.

"You weren't there," Sándor said.

"Once your tongue was loosened you probably gave all kinds of information without even knowing—"

"I betrayed no one!"

"The Nazis are not stupid," Catherine said. Not the force of her voice but the fact she'd spoken at all drew every eye to her. "They already know everything. Who controls what, who owns what, who is or isn't Jewish. They were just verifying."

Catherine's directness doused the argument.

"And you weren't fed?" Ella asked.

"Nothing. Just water."

"But you were allowed a toilet," Ella said.

"We were taken. Twice a day. They stood over me. I slept on the floor of the room."

"Why did they release you?"

"Once I'd established who I was…" A wonder came over his face as he looked at everyone present. "You've all disagreed with me over the contracts to build the trucks. They're what saved me. Peter *is* wrong--"

"I'm not wrong." Peter stepped towards Sándor, Erzsébet grabbing his free arm at the wrist. "You're a fool to deal with them. That's why you were arrested."

Sándor smiled. "I had them contact, Müller, in Berlin. He was irate. Incredibly irate. He had them release me immediately."

For a time, no one spoke. Zeno stood by the door. Catherine focused all her attention on Ella, who sat like a statue in an armchair.

"It's unsafe," Peter said. "We must leave."

He was right, Zeno thought. All of them, including Catherine, himself, and their baby must leave Hungary.

"Peter," Sándor said. "You're not listening. The contracts saved me."

"Not from arrest. They'll inflict tighter and tighter control."

"But where are we to go?" Ella said.

"This is just the beginning," Peter said. "Regent Horthy has appointed Döme Sztójay as Prime Minister."

"What?" Sándor steadied himself.

"The Germans have applauded," Karl said.

Peter smirked. "I thought that might stop you."

"Of course," Sándor said. "He's a fascist. But he's Hungarian."

"We must leave," Peter said.

"No," Karl said. "There's too much to lose."

"It could never happen," Ella said, her voice shaking. "Not here. It could never happen."

"It can happen anywhere," Catherine said.

Zeno looked at all the people in the room. Suddenly they'd all glazed over, lost in their private thoughts.

"There's no option," Sándor said in a faint but determined voice. "We have too much to lose – the plant, property, all our assets. You think if we run now they'll just save all this for us? Hold it so we can come back? Only I've suffered." Sándor looked directly at Peter. "Papa is right. These arrests were just intimidation."

"You think the German army waddles along intimidating people?" Peter said.

"Must I remind you, Peter, of my position in this family?"

"Spare us a tedious Christian parable." Peter glared at him. "It seems that position has changed."

"How can the position of eldest son *change*? You've had your way too long--"

"There's no point rehashing the past," Karl said. He glared from Sándor to Peter then back to Sándor.

"It's done," Sándor said. "The contracts are signed."

"Contracts with the devil." Peter walked to the far side of the room. Erzsébet went to his side.

"We have what they need," Sándor said. "The Hungarian government's resisted. They'll resist further."

Ella clasped her hands to her head. "Isn't resistance the reason they've invaded?"

"We're not Jews," Sándor said with renewed strength. Whilst concerned looks passed between the family, no one actually looked at Zeno. "We are Roman Catholics and have been for many years. If we lose our mettle, all that will be undone. If we falter, everything will collapse, an avalanche. I've not been harmed. We must stay, continue as usual."

Once they'd sought each other's gaze, they looked back at Sándor and with gritted teeth and pressed lips, nodded their affirmation. All except Peter, who remained frozen, his lips pressed tightly together.

"You must all go now," Sándor said, standing up. Zeno moved to support him. "I must sleep."

Slowly, reluctantly, the family drained from the apartment. Ella came to Mr. Steiner and kissed his cheek. Catherine left without looking at Zeno or Mr. Steiner. When they were gone, Mr. Steiner walked on his own to the bedroom. Zeno followed. Mr. Steiner stopped and looked at the bed.

"For the first time since you came to work for me, you've failed me."

Zeno felt panicked.

"What have I done?"

"It's what you haven't done."

He smiled and looked towards his bed. Zeno moved quickly to turn down the bed covers, then retreated from the room.

"Zeno?" he called out.

He walked a few paces back into the room.

"Please don't leave the apartment."

"No, sir. I won't."

"It's just that I may need something."

Mr. Steiner smiled, with some new warmth.

Twice in the middle of the night Mr. Steiner woke yelling. Zeno went to him, assured him everything was all right, made him chamomile tea, and settled him down to sleep. Over the coming days, he regained his strength. The good food brought from the kitchen and hours of sleep reinflated him like a pump on a flat tire, but Zeno didn't get his Sunday off. He was unsure if Catherine had gone to the apartment. He'd heard she was tending to Ella, who'd suffered a complete attack of nerves.

With Mr. Steiner's increased vigor, his secretary came to the apartment to work, his typewriter and piles of paper taking over the small dining table. Mr. Steiner dictated letters and long lists of people who needed to be contacted.

"There's work to do," he said over and over.

And members of the family, his mother and father and sister, visited him. They came to see if he was stronger, came to see if he would still act on the manufacturing contracts with the Germans. After a long discussion, his father accepted his decision.

"It's a sound business proposition," Karl said. "But Peter will never accept it."

Peter never came to visit. Neither did Catherine.

But despite the appearance that life had returned to normal under the German occupation, concerns waxed and waned amongst the staff. One afternoon in the servants' antechamber, Hans told Zeno a rabbi had been to see Peter and his father.

"Why would a rabbi come?"

"I've no idea," Zeno said, and this was almost a truthful answer. "I've never seen one here before."

"Neither have I."

"What did he say?" Zeno said.

"Peter talked about whether the family should leave Hungary. The rabbi told him there was no need. They should wait a while and see."

"To wait and see what?"

"I don't know."

"Why would a rabbi come?" Zeno said.

"I asked *you* that. What's going to happen to us?"

"What do you mean?"

"If the family leaves Hungary, they won't be taking us with them." Hans raised his eyebrows high on his forehead. "We won't have jobs."

Zeno felt a constriction in his throat and did his best to remain calm.

"I'm sure nothing will happen," he said.

Gertrúd came into the room.

"Nothing will happen? The Germans have legalized the Arrow Cross Party."

Zeno stared at her and swallowed. "I guess they had to. They were all illegal otherwise."

"They'll soon take control."

"Is that what Tibi says?"

The bell from Mr. Steiner's apartment rang. They all looked at it.

"Run to your master," Gertrúd said. "While you still can."

He turned back towards her.

"What's that meant to mean?" he said, surprised by his own anger.

"Nothing."

"Then run to your mistress while you can."

He walked quickly through the lower levels of the building, angry with himself for having responded to her cheap bait. The words were Tibi's, not hers. She'd swallowed everything he said.

When he arrived at the apartment, Mr. Steiner was already dressed in a light day suit.

"I've a dentist appointment," he said. "Would you please accompany me?"

"Of course." Zeno hesitated. Although recuperated, Mr. Steiner was still shaken. "But do you think it wise?"

"Wise?"

"Perhaps it would be better next week."

"Nonsense. I'm tired of being cooped up, a small outing will do us both good."

The dentist's rooms were on Andrássy Street.

"See?" Mr. Steiner said, looking out the car's window. "People are still shopping, still going about their business as usual. There's absolutely nothing to panic about. Germany's our friend. They'll do no harm."

Zeno saw a gypsy woman selling flowers on the street corner as she'd always done. Perhaps what Mr. Steiner said was true, on the surface. He sensed only the slightest whiff of change in the city under this new command, just a different set of uniforms on the street. And yet he felt uneasy, nervous, as if some beast moved about unseen, just beneath the streets, something about to tell all the gypsy women all over the city they could no longer sell flowers.

The dentist and Mr. Steiner greeted one another as old friends. Pesti was about Mr. Steiner's age, his rooms filled with the latest equipment, a huge chair he could manipulate to any number of positions. Mr. Steiner said his clients were members of the government, the bureaucracy, the army, the rich, and the middle class. And his poking about in their mouths would often loosen their tongues. People told him things. And he edited a small newspaper, *The Pesti Post*, each week plying a satirical eye over the week's social and political events. Despite most people knowing this connection, it never stopped their talking.

"What have you heard?" Mr. Steiner said.

Pesti raised his eyebrows. "There's much to write about."

It was then Zeno realized there was nothing wrong with Mr. Steiner's teeth. This tittle-tattle was the purpose of the visit.

"There are new regulations coming," Pesti said. "Jews will have to wear a yellow star."

"I see." Mr. Steiner looked down.

"I'm sorry, I forgot."

"That's all right. We're Roman Catholics."

"No…" Pesti's face contorted with woe. "Even converted Jews must wear the star."

Again Mr. Steiner averted his gaze.

"I'm told the Allies are not far," Pesti said.

"Yes." He looked out the window of the dentist's rooms. "It's early spring. I'll walk home."

As they moved towards the door, Pesti raised his hand to Mr. Steiner's arm.

"I hear you were arrested?"

"Nothing serious. They were just flexing muscle."

"These regulations will be like the others. People will find ways around them, lists of exemptions, neighborly agreements. Hungarians are not anti-Semitic."

"You're right. Hungary will survive."

"Don't worry, my friend. These Germans, they have their heads screwed on the wrong way round. They come as if they were going. This won't last long."

Without Zeno's repeating a word of what he'd heard, the rumors of the new regulations spread quickly to the staff.

"Wearing a yellow star isn't such an onerous task."

"These things are only temporary."

But others had heard Jews would no longer be allowed to use a public telephone or go to public places like parks or restaurants or swimming pools. Zeno listened without comment, unsure how much of what they'd heard was gossip and how much the truth.

"Have you heard?" Hans said. He was dressed in civilian clothes with a canvas bag slung over his shoulder.

"What now?"

"This ship is sinking."

"What do you mean?"

"I've quit. I've got a job with a German officer in a house on Andrássy Street."

Hans was leaving? This was something new.

"You won't have a job soon," Hans said. "From what I've heard."

"What's that?"

"Part of the new regulations. Jews won't be able to have servants."

Zeno drew a controlled breath. "The Steiners are Roman Catholic."

"But they converted after 1919. The regulations say they're Jews."

"More hearsay."

Hans shrugged his shoulders and smiled. He gave Zeno his new address and told him he'd be welcome there. If he heard of a job, he'd be in touch. Zeno watched him walk away, the bag over his shoulder like a sailor, something puckish in his gait.

In the servants' tea room nearly every woman on staff sat around a mound of clothes and overcoats, men's, women's, children's, all different styles and colors and cuts.

"What's going on?" Zeno said.

"Can you sew?" the housemistress said.

"A little."

"Then sit down. Hetty, get him a needle and thread."

"But what's happening?"

"All these stars must be sewn on by Wednesday. Then it's law."

"But the Steiners are Christians."

"I'm not here to argue that. I'm just here to do as I'm told."

"Who told you to do this?"

"Ella Steiner."

It wasn't as Tibi had thought, that someone had found something in the house to condemn the family. The laws had changed around them. Their religion didn't matter anymore. They were now part of a race.

"I'll not be a part of this," Zeno said.

"You'd do well not to be so proud."

"I won't support them."

Mr. Steiner was reading when Zeno arrived in the apartment, seated in an armchair they'd moved near the window for the sunlight. Zeno cleared his throat.

"Mr. Steiner?"

He looked up. "I can imagine what you wish to discuss. We must wear the star. I've applied for an exemption."

"They say there'll be no staff."

"This house can't function without staff. Nothing will happen."

"But people are leaving."

"Fools. As Hans has left, you'll now work for both myself and Peter. As you'll have more to do, you'll be paid more. These changes won't last."

"But these awful thoughts are everywhere."

"What do you mean?"

"People talk of the Jews now as if they were an enemy of Hungary."

"People will always talk."

"A friend of mine is full of it. He was never like that before."

"Is he a member of staff?"

"No, I knew him from the lake. What should I say to stop people taking?"

"If you hear staff members talking this way, you must tell me."

Zeno thought of Gertúde spouting Tibi's thoughts.

"Of course."

"You've been good to me, Zeno. You've been good to the family. We'll do all we can to protect you."

Mr. Steiner went back to reading. He seemed unaware of Zeno still standing in front of him.

"You've been good to me, Mr. Steiner. You gave me Budapest." He smiled. "It's transformed me utterly."

On Sunday morning, Zeno hurried to Mr. Steiner's apartment. Still in bed, he insisted he didn't need anything and Zeno should finally have a day off. Without changing from his uniform, Zeno put on his heavy coat and made his way across the city towards Catherine's small apartment. He stopped at the Muvész Café in nearby Andrássy Street to buy some of their famous *túrós rétes*. They'd sweeten the day even more. The place was crowded and busy as usual, more so because it was Sunday.

As he moved away from the cashier he walked straight into Tibi and Gertrúd. He rocked on his feet for a moment, stared at them, first at Gertrúd. She looked right back at him, then turned to Tibi. They were dressed in their best civilian clothes, standing arm in arm. They'd followed him into the shop.

He had nothing to say to either of them so he clutched his package tight to his stomach and made to side-step them. Tibi said nothing until he was past and nearly to the door.

"That's the second time we've bumped into you around here. You must have a girlfriend here."

Zeno paused, only for a moment. He should throw the *rétes* at them, cover them with cottage cheese and flaky pastry. But that was exactly what Tibi wanted, and Zeno wouldn't give him what he wanted. He continued on and left the shop. With decisive steps, he walked away from the small apartment. From the shop door, Tibi yelled out,

"She must be very well-to-do to live in this area."

He continued to walk towards the river, away from Catherine's apartment. To be doubly sure he'd lost them, he crossed the Danube to Buda, walked to the next bridge, crossed back to Pest, then made his way back, all the while checking over his shoulder that he'd not been followed. After nearly an hour's walk, he finally arrived at the apartment. Catherine wasn't there, but she'd left a note.

> *My Darling,*
>
> *I came yesterday to leave you this note. It's very difficult for me to get away. Ella isn't coping. Please wait today as late as you can. If it's possible, I'll come. How sad our time together is chipped away. We must be patient. Hold in your heart that our time will come.*
>
> *All my love,*
> *Catherine.*

He spent the whole day waiting. Damn Tibi and Gertrúd. What did they know? Should he tell Catherine? They were just trying to provoke him. But why did he feel he was being watched? As if the arrival of the German army had turned every set of eyes in their direction, pitted neighbor against neighbor. He'd have to talk with Catherine. After hours of thought, nauseous from eating all the *túrós rétes,* he heard the municipal clock strike eleven. He rose from the chair. This whole situation was impossible --he'd go to her apartment in the morning and speak with her. As he opened the door to leave, he heard footsteps on the stair. He pulled back into the apartment and closed the door. The steps continued to climb, the echoes quickly tripping over themselves in the well. The footfall sounded like Catherine's, soft and yet firm, but would she really come this late? The steps stopped outside the door, then he heard keys jangling.

"Catherine," he said.

"Thank God you're here."

"Where have you been?"

"I couldn't leave. So much has happened."

"What?"

She walked past him into the apartment. She flopped in the armchair, breathed out, and as he walked towards her she lurched forward, raising her elbows to her knees and placing her head in her hands. The act shut him out completely.

"What? What's the matter?"

"The government has passed regulations. All Jews have to wear a yellow star."

"But you're Christian!"

"The Steiner's grandparents were practicing Jews. One grandparent is enough. We are, despite all our efforts, Jews."

"But Mr. Steiner has working contracts with the German Army. He told me they'd protect you all."

"He's still saying that."

"What are the others saying?"

"That it's time to leave."

She looked at him, eyes red from crying. She looked exhausted and wretched. He squatted down in front of the chair and they embraced. He closed his eyes and laid his forehead in the crook of her neck.

"How will they leave?"

"Peter will find a way. Sándor has said he'll stay to run the factory." She pushed him away to look in his eyes. "How dare he speak for me! The family would never take me. Peter has started to plan without us. They'll all leave."

Zeno stood and walked over to the window. His run-in with Tibi and Gertrúd now seemed trivial, not worth mentioning. Instead of thinking about them all day he should have concentrated on finding a way for him and Catherine to leave Budapest safely.

"We must leave," he said. "We must run away."

"How?" She glared at him. "We have no money. No papers."

"And I'll not have a job soon." He refrained from scaring her more. "As it is, I now have to work for two people. You're pregnant. We can't stay here." It was the first time he'd ever raised his voice in front of her. "Perhaps if we went to my mother's in the south?"

She was quiet, considering this possible refuge.

"Perhaps," she said. "But it won't be so easy to hide in the country. Anybody different will be obvious. And your mother... I doubt she'd accept me."

"How can this be happening?"

"The madness of the world has finally come to Hungary."
He turned back to face her.

"I was wrong," he said. "This war is wrong. This fascism is vile and hateful."

"It doesn't matter about wrong and right."

"We have to leave," he said.

"How?"

"If Peter can find a way, we can."

"Peter has an endless stream of money. We don't."

"Then you're content to just sit here and take whatever happens?"

"No."

"Then..." He twisted his hand in front of her.

"Sándor has said we'll stay to protect the business."

"You must tell them you're pregnant."

"I can't do that..." She was lost in thought again. "You're right. We must leave."

"Let's agree on that."

She paused for a moment and he thought he'd lost. Then she nodded.

"We must come up with a plan," he said, not wanting to lose any momentum.

"That will be hard--"

"We must do it," he said. "Now. How will we leave?"

"I don't know." She smoothed her hands over her skirt. "But if we act in haste, we're bound to fail. Be patient. We still have some time--"

"We have *no* time at all."

"Give me time to think." She glanced out the window then back at him. "I'll make some discreet enquires."

CHAPTER EIGHTEEN

The first time Zeno went to Peter and Erzsébet's apartment, the size of the entrance hall overpowered him. Hans had told him the apartment took over virtually the whole floor of the building, but even this didn't prepare him for what he found, a rectangular entrance hall with a high ceiling, almost five or six times the size of his bedroom, with ornate art-deco cornices. Situated on the quieter side of the building, it was another story higher than Mr. Steiner's.

"I'm here to replace Hans," Zeno finally said to Erzsébet when he'd recovered his breath.

"I see." She looked at him as if she'd never seen him before. "Mr. Kresz's not here." She sighed. "I'll show you what needs to be done."

He followed her through the apartment, down a wide corridor. The walls were lined with wood panels, white with gilded borders. There were separate rooms for their three children.

"Peter will often have to travel," she said, passing through a door from the hall directly into his dressing room. Two rows of built-in cupboards lined the space which was as large as Zeno's bedroom.

"In the morning, you'll enter the dressing room from the hall. That door leads to our bedroom." She pointed to a door at the apex of the room. "You'll be able to work here without disturbing us. You'll need to plan in advance, know where he's going. What the requirements of that time are, work or social, and what type of functions he needs to attend." She pointed to the racks of shoes. "All shoes must be polished at all times."

She schooled him as if he had no idea what the job entailed. Rather than be rude and correct her, he let her drone on. This tuition, which pushed so solidly into the future, seemed so unnecessary. If the family were planning to leave Budapest, his service would be really brief.

While Erzsébet continued talking, a low droning noise came over the apartment. Zeno looked towards the ceiling. It was mechanical, some distance off but getting closer. When he looked back at Erzsébet, although she was still talking, she too looked up at the ceiling. She stopped speaking and listened.

"What's that?" she asked.

"A plane."

They listened. Her maid appeared from the bedroom and looked from them to the ceiling and back at them. Zeno shrugged.

"That's more than one plane,' the maid said.

And then the air raid sirens wound themselves to increasing hysteria. Erzsébet's eyes widened with fear.

"It must be a false alarm," she said.

The maid was now standing next to her. "Another drill."

"But what's that noise?" Zeno said, still looking towards the ceiling.

The drone grew more and more insistent. The glass panes in the windows began to rattle. The sirens became more urgent than they'd ever been before in any drill.

"Quick!" someone yelled from the hallway. "Everyone get to the basement."

"It's the Allies," Zeno said softly. "They've come."

"Perhaps you're right." Erzsébet looked up at the ceiling again. "We'd best get to the cellar."

By the time they reached the lower levels of the building, there was a line of people, servants and Steiners alike, making their way towards the basement which had been fitted as an air-raid shelter. Erzsébet and the Steiners were ushered away to the far side of the room, to padded benches. Catherine sat towards the back, next to Ella. She made no acknowledgement of Zeno, her back rigid, her hands held together in her lap.

The servants stood, squatted on their haunches, or sat directly on the earth floor. The basement contained no windows, the only light from an electric bulb hanging from the ceiling. At least sixty people crammed in. The air soon became close and stuffy. People lit a number of nervous cigarettes. Zeno lit one. Some began to talk as if they were waiting for a train.

Catherine wound a small handkerchief around her finger. She adjusted the shawl around Ella's shoulders.

"Sándor is at the factory," Ella said.

No one added anything to this. All factories were obvious targets.

"So is Peter," Erzsébet said.

"They're American planes," a man said. "I can tell by the engine noise."

"What of it?"

The man listened again. "Judging by the strain on the engines, they're loaded with something heavy."

Zeno listened. The sounds of the engines were nothing like the German plane he'd heard with Catherine at the lake. The building shook. A quantity of dust and dirt fell from the ceiling. Then a tremendous sound. BOOM! An explosion. A woman screamed.

"Don't panic!" a man yelled. "It's all right. They're actually falling a long way from here."

The building rocked again and again. Boom! Boom! Not as loud or tremulous, but the dust fell and the air became more and more difficult to breathe. People started to cough. Zeno didn't take his eyes from Catherine. Through the haze she looked straight ahead. With each shock, she barely flinched. Just once she looked at him. Their eyes met and locked. The barest trace of a smile flickered across her face. He flinched from the intensity and averted his gaze--unfortunately too late. Gertrúd flicked her head back and glared at him. She'd witnessed what had passed between her mistress and Zeno.

After perhaps as little as fifteen minutes, the bombs ceased to fall but still the sirens wailed. They must wait until the sirens changed their tune to an all clear. By mid-morning, they emerged from the basement. People left for the upper reaches of the house, dusting themselves off, arms around shoulders to steady each other.

What had only been a brief confinement changed the world. As Zeno climbed back up the main stair, large pieces of plaster and masonry littered the marble floor of the foyer, shaken from the ceiling dome. Gertrúd was waiting for him on the first landing.

"Are you all right?" he said.

"Yes."

There was an awkward moment. She stuck out her chin.

"You know she's pregnant."

He steadied himself, looked around as if she was talking to someone else.

"Who?"

"Catherine. She vomits every morning. You can damn near see it."

He shrugged his shoulders. "How would I know that?"

"I thought the father would know."

Again he took his time, exerting care and control over what he'd say.

"You're a gossip, Gertrúd. Just because he may know doesn't mean I would."

"But when the servant becomes the master…"

"Sándor Steiner is the master."

He walked towards Mr. Steiner's apartment, his mouth dry, legs quivering with nerves and new resolve. Something had to change. Gertrúd knew it all. She'd put the pieces together. She was dangerous. It would soon be obvious Catherine was pregnant. If the building had been hit, God only knew if one or all or none of them would have survived. They'd be safer out of the city. If they could just leave now. But they needed money and, as Catherine maintained, a plan.

In the following hours reports came in that along the main streets of the city, buildings had been hit, their contents and substrate spilling onto the street. The train stations hadn't been hit. The Danube's bridges were all intact. The planes had been inexact, hitting residential property. The Steiner factory hadn't been hit. An oil refinery burned, blackening the air and everyone's mood.

On Wednesday morning Zeno was helping Mr. Steiner into his overcoat when he noticed that a yellow star had been stitched roughly to the fine camel-hair wool of the left-hand lapel. It was ruined. There would always be the mark of a star on the fabric.

"Come now," Mr. Steiner said, shaking his hands behind him. "This star is only temporary."

"I thought you sought an exemption."

Mr. Steiner slipped his arms through the sleeves.

"I was unable to get one." He turned towards Zeno, who adjusted the shoulders. "It feels just the same."

"Does the rest of--"

"The whole family must wear them."

Catherine too had to wear a star.

Mr. Steiner looked towards the window, judging the tenor of the day.

"It's such a lovely morning," he said. "I'll walk and take a taxi."

"Perhaps the car?" Zeno said.

"I'll be fine."

"I've seen people attacked."

Mr. Steiner looked out at him from a heavy brow. "Let's not join the hysteria."

After he'd left the apartment, Zeno grabbed his coat and followed him through the streets. Even though it was early morning, many people on the street wore the star. He refused to look directly at them. Instead he observed the ones without a star. They seemed to be like him, looking anywhere except at a person wearing a star—which only made the ugly yellow badges more noticeable. And was their lack of looking borne from consideration for these poor people or some now un-reined revulsion they'd curtailed up to now?

"Who would have thought he was a pinky pig."

Zeno spun around to see who'd said it. Two men huddled together and laughed like schoolgirls. When they realized Zeno was looking, their expressions became defiant, as if they were goading him to say something. At some distance, Tibi stood, almost at attention, observing what had happened. Zeno watched him, but his expression remained impassive and mute. He could read nothing. Was this another chance encounter? No. Tibi was following him. Or Mr. Steiner. He turned to see where Mr. Steiner was. He was gone. Zeno walked away from Tibi. He didn't want another cut eye or to see someone else thumped about.

As he now worked for both Peter and Sándor, his days were doubly full. He started work at 5 am which meant rising from bed by 4:30 at the latest. After washing his face with cold water and dressing, he went to Peter's apartment. He'd enter the dressing room from the hall and prepare Peter's clothes for the day, lay them out on the bench, hang the ironed shirt, and brush down a suit on the clothes rack, the polished shoes for the day on the floor.

By 6:00 am, he'd descend to Sándor's apartment to prepare his clothes and be ready to wake him at 7:00. Upstairs, Erzsébet stepped into the breach and woke Peter, made him tea, helped him dress and prepare for the office. Both Peter and Sándor were appreciative of his efforts and neither of them remonstrated if he missed something or failed to anticipate in advance, which he did now with some frequency.

"We all must make an effort," Peter said. "We'll settle into a routine."

The increased work meant no Sundays off. He was paid for the overtime, which he appreciated greatly, but his time with Catherine was reduced to an hour at the most in the late evening. Talk spiked with fear about everything that was happening replaced their lovemaking. Catherine's coat bore a yellow star. But in some grand act of defiance, she also wore the crucifix.

"I worry about you out in the streets wearing the star."

"Please don't. I go out as little as possible. I walk quickly and stay in the shadows."

"But you shouldn't wear the cross. It'll make people angry."

"Let them think what they want."

"Gertrúd knows you're pregnant."

She sighed. "I suspected she did."

"She also knows about us."

Her eyes opened wide. "How?"

"In the cellar, she caught us looking at one another."

Catherine sighed heavily. "She's not a stupid girl."

"We must leave. We have to. It's all too risky."

"I know. We'll talk."

"Catherine, we *must* talk now."

"I have no time now."

"She could destroy everything."

"No."

She narrowed her gaze.

"I…" he said. What was he to say? Not only did Gertrúd know everything, he'd slept with her and rebuffed her, spurred her jealousy.

"What?" she said.

"I think… Gertrúd likes me."

Catherine's eyes wandered from his.

"Have you given her any cause to feel this?"

He hesitated, aware a moment's hesitation was tantamount to admission.

"Not really." He sighed. "Perhaps when I first came to Budapest."

"I'll speak with her."

"She's seeing a man who's a member of the Arrow Cross Party."

Catherine rubbed her forehead, smoothing away worry lines.

"We can't just go on hoping," he said.

She straightened herself. "Gertrúd is faithful."

"Are you so sure?"

Catherine flinched. "Why are you so unsure?"

The municipal clock struck eleven.

"Okay," he said. "You speak with her. But we must talk soon, make a plan."

"I've made some inquiries."

"How?"

"Someone I know. In the Jewish Aid and Rescue Committee. I'm meeting him soon."

She walked to him and kissed him.

"I must go," she said.

"I'll follow you back to the building. But you must promise me we'll talk of this again as soon as possible."

"Of course we will." She looked away from the intensity of his gaze. "We will."

Not only were the days hectic, but no sooner had a routine been found than something changed it completely again. One morning, after he'd cleared up Mr. Steiner's apartment and completed his chores, he left to return to Peter's. Catherine crossed the mezzanine foyer as he did. She came down the stairs, on her way out of the building. She wore a long grey overcoat without a yellow star. If Jews were caught without the star it was mandatory deportation to a labor camp. He ran towards her. She shook her head, the action only slight but of sufficient gravitas. He stopped. He pushed the wooden panel that sprang open to the staff stairs. He motioned for her to enter. She glanced around and stepped into the well.

"You're not wearing the star."

"There's an exemption. Sándor took my French papers to one of his German cronies and they accepted them. I don't have to wear the star, and because we're married, he's exempt."

Zeno sighed. "That's good, then."

"How life's filled with petite irony. Suddenly I'm the savior of the family. Now Sándor is certain we should stay."

She slipped back out the door. He waited while he heard the sound of her heels disappear on the main stairs. If Catherine and Mr. Steiner were exempt, then at least his job was safe and he could keep living near Catherine, keep earning money, keep looking for the window of escape.

When he arrived at the upstairs apartment, Peter was still there, seated at his desk in the library. Normally by 7:30 he'd left for work.

"I'll come back," Zeno said.

"Do what you need," Peter said. "I've a meeting here this morning. "

Zeno moved through the apartment. Erzsébet had taken the children to school. Now that Jewish children were not allowed to attend a school, each day she took them to a Jewish teacher. Since Jews couldn't teach, the Steiners and several other wealthy families had set up a makeshift classroom at the factory.

Later in the morning, there was a knock at the main door. As he was the only servant, Zeno went to answer it. An SS officer stood at the door, dressed in the black uniform which seemed to shine like patent leather.

"I've a meeting with Peter Kresz."

Zeno opened the door wider. As he stepped back, Peter walked down the hallway towards them.

"Lieutenant Becher," Peter said, holding out his hand.

The lieutenant lifted his hand high. "Sieg heil."

Peter seemed taken back by the sign. "If you'll follow me to my library." Peter motioned towards the library door. "Zeno, will you bring us tea?"

What the hell was an SS officer doing in the house with Peter? Did Mr. Steiner know about this? Did Catherine? When he carried the tray to the library, Peter was seated behind his desk, Lieutenant Becher opposite him. Becher had taken off his cap, his fair hair combed back over his head, revealing a bold, intelligent forehead. Zeno went to place the tray on a side table.

"Leave them here." Peter pointed to the side of his desk. "Leave the apartment."

Zeno bowed his head and left the library. Outside in the hall, he flattened himself against the wall. His heart raced. Peter had never spoken to him so abruptly. Something was happening.

"When did you arrive in Budapest?" Peter said.

"Towards the end of March. The cavalry needs horses. I'm here to engage them."

"I see."

Peter seemed to be stalling, no doubt waiting to hear that Zeno had left. Zeno walked quickly to the apartment's main door, closed it heavily, and crept back to the library door.

"It's good of you to come at such short notice," Peter said. "If we're going to advance, the sooner the better."

"What are you proposing?"

"We'll sign over the ownership of the whole factory to the SS. In return for this, you'll provide a plane to fly the family to Switzerland."

There it was, Peter's escape plan, so grandiose, so bold, so financed, everything he and Catherine couldn't manage.

"I see."

There was silence. Perhaps Lieutenant Becher contemplated, perhaps he sought to make Peter uncomfortable. Zeno held his breath.

"You're prescient," Becher said at last. "Let me be frank. Your offer to sign over the factory is wise. Shrewd."

"We want our freedom. I know the price will be high."

"As generous as your offer is, what you're asking is gigantic. Such a request will meet resistance."

"What would provide the necessary lubrication?'

"Cash, valuables. For each person."

"How much?"

"Name a price."

"I can't put a price on such a thing."

"If the price is right, people can be made to do almost anything."

"If we are also expected to pay for each individual, we must be allowed to take possessions with us."

"It's a plane, for god's sake. There's a limit to space."

"I'm not proposing furniture. Small pieces of jewelry. Clothing."

"How many people do you propose?"

"My wife, my children, her mother and father. My parents. Sándor is intent on staying. He has negotiated contracts."

"Good. We need someone who knows the factory."

The main door of the apartment opened and closed. The voices in the office fell silent. Erzsébet stood at the door. She swallowed hard, as if she'd just resigned herself to something, and walked into the apartment, unaware of Zeno flattened to the wall. Zeno heard Peter's footsteps circle the desk, heading for the library door. On his toes he scurried to the main door. As he closed it, he heard Peter yell out, "Darling, is that you?"

In the outside hallway, Zeno stood still. He exhaled. The family was going to leave Hungary. What was he to do with such information? So easily the SS had been bribed. But what a price. The lives of everyone in the house would be affected. Should he tell them? Should he tell Mr. Steiner? He didn't know. But he must tell Catherine.

On Sunday, Zeno spilled the details of the conversation to Catherine as if he were up-ending a pail of water.

"I know all of this," she said. "There was a family meeting to discuss the proposal."

"The Gestapo was so easily bribed."

"If the factory is legally signed over to them, if anyone in the future should question their dealings, they'll argue this as an example that they'd always acted legally."

"I don't understand."

"They know they're losing the war. Despite what we all may think, the men of the Gestapo are human. They're only looking after themselves. They want money. Like us, they'll need to escape. Peter's prepared to pay them."

Zeno felt chilled. "So you'll leave with them."

"Sándor is against it. He says he's negotiated to run the factory. He'll work with the Germans. He sees no need to flee."

"So the rest of the family will go without him."

"And we'll stay. My papers have fooled people. Sándor says that will protect us both, but for how long? The Germans change the rules every day. How long can this deceit be maintained?"

"Hasn't the family asked you to go?"

"They wouldn't take me even if I asked. I've failed them."

"But if Mr. Steiner wanted to go?"

"He's driven by something, something new. He competes with Peter in a way I've never seen before. That's what this is about—a difference of opinion that's been reduced to a joust. I think he's mad."

"What do you mean?"

"This insane need he has to prove himself better than Peter." The two were silent.

"I know what you're thinking," she said, finally. "You're completely right. We must leave."

Zeno rocked. It was the first time she'd suggested such a thing.

"How the hell are we to do it?" he said.

"I'm not sure, but we have to do it. For the sake of the baby."

"Yes. Now, if we--"

"I've to go," she said. "Return to the house. I've met with my contact. He's hopeful to find a way but we must do what we can. Bring things here to the apartment. Collect them here. We need money, some food. Different clothes. At least it's spring. Bring things here and we can start to plan."

CHAPTER NINETEEN

In a cupboard in the servants' hall Zeno found a small spirit lamp. It had remained untouched the whole time he'd worked at the house and it might come in handy, so he took it. In another cupboard he found a travel rug with a similar history so he took that as well. That evening after he'd finished work, he took these supplies and his heaviest jumper to the small apartment.

The following day he lingered in the kitchen to see if there was anything he could appropriate. But food perished quickly. They still had no idea when they'd leave, so anything he took, fruit, bread, even cheese, would be rancid. And food was heavy. As he walked back through the house to Mr. Steiner's apartment, he thought Catherine was wrong and rather than food they'd do better to carry a good quantity of money. As he'd heard the SS lieutenant say to Peter, for a price people can be made to do most anything.

When he reached Mr. Steiner's apartment, Father István was standing outside.

"There you are," he said. "It's no wonder I can't raise anyone."

"Mr. Steiner is there."

"He's not answered."

Zeno opened the door.

"You seem very well," Father István said.

Lack of sleep, worry, and too much work made Zeno feel far from well but he said nothing. He escorted the priest to the lounge room and Mr. Steiner seated in the sun.

"What a beautiful morning it is," Father István said.

Mr. Steiner rose to greet his cousin. "It would seem the occupation has even augmented the weather."

"Indeed."

Mr. Steiner handed Father István his monthly cheque for an orphanage run mostly on the family's behest. Father opened the envelope and smiled.

"Your generosity knows no bounds." He looked from the cheque to the vase of flowers on the mantle. "And what beautiful flowers…"

"Yes."

Mr. Steiner's tone was curt. He wanted Father István to stop with the compliments and get to the point of his visit.

"I've written to the pontiff," Father István said, "concerning the deportation of Jews to ghettos and labor camps."

"Zeno, will you bring us coffee?" He looked back at Father István. "And what was his reply?"

Zeno bowed his head and retreated to the small kitchen. As he prepared the coffee, he realized he'd been so intent that morning on what he could steal from the kitchen he'd not brought fresh milk up. He walked back through the lounge.

"And it's with great happiness," Father István said, "that I congratulate you."

"Congratulate me?"

"Oh dear, perhaps I've spoken out of turn."

"Not at all. I'm just not sure exactly what you're referring to."

Father István's eyes twinkled. "Well, now--Catherine's pregnancy, of course."

Zeno spun towards them. Mr. Steiner's face was frozen, his body held still and tight. He'd not noticed Zeno staring at him. Suddenly he wiped his hand over his forehead and sat down.

"I'm so sorry, I *have* spoken out of turn."

"No…" Mr. Steiner rested. He realized that Zeno was staring at him. "The coffee."

"I have to go for milk," Zeno said. "I won't be long."

He walked into the apartment's entrance hall.

"It's just that we haven't told anyone," Mr. Steiner said.

"Such a blessing. Finally."

"Yes. A blessing."

For a few moments no one spoke. Zeno's mind coursed over what he could do.

"We'd rather keep this a secret. How did you hear?"

"Many things are said, not in confession you understand, but in passing."

Zeno left the apartment. For a minute he stood still in the hall, fighting off the adrenaline to find some clarity. Then he ran to Catherine's apartment. He knocked on the door. When no one answered he thumped. The door opened.

"Why are you here?"

Gertrúd stood before him.

"I must speak with Catherine."

"Does she know you're coming?"

"I've a message from her husband. I must speak with her."

He made to pass her but she blocked his way.

"That's quite irregular." She looked him up and down. "I'll see if she's in."

She walked down the hall. Zeno took two or three paces with her. She turned and glared at him. He stopped. She disappeared into the lounge room. She spoke to Catherine in French. Catherine appeared in the hall, her expression as neutral as she could make it. Gertrúd stood behind her.

"I must speak with you," he said. "Your husband asked me to."

Catherine looked over her shoulder at Gertrúd.

"I see." She looked back at him. "Follow me."

He followed, taking care not to look at Gertrúd. Catherine walked through the lounge and straight to the bedroom. For a moment he was unsure if he should follow but she motioned for him to join her. She closed the door, the intensity of her perfume overpowering. Now her face was stern. She remained at a distance.

"He knows."

Catherine closed her eyes, took a deep breath and let it out slowly.

"How could he?"

"Father István congratulated him."

There was a quiet knock at the bedroom door. Catherine looked at the door and then at Zeno.

"Yes?"

Gertrúd walked in. "*Votre mari est ici pour vous voir.*"

"*Je vais le recevoir,*" she said. Catherine ran her hand over her belly and sighed deeply. "Does life never let you suffer just one emotion?"

"What's happening?" Zeno said.

"Sándor is here."

She composed herself and left the room. Whether she purposely left the door ajar or not Zeno had no idea but from his vantage in her bedroom he was able to hear everything in the lounge, even see some of it reflected in a large mirror hanging above the fireplace.

"I'm sorry to disturb you," Sándor said.

Catherine dropped like a stone onto the sofa opposite the mirror. Sándor was outside Zeno's field of vision.

"Gertrúd," Catherine said.

She appeared too quickly in the room. Zeno couldn't understand what Catherine said to her in French, but Gertrúd looked towards the bedroom door, then left the apartment.

"What is it you want?" Catherine said.

Mr. Steiner took two measured steps, the sound of his foot firm on the parquet floors. With the last step, he came into Zeno's view, facing Catherine, looking at her with a vile half smirk.

"Come, now, Catherine. At some point, civility must reenter our relationship." He paused. "Now that we're to be parents."

Zeno's eyes darted to her face, reflected in the mirror. She remained composed, sat up straight, leaned slightly forward toward her husband.

"Do you bribe everyone in this city?" she said.

"You're too coarse." He spat the words, his face pulled tight. "Let me just say there are those faithful to the family, overjoyed we'll finally bear issue."

She said nothing.

"Who *is* the father?"

He stepped out of Zeno's view. Catherine stood, circled the sofa, and stopped in front of the mirror. She glanced towards the bedroom door. Out of sight, Mr. Steiner waited for her response. When none came, he spoke.

"Come now," he said. "Unless we have another immaculate conception, it's clearly not me."

Still she remained silent.

"Why didn't you tell me?" he said. "Did you think it would all go unnoticed? Can you imagine the embarrassment when I was congratulated?"

She said nothing.

"Come," he said, his voice laden with faux joy. "You simply must tell me who it is."

Catherine held her mettle and remained silent.

"Thrill me," Mr. Steiner said. "Was it my driver? No... a friend of mine... Zsigmond?"

Her expression hardened. Zeno was sure she'd lose her nerve.

"Ah…" he said. "I know who. Zeno. Yes. Zeno."

Zeno stopped breathing. Mr. Steiner had recognized her in the cuts of film. He'd put two and two together. She was going to lose her cool.

"How dare you ask such a thing?" Her voice hissed as she spun to face him. "How many years have you paraded your chorus line of whores in front of me, and have I ever said a thing? No matter how public it was--"

"Chorus line of whores... I like that."

"Couldn't you have chosen women less cheap?"

"So I am to deduce that *your* lover, if there's only one, is nobility?"

"You've no right to know."

"Perhaps from the lower ranks of royalty... a relation of Horthy--"

"You've no right to ask."

Now he was silent. "There's no need to be so testy. I've already publicly claimed the child as mine. It will have all benefits--"

"How dare you!"

"And what were you going to do, exactly? Run away with this man and have the child?"

Now she walked away from the mirror and Zeno couldn't see either of them.

"Life's full of irony, isn't it?" Mr. Steiner said. "You were brought to Hungary to bear children, Jewish children. And you failed at that."

"*I've* failed? Despite what you may think, I haven't had endless affairs. This is the first. You're the one who's failed, though I know how much that shatters your self-image."

She walked back into view and sat down on the sofa.

"This conversation is of no consequence," he said.

"I thought you might say that."

"By claiming this child as mine, I've actually done you a favor."

"I don't see how."

He was quiet for a moment. "Yesterday, I saw a friend. He crossed the street to speak with me. He told me to leave Hungary, immediately, that day. Two men, Slovakians, have escaped from Auschwitz. They have written a report. They detail the killing of Jews by gassing."

Catherine gasped, then held her breath. "What? That can't be true."

"The men have been interrogated. The labor camps are death machines. Jews are gassed and burnt. They report the recent construction of vast new facilities. That can only mean one thing: they're preparing for Hungarian Jews. The Germans plan the annihilation of all Hungarian Jews."

"Why hasn't this been made public?"

"It can't be. Not at this stage. It would cause panic."

She was quiet. "That's obscene."

"I'm sure what I'm about to say will bring you great joy. But you should consider it before you respond." Mr. Steiner steadied himself. "Peter was right. I was wrong to deal with these people. They're killing machines. We have to escape, and you've provided us with the ticket."

He turned to leave, walked some paces towards the door and turned back.

"Who *is* your lover?"

In silence, Catherine stared at him.

"You won't tell me, will you?" Mr. Steiner was quiet for a moment. "Come to think of it, I don't actually give a tinker's damn. I hope it makes you happy, Catherine. You rather got the bad end of all of this. I'm sorry you were ever dragged into this fucking family."

When Zeno heard the apartment door close, he left the room. Catherine was standing at the fireplace, pale and shaken. Wordless, she looked at Zeno but couldn't maintain the contact and looked away. He too was speechless. What could they say? He wanted only to hold her, kiss her. As they stood so apart, the door of the apartment opened. Gertrúd now stood between them. She looked from Zeno to Catherine and back to Zeno. For a moment, as if time stood still, Zeno continued only to look at Catherine.

"*Prendriez-vous du café,*" Gertrúd said.

Zeno had no idea what she'd said but from the scowling look on Catherine's face something vexing had passed between them. Zeno left the apartment without saying anything.

Over the next few days, the joy of Catherine's pregnancy filled the house. The endless delivery of flowers packed every vase and every available space in the house. One evening, Catherine and Mr. Steiner appeared together in the main lounge room. Surrounded by his parents and the rest of the family, they toasted the health of the child.

On Sunday morning, Zeno arrived at the apartment early to find Catherine already there. She'd brought a small carpet bag that sat unattended in the middle of the floor. Were they to leave today? She stood by the window, quietly looking out at the city. She didn't turn when he entered the room. In an instant, he recognized that stance, that particular arrangement of limbs and torso that reflected her pensive state of mind.

"Those poor men," she said without turning towards him.

Zeno walked towards the window.

"Who?"

"Those Slovakian men Sándor spoke of. They risked their lives to escape Auschwitz. To confuse the search dogs, they sat for three days soaked in petrol--to tell the world what's really happening. And no one's doing a damn thing."

"Their story's very hard to believe."

"It's not hard to believe at all. Now everything make sense. Everyone who's missing is dead." She stopped herself. "They've suppressed the information."

"Who?"

"The wealthy Jews of Budapest. Lieutenant Colonel Eichmann said it's not true and they believe him, but even that's not true. They don't believe him at all. They want to buy their escape before the death camps are known about and everybody without money panics."

Zeno thought about what she'd said. Could it be true that this was happening? The Jews supposedly had been transported to labor camps, centers from where they were to be taken to their own land, their own country, and resettled. Was that really just what people wanted to believe?

"I love you," she said, still looking out at the city.

He went to her side, caressed her shoulders.

"I know," he said. 'I love you too."

She turned her face towards him. She smiled. A simple smile, her eyes so brilliant and clear.

"I've lost so many people," she said.

"We'll not lose one another."

"You once asked how my father could be so heartless to send me here to marry Sándor."

"I've never understood."

"I was heartless when I responded to you." Her glistening eyes darted to his and then returned to the window. "When I was eighteen, my brother... interfered with me. My father caught him."

"Catherine--"

"My father took his side, said I'd tempted him. I was old enough to understand the gravity of what I'd done. I was banished before a scandal erupted."

He had no words, for they all suddenly felt inadequate. But now he understood.

"I lost all my family, my sisters, my mother, everyone. I can't lose you." Her voice wavered. "I simply can't lose you."

He turned her towards him. She laid her head to his shoulder and began to cry. What could he do to salve such a raw wound? What could he do?

"You're so tender," she said. "I've never felt such care." She pulled away from him. "The Steiner family is to leave Hungary in three or four day's time."

"Mr. Steiner has made no mention of it."

"And he won't. This is all very secret. The Gestapo will fly them to Switzerland. Everything's been arranged."

"And you?" he whispered.

"I've had enough of the Steiners. My future's with you."

"Then we must leave together."

She nodded. Feeling overwhelmed, he sank onto the single chair at the table. His plans seemed so skimpy.

"First we need to think of what we have in our favor," he said. "We have some money."

From his wallet he took a few thousand pengő he'd managed to save and placed them on the table. His mother and sister would just have to make do without it. From her carpet bag she took a greater wad of notes.

"I can get more," she said. "I just didn't want to arouse suspicion."

"Are your papers still valid?"

She nodded.

From the bookcase he took a book that contained a rough map of Europe.

"We'll travel south." He ran his finger over the map, running from Budapest down to Lake Balaton, along the eastern shore and further down to the Yugoslav border. "We should have no trouble, this far. We can travel on trains."

"As long as we were in sight of one another, we could travel separately."

"Yes. We'd be less obvious. But from the border…"

The border, a line on the map, seemed as high as the Great Wall of China. There were checkpoints, soldiers patrolling both sides. And he had no idea of the terrain, no idea how to move with a map in the pitch of night.

"I've a contact," she said, "in the Jewish Aid and Rescue Committee. For a fee, I'm sure they can help us over the border."

For a price, people could be made to do anything.

"From there," he said, "we'll make our way to Dubrovnik." He moved his finger on the map, further south. "We'll buy a boat. If we can't, we'll steal one, and sail to Italy. If the weather's fair, we won't need a large one. The distance isn't so great."

He ran his finger over the Adriatic Sea. It looked about twice the length of Lake Balaton. He'd sailed this distance many times in fair and foul weather, but…

"You're a good captain," she said. "We can sail through the islands."

"Once we're in Italy, we'll surrender to the Allies. We'll be free."

For some time, Zeno was quiet. He thought through the intricacies of the plan.

"We'll leave no trace on the skin of water." She ran her finger over the Adriatic Sea. "I'm positive of this."

"When?" he said.

"The family will leave on Thursday or Friday night. Everything must be ready by then. Just as the family's leaving the building, I'll slip away and meet you here."

CHAPTER TWENTY

"Will you please have Peter's dinner suit ready for Saturday evening?" Erzsébet said.

Zeno nearly dropped the clothes brush he was using.

"Saturday evening?"

She'd always given orders well in advance but the family would leave Hungary on Thursday or Friday night.

"We're attending an opera," she said.

This was a charade. A game. And it continued over the next few days, all through the house. In the morning, Mr. Steiner rose at his usual time and left for the factory by 7:30. He went to dinner on Monday night and stayed out very late Tuesday, which often meant he'd slept somewhere else. The rest of the house functioned like clockwork, albeit with reduced staff and not quite the usual attention to detail. No requests for traveling trunks to be pulled out of storage, no clothes packed, nothing especially laundered, no sign of anything but the day to day. If he hadn't known what was really going on he'd have perceived no change at all.

In all this usualness he did see Catherine more frequently in the public areas of the house. She went out often. And though he didn't speak with Gertrúd, she also went about her tasks in much the same manner. Perhaps the few remaining staff detected nothing, the masquerade visible only to the informed eye.

At eight on Wednesday evening after dinner had been cleared, Karl and Ella appeared in the servants' antechamber. They stood together, motionless, at the center of the room, dressed in warm coats, not elegant, just functional. They carried nothing. She had her arm linked through his.

"Is there anything you want?" the housemistress asked them.

"No," Karl said, his voice stern. As a pair, they looked straight ahead and said nothing to anyone.

Then Peter and Erzsébet and the children joined them, similarly dressed and also carrying nothing. The children were unusually calm, as if they'd been administered some soporific medicine. Next Mr. Steiner and Catherine came to the chamber, followed by Karl Steiner's brother and his wife and their children.

"What's happening?" the housemistress asked Zeno.

"I don't know," Zeno said.

The family stood in a tight bunch. The children looked down at their shoes and made no sound. Peter looked at the wall clock and walked down the corridor to the rear lane. One of the servants went to Karl to ask what was happening. Karl shooed him away.

"They're here," Peter called out. He came back to the antechamber. The family exchanged glances, their expression more concerned now.

"I can't explain what's happening," Karl said, still looking straight ahead. "We wish to thank you all."

And then, in single file, with rehearsed precision, the family walked down the thin long corridor to the rear lane.

Zeno watched Catherine. As she passed in profile her expression was cold, set like stone, her face turned down to her feet. Despite all this, he felt close to her. Amongst the line of others, the back of her head appeared and disappeared. This part of their life together was over.

When the family was gone, the remaining servants looked at one another in disbelief.

"What's going on?" someone half whispered.

Someone walked down the corridor and returned.

"They've gone. German military cars came for them and they've gone."

"German?"

"Why would he thank us?"

"Where have they gone?"

A hush fell over the servants. They looked at one another, their expressions blank, the scene they'd witnessed leaving them without words.

From the northern hall, footsteps, running loud, came towards the antechamber. As the other servants turned, Zeno seized his opportunity and moved unnoticed towards the eastern hall, which would take him to the servants' stair. His footfall was silent but as he reached the hall, he turned back to see who'd run so urgently to the antechamber. Gertrúd stood at the north, her faced flushed, her hair disheveled. Silently, Zeno moved on towards the stair.

"Where's Zeno?" she yelled.

No one in the antechamber could muster any voice. He didn't stop for a second. There was no time for delay. He took the stairs two at a time but without making a sound, winding quickly up the small circular stair.

"Where the hell is he?" Her voice rang with hysteria. "I have to speak with him."

He pressed on and took the panel door to the empty main entrance hall, ran up the grand staircase to the mezzanine and along the hall to Mr. Steiner's apartment. In his small office he removed his uniform and changed into the dark jumper and woolen pants he'd hidden there. Although the family's escape had happened ahead of schedule, everything was in order. Thank God that morning he'd completed the last of the preparations and mailed all his precious film back to his mother. His projector, all his clothes, he'd just leave in his room. He was leaving the Steiner building and he'd never come back.

He slung his camera over his shoulder, newly surprised at its weight. This would be a burden. It was still broken from its crash to the ground. It was old. He could buy another camera. His own eye would be the lens through which he dissected the world. He took it off, placed in on the floor.

"Goodbye, old friend."

He looked around the apartment one more time. He'd always remember the visual play between the two windows, the scent of the polished floor, the click of the door's latch.

The hall was empty. If Gertrúd was looking for him she'd have gone to his room. Quickly he ran towards the main stair. The air was quiet. He'd never heard so little fuss in the house. Perhaps the others had started to put together what had just happened with some of the odd events of the last few days.

His quickest route from the building was straight down the main stair and out the front door. Other than that, he'd have to return to the lower levels of the house, where he'd almost certainly encounter other staff and be delayed. He pricked his ear. He could hear someone's step echoing higher on the stair.

He ran. His footfall echoed through the building but it no longer mattered. He had to be free. He ran across the entrance hall to the door. He slid back the huge bolts. With no turning back, he swung the door open, leaving it wide open, and started to run. His instincts told him to remain unseen, to stick to the edge of the building, but his urgency forced him to run the shortest route, directly across the courtyard to the street. He ran hard.

A fleet of five or six roaring German military trucks passed him headed in the opposite direction. He stopped and looked back towards the building. In a well-oiled formation they snaked into the courtyard. It was happening. They were taking over the Steiners' lives. The past, with all its grandeur, was over. This was the future.

He ran, as hard as he could, through the streets and across the river. Pest was awash with soldiers, troops moving everywhere for no reason he could discern. Two German SS strolled down the street. Something told him to avoid them. Another truck roared by. He was so out of breath he feared he'd draw attention to himself, and they were happy to arrest people for less. He took to the shadows, slipped through the city by longer back routes until he'd reached the small square of the apartment. He looked up at the windows and felt a bead of sweat run down his spine. The apartment was dark. He steadied himself, then walked the last few steps to the building.

As he climbed the main stair, he caught Catherine's perfume. God knows how she'd done it, but she'd escaped them. He fumbled the key but the door was already unlocked. The apartment was dark. He walked towards the main room.

"Catherine?"

He turned on the light. At the center of the room sat her carpet bag, full of things they'd readied. He took two steps into the room. Her perfume was overbearing.

"Catherine?"

He looked down at her bag. On top was an envelope with his name, in her hand. He tore it open, turned it to read.

I'm sorry. Forgive me. I couldn't. Please think well of me.

His breath clogged in his throat. What could this mean? She wasn't coming. The floor felt insecure. His viscera tightened. He needed to shit, water, his whole being was going to run out of his body. A noise came from the other room.

"Catherine?"

Unable to move, he looked at the door to the bedroom. A foot scraped over the floor. He smelled her perfume. Gertrúd moved into the light. She was wearing Catherine's perfume.

"What… what are you doing here?"

She looked much as she had a few moments ago at the main house, her hair tousled. But she'd lost that blush of exertion, her skin now pale and drawn taut.

A blast erupted behind him. Zeno spun towards the apartment's door just as two SS soldiers kicked it open. They stood in the doorway, guns drawn. He turned back to Gertrúd. Tibi now stood behind her.

"What are you doing here?" Zeno said.

Tibi was dressed in a suit and tie and a long gray coat. He made no response, his face passionless. A Gestapo officer walked from the dark behind them into the room, his heel slow and firm on the wooden floors. He sat in the armchair.

Zeno looked towards the bedroom. He felt ice cold air on his skin.

"Tibi," Zeno said, trying to make light of his voice. "What are you doing here?"

Tibi looked Zeno directly in the eye.

"What am *I* doing here?" Tibi said.

"Arrest him," the officer said.

Zeno turned back towards the door but the soldiers advanced, grabbed him, yanked him back into the room.

"It's illegal to have intimacy with a Jew," the officer said.

"She is a Catholic."

"She *is* a Jew."

"I work for her husband."

The officer looked at Tibi, who walked to the note which had fallen to the floor. He read the note, then waved it in Zeno's face.

"I think with such a letter," Tibi said, "it's hard for you to deny the intimacy."

"Where is she?"

The cool eyes of the officer and Tibi stared him down and gave away nothing. He turned to Gertrúd. She averted her eyes.

"Gertrúd?" he said, but she wouldn't look at him and moved away, back to the dark of the bedroom.

Zeno glared at Tibi's cold eyes. Why could he now, only now, detect the depth of corruption in that cold blue with pins of black at their center? He sucked in a long breath. Something roused in him. He spun, with all his force, back towards the apartment's door. The soldier's grip faltered. He was free. Two or three more steps and –

He felt something crack across the back of his head. He raised his hand to the pain but it struck again. He felt his strength go, somehow the drain felt sensual as he collapsed. He lost his sight.

CHAPTER TWENTY-ONE

Tibi sat behind a large wooden desk.

The welt on the back of Zeno's head still ached without mercy. He'd lost track of the days. Could it be weeks? This room was light, on the second or third story of a building. Zeno looked at the light, the first direct sun he'd seen in… he had no idea how long. His clothes, the clothes of his and Catherine's escape, were stained and splattered. He'd lost his shoes. His hands were black, dirt under his nails.

Tibi wore a military uniform, the dark green of the Arrow Cross. Behind him from a floor stand hung the red Arrow Cross flag. Both the flag and the armband bore a set of crossed arrows. Zeno thought the flag hung rather limply. Tibi's blond hair was clean and oiled and combed. To his side stood another man, also dressed in the Arrow Cross uniform. No sign of the Gestapo.

"Again," Tibi said. "You're charged with having sex with a Jewess."

The hammer of a typewriter behind him caused Zeno to jump and turn his head. For this investigation, he received a slap across the face from one of the men who'd dragged him from this cell. Zeno looked back at Tibi. He dug his nails deep into the flesh of his palms. It calmed him.

"You must answer this charge."

"Why are you doing this, Tibi?"

It was the first time Zeno had spoken since his arrest. His voice sounded gruff and unfamiliar. Tibi leaned back in his chair, away from the desk.

"You've slapped your country across the face."

"What are you getting out of this? Some miniscule promotion?"

Tibi stopped. He glanced at the others in the room.

"Nothing is miniscule anymore."

"And what did Gertrúd get out of it? Did she steal a bottle of Catherine's perfume?"

Tibi's hard face softened. He laughed.

"Stop typing." The noise behind Zeno stopped. "She took far more than that."

"The Steiners have paid off the Gestapo," Zeno said. "That's real wealth, real power. That's what money can do. They're free."

"Do you think the Gestapo is a cheap whore?" Tibi raised his eyebrows. "It would cost more than the Steiners could muster to corrupt them."

"I heard the negotiations--"

"They were arrested."

For some moments he stared blankly.

"The Gestapo drove the lambs from their house to a processing center. They couldn't have been more compliant."

The blow felled him to his knees. They cracked on the hard floor and the pain shot up his thighs.

"In an effort to save herself she confessed everything of your affair."

This thought looped around in his head. This all seemed so trivial.

"What will happen to her?"

"The whole family has been sent to a labor camp."

Zeno's eyes bulged as he looked up at Tibi. "They're death camps."

"Perhaps. What does it matter?"

Zeno slumped his buttocks back onto his ankles and lay his forehead on the floor.

"You must release her," Zeno said, calming his voice as much as he could. "She's pregnant."

Tibi stood up, walked around the desk, paused, then kicked Zeno in the ribs. Oddly he felt no pain, as if the kick had been fake, delivered in a movie. But the momentum swung his body over. He righted himself against the force.

"You're in no position to bargain," Tibi said. "You've betrayed the laws of your country." He kicked again, hard into the ribs. This blow rolled Zeno on to his side, winded him. "You stuck your dick where a man wouldn't put his walking stick. You need to be contrite."

He closed his eyes, no longer wanting to see the black boots on Tibi's feet. The act of breathing hurt. He held his breath to relieve the pain. But he gasped. His lungs seared. He heard Tibi turn and walk back to his chair. He gulped air again and writhed in pain, then settled for light puffs in the upper reaches of his lungs. He clutched his arms around his body. With excruciating effort, he stood up.

"What is it you want from me?" Zeno said.

"You must confess to what you've done."

"This is petty. I've done nothing wrong."

"You've broken the third Jewish law of your country, passed in 1941."

Catherine had been arrested. Everything was lost. Nothing mattered anymore. He wanted to be away from Tibi, more than anything else. As best he could, he raised himself to his full height.

"All right," Zeno said. "I confess. I had sex with Catherine Steiner. Many, many times. Do with me what you will."

Tibi smiled.

"I blame myself," he said, looking at Zeno. "It was obvious at the lake you were hell bent." Tibi looked at the man beside him. "If the right pressure is applied, we'll arrive at the truth."

In isolation, Zeno's days became a series of bowls of thin gruel, no words, no conversation, moonlight after daylight. He gave up the idea of time. The pain in his ribs retreated or he'd grown used to it. He tried not to think of Catherine, of himself, of Tibi or Gertrúd or Mr. Steiner or anyone. But without distraction his mind was prey to easy anxiety. He'd drift away from what Tibi had said, tried not to imagine Catherine in a camp but imagined them both as they should have been, sailing across the Adriatic.

His stomach turned when he heard someone coming. Whilst he had to close his eyes to eat the gruel, its arrival relieved the boredom, its ingestion eased his hunger pangs. But this footfall was different, swift and intent. He stood up. The bolts slid back and the door hurled open. Two guards advanced on him, shackled his wrists and ankles, and hauled him from the cell to the courtyard of the building, corralled with other men in bare feet and stained rags and chains and hollow faces. Was he looking at himself? In horror he realized these tattered men were his mirror. They were marched to the street.

The outside sun blinded him. The air was warm, the pavement warm under his bare feet. Summer had arrived. That meant two months, three months of incarceration? The sunlight forced him to close his eyes but he had to walk. They were near the Danube, on the Buda side of the city. He'd been held in a building near the river.

From the other direction, Arrow Cross soldiers marched another group of bedraggled people. They were civilians, men and women, some children in their teens, a dozen or so in all. Some wore yellow stars. Some wore not much at all. All wore terror on their faces.

"Stop," the guard controlling Zeno's band commanded.

The men rattled to a halt. The other band were marched to a set of steps that led down into the Danube and lined up along the lower step. A guard lifted a gun and shot each person in the back of the head, advancing along the line, which showed no real sign of dissent. The people capitulated, slunk weak at the knees towards the river. A woman cried out "In the name of God!" Those bodies that hadn't slipped into the Danube were kicked down the steps. This was madness. The bodies hung in water. The blood drained from these torn orifices. The red Danube.

Zeno lowered his head towards the pavement. He didn't want to see any more of the world. He didn't want to go on. He searched his mind for feelings of angst and pity and remorse but he felt calm. He was to be shot and kicked into the water. He'd make no display of emotion. He wouldn't give them that. The people before him hadn't suffered. The bullet entered their minds and destroyed all memory, all thought, all humanity in less than the blink of an eye. Who was he to fight? Why would he fight?

"Move," the guard said.

Zeno shuffled towards the steps, but the chains tightened and pulled him away from the river. A sense of regret washed over him. He wanted to walk back, slide with the bodies into the water of the Danube, float away, sink, drain, anything was better than this creeping walk. But he was in chains, pulled like a roll of film through a projector's sprockets and shutters.

They marched for two days. At night they slept in open fields. He found a jewel, a small potato in the tilled earth. He spoke with no one but listened to all. They were being marched to a temporary prison outside Budapest. And on the third day they arrived at a school, the gardens grown wild with weeds, rolls of barbed wire hung over the hedgerows, large guns the size of small cannons mounted in the clock tower, huge lights from the roof.

And here he stayed with no information, much deprivation, and great anxiety. With nothing else to think of he was swamped with thoughts of Catherine. Why hadn't she come to the small apartment? If they'd arrived at the same time, maybe they'd have known what was going on and that Tibi was there. Maybe they'd have just left? Maybe they'd have escaped? He thought of his mother and sister. What had the war brought to them? Did they know where he was?

Bombs rained on Budapest, the Americans by day and the Russians by night. The Arrow Cross Party, backed by the Germans, forced Regent Horthy to resign and were now in power. Once a day in the late afternoon they ate a bowl of thin soup. Despite the fact he ate almost nothing, he couldn't stop shitting. His clothes fell apart and he tied them back together. He slept in a room, once a classroom, with at least fifty others. As the winter came close to Christmas, they slept closer together. Every day there was talk of escape, of the breaches of the Geneva Convention, of an armistice off in the future. Every day he acted as if he didn't listen.

As they passed through Christmas and into 1945 with little cheer, Zeno was sure he heard bombs without the laboring of the planes attached. He said nothing to anyone. And there was gunfire. Day by day it grew closer and closer until one day a band of Russian troops walked into the school and the Arrow Cross soldiers simply lay down on the ground like lambs. The Russians let all the prisoners go, they just opened up the gates as if it were finally the end of term.

The roads were dangerous, filled with bands of people. He walked along the rail tracks to Budapest. When a train approached, the tracks would rumble beneath his feet and he had some time to hide. He stole some clothes from a village clothes line, some shoes from a shed, some eggs from a startled hen. He ate them raw. It was cold.

Budapest had fallen to pieces, building façades crumbling and teetering, streets broken into potholes and cracks and ravines. Pieces of bodies—arms, lower legs, hands—lay discarded in the street. Pockets of German resistance spluttered for control of smaller and smaller areas. Gunfire, near and far, rattled the air. He kept to himself and made his way to the Steiner house only to find the building no longer there-- in fact so much had been destroyed it was hard to tell exactly where it had stood. But it didn't matter. It definitely wasn't there.

From there he crossed the city. The Germans had bombed all the bridges but he found a small dinghy at the base of some stairs along the Danube wall and rowed over to Pest. The square of Catherine's apartment had also been hit but the building still stood, at least the skin of it. The entire center was gutted. The glassless windows looked vacant to the square like unblinking eyes.

For days he avoided anyone, guided only by moving away from the sound of gunfire. One day he sat in the sun on the steps to a building and fell asleep, only to be awakened by someone calling him.

"Zeno?"

He turned towards the voice. The face eclipsed the sun, nothing but a bright halo.

"My God," a woman's voice said.

He squinted, placing his hand over his eyes.

"Gertrúd," he said.

She offered her hand but he waved it away with all the brutality he could muster. He stood. For a time they looked at one another. She was thin, her hair lank and tied back behind her. Her skin had lost any touch of youth. Her clothes were intact and she seemed healthy enough. He wanted to strike her. He wanted to hold someone familiar. He wanted to ask her a thousand things. She smiled.

"We can't talk here," she said. "I've a room nearby."

At a distance, he followed the sound of her heel. She'd stop, beckoned him to follow. He couldn't look at her. After two blocks she held open a door but he motioned for her to go ahead and despite no reserve of energy pushed open the heavy door himself. They climbed three exhausting flights of stairs. She waited for him on the landing, the apartment's door open. The room was not unlike his and Catherine's. In silence, he sat at a small table in the morning sun. She made tea, moving swiftly about the kitchenette with energy he no longer had. She cut some bread. He sipped the tea.

"You look dreadful," she said. "You must stay here."

He peered into the clear tea.

"Tibi has been forced to flee to Austria." She looked at Zeno as if she expected him to say something. "It's quite fortunate, with everything that's happened, we've not been able to marry." She hesitated for a moment. "I'm not sure I want to."

"What happened to Catherine?"

She placed her cup heavily on the saucer and looked out the window.

"They were arrested at the airport, deported. I can only guess…"

"Why did you do it?"

"Tibi wanted evidence against them--"

"And you gave it?"

"I believed what he believed. I saw nothing wrong."

"Nothing wrong in killing an entire family?" He lurched towards her, grabbed her with both hands around the throat. "You fucking bitch!"

His teacup smashed on the floor. Their eyes met. She didn't flinch. Despite the fury in his eye, his weak grasp was merely symbolic, a caress. She trembled. She breathed easily.

Her eyes dilated and moistened. He released his grasp. She shuffled back in her seat, soothed her neck with her hands, regained herself.

"I came back to the house," she said, "to tell you if you went to the apartment they would arrest you. No one knew where you were. I went to the apartment to warn you but they were already there."

Zeno sat down again. Gertrúd looked out the window. With her right thumb she fidgeted with the quick of her left thumb.

"I know you won't believe me," she said, "but for months, I'd known she was having an affair. I knew she was pregnant and that day in the air raid shelter I realized *you* were her lover, *you* were the father. You'd slept with me when you were her lover."

"Who did you tell?"

"No one. Just Tibi."

"Tibi?"

"A Gestapo officer told him about the family's escape. He was repulsed and wanted to stop it. The Nazis were God to him. This defiled them. He wanted the officers court-martialed. By the end he hated everyone."

He thought back to Tibi at the lake, lying naked and listless on his bed, filled only by the desire to find another woman. When had he learned to hate so furiously?

"Why did Catherine change her mind?"

"We never spoke of this. I resented that. We'd always spoken of everything."

"You were her maid."

Gertrúd sucked in her breath. "Yes, her maid." She glared at him. "One shouldn't rise above one's place." She stopped. "In those days leading up to the family's escape, nothing unusual happened. She had no meeting with Mr. Steiner or anyone else in the family. I had no idea."

He looked at her as she looked down at her lap and played with the quick. What had he meant to her? He had her because he could and as a consequence he lost Catherine. But he'd been young. Young? It was only a year or so ago.

"I miss her," she said. She waited as if she expected him to agree with her. "She treated me well. She took me places, taught me things, French. Like I was important. I mattered."

A tear ran down her cheek. "But when she no longer trusted me.... I told Father István she was pregnant." She stopped, waiting for a recrimination he couldn't give. "Tibi was always a poor second. You see, I fancied I loved you. But it was all rather solitary as it turned out, so I tried to hate you. Both of you." She paused. "How close they are, those two things. But in the end, I tried to save you."

Zeno closed his eyes. In the dark he breathed deeply. The sun was lovely. Indeed, how close they were.

"I'll leave you," he said.

Despite the age he felt, he stood up.

She looked up at him. "Stay and eat something."

He touched her shoulder and made his way out of the building. For some time he stood on the pavement looking up at the sun.

What had he ever meant to Catherine? She'd said over and over she loved him. Did he doubt that now? All that fucking. All that fucking... Even now with all his weakness if she were in front of him, he'd take her. He felt no arousal for Gertrúd. Had he mistaken that feeling for something else? Was that all love was? Some trick had been played upon him, some spell cast over him by something deep within himself. Had it ever really had anything to do with Catherine? Had he seen only what he wanted to see?

He walked back through the blighted streets of Budapest he'd once run with energy and expectation and zeal. When he arrived at the square of the small apartment, he walked into the hollow and burnt shaft of the building. Five floors above him where the piano had been there was blue sky. He looked down at the jostle of broken bricks and broken wood and shattered glass. He moved his foot. He found a white piano key, the note still intact but the long rear mechanism snapped off like a spear. He ran the tip of his finger over the ivory. It was a D, a G or an A. He balanced it in the palm of his right hand and with his left index finger played the note, the remains of the mechanism waggling in the air, the clarion sound only for his ear.

He could make a shelter here, in the rubble. He'd stay here. If it all fell down on him, what did that matter? The talk on the street was that the Russians had liberated the concentration camps. If Catherine were alive, if Catherine wanted him, she'd return here.

CHAPTER TWENTY-TWO

Manhattan, New York City, Summer, 2010.

"The meniscus is damaged. Torn."

Zeno ran his hand slowly over Zsuzi's head.

"It's common in dogs her age," Peter Blacker said.

Zeno had been bringing Zsuzsi to Peter for at least ten years.

"What's the meniscus?"

He looked at Zeno, hard. "Well… it's like a type of cartilage, in between the bones in the knee. It helps stop the bones wearing one another away."

"And if it's torn? What happens?"

"It may tear more. Become entangled in the joint. And the joint will continue to degenerate."

Again, Zeno soothed her dark head with his hand.

"You can fix it?"

"I'm hoping with a stitch it will hold. If it's more damaged, I may have to remove it. Not an ideal solution, but she'll walk better than she is now."

"You'd have to operate?"

Cutting filled Zeno with fear.

"It's not such a big thing. She's fit, generally." Peter Blacker paused. "We'll take extra care of her."

"No, no... I know you will. It's just... I thought she had arthritis, like me."

"It's not that. We can fix this, nearly a hundred percent. I'm hoping. It'll take a stitch and time."

Zeno looked at the vet for a long moment. What was he to do? He simply couldn't make such a decision so quickly.

"It's not so expensive..."

"It's not a question of the money. I just don't want her to suffer."

"Truth is, she's suffering now."

"I'll have to speak with my daughter."

Peter held himself tense for a moment, then nodded. Outside in the waiting room, Manhattan's dogs and cats and birds were howling and meowing and twittering to be seen.

"I could operate tomorrow afternoon," Peter said.

The city radiated like a griddle under Zeno's feet. As he walked, Zsuzsi hobbling along behind on three legs, he looked about him. For weeks he'd had this feeling someone was watching but there was never a face he recognized. Every few steps Zsuzsi's bad back leg touched the pavement and she let out a little yip from the pain. She stopped and looked at him, no spirit to go on.

"*Sajnálom*," he said, because Zsuzsi spoke Hungarian. "I'm an old man, I've barely strength to carry myself, let alone to carry you."

He passed his hand over her head. He looked around, then to the other side of the street. There were just people rushing by, no one he knew. It wasn't that much further and they could rest at the bench outside Schonberger's.

Outside the brownstone, he squatted down beside her, placed one arm under her chest, scooped in her tail around her rear and summoned all his strength. Her weight, only thirty-five pounds, nearly sent him reeling. A few years ago, when he wasn't paying attention, his sturdy old limbs had been replaced by these frail ones. They'd no power and some days ached to the bone. Zsuzsi collapsed like a sack of flour, dead weight.

"Come on, old girl," he said. "We can't stay here all day."

With frequent pauses, he managed to struggle her up the steps into the foyer. His apartment was on the ground floor, a wise decision he and Panni had made when they moved to this building some five or six years ago. He opened the apartment's door. The air was cool. His daughter had the air conditioning declaring war on the height of summer. Zsuzsi walked with all four paws on the floor into the cool.

"What the fuck?" he said. The entire contents of the hall cupboard were strewn across the floor. There was a moment's silence.

"Dad?" Kati yelled from the other end of the apartment. "That you?"

She came into the apartment's small entrance hall. Her chestnut hair was tied up in a scarf, one of her mother's. As a child she'd had his body, lean and sinewy, but now she was older, her life had drawn her completely away from the swimming pool of her youth. In the last few years, she'd put on a deal of weight and he didn't think it suited her.

"Why didn't you buzz me?" she said. "I'd have come to help you."

"It's all right."

"It's not. You look beat." Through the cupboard's contents she picked her way towards him. "What's happened to Zsuzsi?"

She knelt down beside her.

"What's going on here?" Zeno said, looking at the mess.

"Now Mom's gone, I thought it was time to clean up."

"Cleaning up, you say?"

She caressed the top of the dog's head. "What happened with Zsuzsi?"

"You're not to throw anything out."

"I haven't. I won't. Come. Sit down. Tell me what happened at the vet's"

Zsuzsi half-hopped into the living room, curled up on a blanket on the floor since she could no longer jump onto the sofa. Zeno sat down and told Kati everything the vet had said.

"Katalin, do you think I should send her?" Zeno said when he'd finished.

"It's a tough call. Apu, she's old…."

"She isn't so old. Vet says he can fix her."

"No, she's not so old."

"I just don't know what to do."

"When do you have to decide?"

"Not right away."

"Then take your time. I'm here for a few more days. We can struggle on with her as she is."

"If she has the operation, she won't be allowed to walk at all for ten days. Will you stay some more?"

Kati took a deep breath, held it, and let it flow out.

"I can try, Apu. Robert rang this morning and they need me back in California. We have to cut a whole lot of scenes."

"I need you here."

She smiled warmly. "I'll see what I can do."

Zeno looked around the room. Nearly every cupboard was open.

"Don't throw anything out. Nothing of your mother's."

"I won't. Not till I ask you about it. But you've never thrown a thing out. Ever." She looked around the mess. "What are all those reels of film?"

"Film?"

"I found them, right up the back of the hall cupboard. There's an old projector too."

Zeno grunted, trapped. "They're some films I made."

"When?"

"During the war. Nothing of interest."

"Well, that's just not true. I'm interested. I never knew this. How can you never have told me you'd shot films? Can we watch them tonight?"

"No."

"Papa. Don't be like that. Why can't we watch them tonight?"

"I don't want to."

After dinner, Kati spread Zsuzsi's blanket in the middle of the sofa. The dog looked around, pleased to be part of some activity. Kati picked her up and placed her on the blanket. She hobbled a mandatory circle and collapsed.

On a small coffee table, Kati set up the projector, an old Kodak.

"Wow. I don't think we even heard of these in college."

"Just because you work in Hollywood doesn't mean you know everything."

"I wasn't suggesting that."

Kati unwound a small section of film, holding it up to the light.

"You're right. I think they're Budapest." She moved her fingers over the film stock. "These films are nitro. They're dangerous. They can burn."

"We can only hope that after sixty years they'll explode."

Kati put down the film and looked at her father.

"Don't be like that, Apu. If you don't want to look at them we don't have to."

"You want to."

"I take it that means you do too." With care, she wound the film through the shutters and sprockets. "We're ready."

She walked over to the room's lamp and turned it off. A small shaft of light spilled into the room from the hall. The projector started. Black at first and then an image, the camera's eye running along the second story of a building and down to the level of the street.

"It's Budapest, isn't it?"

"Near Vaci Street."

"What year?"

He turned to look at her. "What year you ask? It's 1944."

"The year of the occupation…"

"It's the morning of the occupation."

Kati sat forward. Zeno too felt engaged with a part of his life he'd not thought of for too long. Despite the rattle of the projector, he could feel the rumble of the tanks that morning, hear the sporadic outcrops of fire, feel the weight of Catherine resting between his thighs.

At that moment, the image on the screen shook and filled with cobblestones--Zeno was running and had left the camera on. He must have steadied himself and raised the camera, for the next shot seemed to be from a small alley, looking out towards a street. Dark high walls framed each side of the shot. For some moments the scene was static, then a tank rolled by.

"My God," Kati said. "You were so close."

"So much noise..."

"Was this actually *during* the occupation?"

"I'd been at a friend's apartment," he said, "when we realized the tanks were in the street. I was trying to get back to the... to where I lived." Zeno sat forward and looked closer at the image. "If I'm not mistaken... Yes."

At that point the camera moved slightly forward, out of the alley, looking down the street. There was a line of tanks now where before there'd been nothing. And soldiers were on foot, soldiers with large guns.

"Apu, you were so close--"

"Don't speak. Let the film speak."

People moved about the street, walking normally past the tanks.

"My God," Kati said. "What're all those people doing?"

The tanks were moving slowly, forcefully, despite the jerky nature of the old film. A woman in a stylish suit came from behind the camera, stared directly into the lens, then walked to the other side of the street and out of view. Zeno gasped but Kati didn't notice.

"It's as if nothing is happening," Kati said.

People moved around the tanks, some nodding to the soldiers, none of their faces showing the slightest trace of fear

"You see what I saw," Zeno said. "Life always goes on. Even during the invasion, people went about their business as best they could."

"It's as if the Germans were expected."

Zeno looked at her again. "They were welcomed."

The film came free of the spool and clattered in the dark, the screen exploding to light. For a time, Kati remained staring at the white screen.

"Have you ever shown these to anyone?"

"Why would I do that?"

"They're amazing images. Not at all what you'd expect. They should be in an archive." She turned to face him. "I can't imagine… Why haven't you shown me them to me?"

When he didn't answer she shook her head and wound back the first spool and loaded another film. This started with a scene in a forest.

"Now for something completely different," Kati said. "Where are we?"

Zeno wished she hadn't found this film. The camera panned about the forest, up into the canopy of the trees and then down. The scene cut to a path.

"An edit," Kati said.

"What edit?"

"Don't tell me my craft. That was intentional. You've edited this one together."

"Why are you so surprised at your old father's ability?"

The camera traced the walking trail through the forest, swung from one direction to another, from where it came to where it led. The scene cut again, away from the path, at some distance. Another shot, panning from the path but moving back towards it. Suddenly there was a woman, standing, looking left and right, back and forth along the path. The image trembled.

"No tripod, huh?"

But Zeno was lost. The woman stood, strained her ears. She scuffed off her shoes. She hesitated again, looked about her, the eye of the camera tracing her view.

"That's quite sophisticated syntax," Kati said.

"Syntax?"

"The camera angles, the way it's cut together."

"Such fancy words you have."

"You're a master at it. A master editor."

And then, the woman began to run. The image cut to the path, running as well. It looked further ahead, then further, no sign of the woman on the path. Occasionally it would stop, pan about the forest and run again, jolting slightly. Zeno's pulse raced.

"You filmed this part later, didn't you? The light's different."

Then the path rose, up to a bluff, the image rising, the intensity heightened by the quickening jolts, until the image went over a cliff. And there the quality of the image changed as it spiraled down, towards the sea.

"You refilmed that."

"It needed some movement. I projected it and filmed it again."

"It's like something out of *Vertigo*."

"Don't be silly."

"It is. Those scenes looking down the tower of the Spanish mission."

"You remember I took you to *Vertigo*?"

"Apu! Of course I do."

So many years ago, her small hand in his, he'd taken her to that film, a landmark, but never said a thing of his own desire and loss. The last of the film slipped through the shutter. Kati was still. Despite the harsh light on the screen, she remained absorbed.

"What happened to her?" she said finally.

Zeno looked at Kati. "I don't know. It was just a small story."

"No, it's not. It's the same woman."

He tensed. "What woman?"

"She was in the other film. She crossed the street in Budapest. She came from behind you. She looked right into the camera. She was with you. Who is she?"

Zsuzsi struggled to her feet and laboriously rearranged herself in another ball on the sofa.

"I could never keep anything from you."

"You seem to have done a pretty good job with all this." Kati stopped a moment. "Now I'm completely intrigued. Who is she?"

Long gone were the days when, despite all his effort or fatigue or distractions, she came to his thoughts at least once a day, if not once an hour or minute.

"We're all so many things--"

"What was her name?"

"Her name..." He shuffled in his seat. "I don't really know."

"Apu, of course you know her name."

"What's this? Some kind of interrogation?"

Trapped, he starred at the blank screen. Images came to his mind, Catherine's bare breasts, the nipples dark and erect, the baby grand piano, its clear sounds under her precise fingers, fingers that played upon his spine. Her scent. Her scent. An abyss opened. He felt the old pain in his ribs, in his heart, his soul. He reached out his hand to touch Zsuzsi. Her tongue lapped at him, once. He turned to Kati's eyes.

"I loved your mother with all my heart."

Kati's face tightened.

"I know..." She shook her head. "I know that. I've never met another couple like you." She looked back at the screen. "I don't doubt that at all. We all have histories. No doubt there were people before Mom." She motioned towards the screen. "Who was she?"

Who was she? How often he'd asked himself this question and never arrived at an answer and now these flickering films had taken him back to meet her. He'd never spoken of this with anyone.

"Have you ever had an affair that broke your heart?" he said.

At first he hoped this would distract Kati. The young like most to talk about themselves, and he could remain quiet while she spoke of her first love, but she said nothing, just stared at him.

"I don't mean an affair that made you feel good," he said, so pushed he'd lost all control, "and then sad for a few weeks. I mean... left you so weak you couldn't draw breath?"

He felt a tear roll down his cheek.

"Apu..."

Kati moved over to him.

"You do, of course you do." He paused a moment. "Life always has plans apart from our own. But the person stays with you, the promise they held, the excitement they contained."

"I suppose so. But if this happened in 1944 you'd have only been... what? Seventeen."

"I turned eighteen that morning. She was much older, much wiser, perhaps."

"What was her name?"

He looked at her. What would Kati feel if he told her Catherine?

"Eva."

CHAPTER TWENTY-THREE

In the taxi on the way back from the vet, Zsuzsi had a half-pant half-smile on her face. Kati bribed the driver to carry her. She wasn't allowed to walk for ten days. On the pavement outside the brownstone, they placed her on the ground and she hobbled a few steps and, as best she could on her steady rear leg, squatted and urinated, a long pale-yellow stream running out over the footpath.

"Good God," Zeno said.

"She's been on a drip. They've pumped her full of water."

Once she'd finished, Kati carried her up the apartment's stairs. They prepared a bed for her, on an extra piece of foam rubber on the floor so she wouldn't jump down from the sofa and hurt her leg.

"Thank you for staying."

Kati smiled. "Happy to do it."

She cooked chicken soup the way her mother had, Hungarian style with absolutely no concept of fat-free. Yesterday she'd boiled the whole bird in a pot until it fell apart and the aroma filled the whole apartment building and spilled out onto the street.

"God only knows how you stayed so thin," she said, clearing some of the dishes to the kitchen.

He looked at her with no understanding. Kati's chicken soup even rivaled Panni's.

He held a half a bowl under the table for Zsuzsi, felt the strength of her tongue lapping up the soup.

"Good," he said. "It'll do your leg good."

"Careful," Kati said. "She'll lick the pattern off the bowl."

Zeno set the empty bowl back on the table.

"Apu, I'm going to have to leave tomorrow."

"I know. You must get back to your life."

"I'm sorry."

"There's no need to be sorry.

"They can't spare me any longer. The editing's at a crucial stage."

"It's okay."

"I've arranged for the Puerto Rican girl upstairs to come twice a day to carry Zsuzsi back and forth from the street."

"I can do it."

"No, you can't."

A silence fell over their meal. Zeno knew exactly what Kati was thinking.

"Don't you know what happened to her?"

"Happened to who?"

"Eva. Eva Steiner?"

Zeno finished chewing his mouthful of bread.

"I waited for two months, sleeping in the rubble of the apartment. If she was alive and she wanted to see me, she'd have come there. She never came. I think she died--"

"But they were a wealthy family."

"--or she didn't want to see me."

"There must have been some trace."

"Trace? There was nothing but chaos. Our charming Russian liberators arrested nearly every man in Budapest. One morning I was hauled into a bank, then put in jail. For no reason."

"But after that, did you look for her?"

"After... I was held for eighteen months. The communists were taking power. Sure, I made some inquiries about the family but no one knew what had happened to them. The factory had been taken over. The man who operated the gate was now the manager. It was a time of collectivization. It wasn't a time to ask a lot of questions about former industrialists. And they'd cooperated with the Nazis."

"How?"

"Mr. Steiner had bought trucks for them. They'd paid the Gestapo huge amounts of money for their freedom. Many Jewish families did. Their money helped keep the whole war turning for nearly another year. I didn't want to connect myself with that."

"So you never found Eva?"

He glared at her. "Has it ever occurred to you I don't want to know?"

"What? You can't mean that."

"I don't want to know."

"You should find out. It would help you."

"Help me?"

"You need closure. Knowing what happened would--"

"Closure. Such words. Do you think they just went to a holiday camp? I don't want to know how she suffered."

"But don't you want to know what happened to her?"

"You're not listening to me. She left me. That part of my life was over. After I was released, I went back to my mother. Life just had to start again."

"I know."

"My memories of Eva faded. And then I met Panni. I felt young again. We started our life together."

"You can't have just forgotten Eva."

"I didn't. But I stopped aching for her."

Kati sighed.

"Panni and I had greater things to worry about. Food. Money. We had to leave Hungary. That took us years of planning. Can you imagine what it was like to smuggle her and you out of Hungary under the nose of those communist bastards, all the way to America?"

Kati looked at a photo on the mantlepiece. It was the three of them, taken on Ellis Island in 1958. She was eight months old, held in a wool blanket in her mother's arms.

"You've told me those stories."

"And then we had nothing. Miss Liberty may have given me a whiff of freedom but she didn't help me work."

"I know."

"Sixteen hours a day. Do you think that restaurant ran itself? All those bloody Hungarians to feed…"

"Apu, please. I worked too. I was there.'

Zeno stopped. He wasn't being fair.

"Yes," he said. "I remember your little hands were red from the washing-up water. You don't know the dreams I had to kiss goodbye."

"No, I don't."

"I'm sorry, Katalin, but I had no time to think about the past. And I'd married your mother. Catherine Steiner was dead…"

"Catherine?"

Zeno closed his eyes. He'd almost argued his daughter in to a corner. Now he'd thrown gasoline on to the smoldering ashes.

Early the next morning, Kati left for L.A.

"I'll call you tonight," she said. She already had one foot in the taxi when she walked back up the steps to Zeno and kissed his cheek. "Don't worry, Zsuzsi will be fine."

"Of course she will. You take care."

Over the next ten days, Zsuzsi hardly moved. The Puerto Rican girl came every morning and every evening, and Zeno gave her biscuits and coffee once Zsuzsi completed her business on the street. In the morning Zeno would cook and in the afternoon he and Zsuzsi dozed in front of the TV. After ten days, the girl and Zeno helped Zsuzsi into a taxi and together they took her to the vet. Peter Blacker moved her leg this way and that.

"She's better than I expected." He smiled at Zeno. "She should be fine to walk home today. But slowly."

"It's the only way I walk."

And so the three of them walked down East 11th Street. Zsuzsi stopped every few metres to sniff. Zeno smiled at her.

"You've been out of circulation," he said. "There must be lots of messages."

As they walked, Zeno resumed his old habit of looking at faces. So many times, so many years ago, he'd walked Manhattan, uptown and downtown, and thought of her, thought he saw her, the cut of her waist, the color of her hair, and rushed to touch some woman's arm who turned and was never her. He'd looked in every Hungarian pastry shop or restaurant on Second Avenue. Catherine was dead, even if she'd survived.

Zsuzsi and he and the Puerto Rican stopped at Schonberger's café. They sat at their usual spot, an outdoor table. Without his ordering, the waitress brought him a strong coffee and a bowl of water for Zsuzsi. The Puerto Rican girl ordered a cola.

"Wow," the waitress said. "She looks great."

"Except they shaved all the hair from her bum," Zeno said and laughed. "She looks like a baboon from behind."

"It'll grow back."

While Zsuzsi drank her water, Zeno felt overcome by the past. The waitress had a box of cigarettes in her shirt pocket.

"Could I have a cigarette?" he said.

"Didn't know you smoked." She pulled the box from her pocket.

"I haven't. Not for years. Would you have one with me?"

When they arrived home, there was a message on his answering machine. The message was brief.

"Call me."

It was Kati. It was only mid-morning in Manhattan so it was early in L.A.

"I've got something to tell you, Papa," she said.

"And what would that be?"

"I've found her."

"Who?"

"Catherine. Catherine Steiner."

Zeno sank down in the chair next to the phone.

"That can't be true. She must be dead by now."

"She is."

Zeno sighed.

"Apu, you said yourself she must be."

"I know. But it's another person I must farewell."

Tears swelled in his eyes and once they'd formed he had no way to stop them from rolling down a cheek.

"Where did she die?"

"They survived, Papa. They made it to Israel." Her tone was gentle. "She lived a long life. Don't be upset."

"I don't want you... How did you find her so easily?"

"The internet."

Zeno said nothing.

"I searched her name and didn't find anything but then I looked for her family name plus Budapest. There were some references to their family and the Kasztner train. It was a train of people..."

"I know who Rezsö Kasztner was."

Zeno rocked back and forth. He felt angry, really angry with Kati.

"At the library, there was a reference to an interview with the Steiner's daughter, Eva."

Zeno's heart rate increased. His breathing became shallow. He was in too deep, over his head, out of his depth.

"That was just too much of a coincidence," Kati said, "so I followed it up. It seems they only had one child. End of 1944."

"They?"

"Her and her husband, I forget his name."

"Sándor."

"That's right. Her daughter still lives in Israel." There was a long pause. "She's yours, isn't she?"

"No." Water rose around him. Warm water flowed over him. "She can't be my daughter..."

"Apu, I did the math. Catherine must have been pregnant when she left Budapest. She left a month or two after the occupation. I think she's pregnant in the film during the occupation."

Zeno rocked back and forth. "I guess I was right. You see everything."

"Did you know that?"

"Of course I did. She'd just told me."

They'd survived. The child was alive. He placed his free hand to his forehead. He felt hot. This was too much.

"Do you want to meet her?"

"No." Zsuzsi wriggled forward onto his feet. "There, there. It's all right," he said, caressing her ears. "Sorry, Zsuzsi wanted comforting."

"I do."

There was a long silence.

"Why? What do you want from her?"

"She's my sister. I'm going to contact her."

CHAPTER TWENTY-FOUR

Zsuzsi bounded down the stairs of the brownstone to the open taxi door.

"Look at you," Kati said.

Zsuzsi jumped up on her rear legs. Kati caught her front paws in her hands and Zsuzsi extended her neck and nose as close as could be to Kati's face.

"Apu!" Kati looked up at the stairs towards Zeno. "Look at her. She's like a puppy."

"I wish my legs were so good," he said.

And then Zsuzsi caught Kati off guard and licked her across the mouth.

"Oh…' Kati pulled her hands away from the paws and laughed. "All right, you got me."

Zsuzsi ran back up to Zeno's side. Kati carried her small travel bag up the stairs.

"You look well too," she said.

"I've lost a little weight, I think." He kissed her cheek. "Now we can walk again."

"Like you need to do that."

Kati left her bag in the spare room. Zeno had coffee ready in the kitchen.

"How long are you staying?" he said.

"Just a few days."

"When does she arrive?"

Kati turned and looked at him. "You always cut to the chase, don't you?"

"I don't have time enough left to muck around."

"Eva's already here, Apu. She's been in New York City the past few months."

He swallowed hard. "Does she know where I live?"

"She's not been spying on you." She looked out the window. "She's been trying to find you for years."

"I wasn't so hard to find."

"She only knew your name started with a Z. In her journal, Catherine only called you Z." She scowled at him. "If you don't want to meet her, that's fine. But I do."

Zeno looked away from her. An ultimatum, delivered just like her mother.

"I'm going to take Zsuzsi out." He stood up from the table and took the lead and collar, which sent the dog running in tight circles towards the front door.

"Fine," Kati said. Her voice snapped like a whip. "I'm leaving at two-thirty. If you want to come, be ready then."

"I'm not confirming--"

"Apu." He stopped and looked at her. "All my life I've wanted a sister. Now I have one."

"And what is it you hope to find?"

She just stared at him for a while and shook her head. "Whatever. I'm leaving at two-thirty."

When they were a block away, Zeno took a packet of cigarettes from his pocket. Kati would have a conniption if she saw him smoking. But how the fumes felt like memory. As Zsuzsi went about her rituals, he looked at faces. It was habit, again. One he'd broken long ago. But he couldn't stop himself. Was that her? Could that be Eva? What would she have inherited from her mother?

The taxi pulled into the Waldorf Astoria. With no words, they walked through the hotel lobby to the lifts. Even in the lift they said nothing, just listened to the Musak .

"Christ," he said.

"What?"

"It's Chopin."

Kati tilted her head. "Chopin?" She raised her shoulders to question him as the synthetic string of notes rose and descended to hell. His legs jittered. He placed his palm on his thigh but when he took it away the leg jittered some more. He wore a dark suit with a cobalt-blue shirt and blood-red tie. Now that his hair was completely white, the boldness of the blue made him feel less washed out.

"It's this way," Kati said, pointing down the hall towards the left. She was as he'd always seen her under pressure, overly focused and removed. At her mother's funeral she'd not even cried. Kati looked at all the numbers on the doors, checking them off one after the other under her breath as they followed their normal sequence. She moved ahead of him but he still felt a reticence. He could just as easily turn and go back to the foyer, take Zsuzsi to the café and forget all this. Kati stopped. She faced the door, square on. He stepped back.

"Apu," she said, still facing the door. "I love you."

She knocked, rather lightly. The hotel halls hummed. After some moments there was a rustle behind the door. It opened. Blocked by Kati, Zeno couldn't see who had answered.

"Katalin?"

"Eva?"

No one moved. For a moment, no one breathed.

"I guess he didn't come."

She had an American accent.

"He's here."

Finally Kati stepped aside.

And there was Eva. She moved slightly forward, then froze, her expression open but her mouth locked ajar without breathing. She was small, short. She could dance on water. A water nymph. Her hair was her mother's. Zeno had no time to see anymore. Her arms were around him. She pressed her head into his shoulder. He caught a scent, something he'd not smelled for a life-time. Eva smelt of the pillow he and Catherine had shared in the small apartment above the bookshop.

"Let me look at you," he said.

He pulled away but she resisted, clung to him, her face nestled down in his chest. He breathed, caught again that scent. His viscera heaved and flopped about. A wave of attraction followed by a severe wave of repulsion crashed over and around him. With all his strength, in a firm, slow gesture, he prized her away from him.

Though worn much longer and fuller, it was the same hair, the exact same color, each strand thick and lustrous. Her eyes, that fiery violet, the dark lashes held glistening together by tears, they were Catherine's. He studied her face. The cheekbones were his, perhaps the lips, but the skin, the translucent porcelain, was hers. She had none of his height, but her frame, the shape of her body, was Catherine's on a small scale.

"My child," he said, his jaw shuddering over the words.

Her eyes widened as she looked into his eyes.

"I can't believe I've found you," she said. She started to cry, no sound, no tremor, just a flow of tears. Her lips quivered. He felt himself weaken and Kati stepped to his side and grabbed his elbow and forearm. Eva slipped to the other side and together they helped him to the sofa. Her hand held his, the grip firm, the skin warm.

He could say nothing. Eva sat next to him and they looked at one another, silence the only appropriate intimacy. Kati had started to cry, tears streaming down her cheeks which she made no effort to stem. For some moments she stood in front of them and then turned and sat in an armchair opposite and looked at Eva.

They remained so for what seemed like hours. Zeno met Eva's stare. His heart raced as he looked for more traces of Catherine. She was impeccably groomed, each detail perfectly placed. He stood at a fork in a road, caught between two paths, two lives, what is and what could have been, a life lived and a life lost. But then he shook his head. This wasn't a matter of choice. This just was.

"I think we need some tea," Kati said.

Without averting her gaze, Eva nodded. Kati went to the phone and rang room service, her voice soft and watery. In front of him, imperceptibly perhaps, Eva reined herself in, control coming over her.

"I'm sorry," Eva said. "I'm not usually so emotional."

Zeno smiled.

"You're very handsome," she said. She coughed to clear all the emotion. "I guessed you'd be."

Zeno looked away from her. "I don't know what to say."

"I'm glad you came. I didn't think you would."

"I wasn't going to. I'd put your mother out of mind."

"Apu…"

"It's all right," Eva said. "I understand."

"I had to let her go."

"I understand."

Zeno felt he should remain present in this room but his mind drifted to the moment Catherine walked, her arm linked through Sándor's, for the last time from the Steiner household.

What would he have done, if he'd known?

To know happiness, there must be knowledge of sadness. To know trust, there must be a modicum of doubt. But at that moment he'd felt no doubt, not a drop in his heart. At that moment he'd felt completely with her, despite the physical distance between them, the many sets of judging eyes, the reality that lived in her heart. That was how he'd felt. How that second in time could have become poison.

"I couldn't have lived otherwise."

The silence came on them again. Kati sat down.

"When did she die?" Zeno said.

Eva swallowed hard. "Ummm… It was the summer of 1991. She was 86."

"How?"

"She died in her sleep. Very graceful. Sándor had died two years before. She taught piano. She stopped after he died. She lost the will to go on after that."

"So they were happy?"

"Happy?" Eva appeared to drift back into the past with Catherine. "I'm not sure anyone is happy for that long. They were… content, very content. Amiable, nearly always amiable."

Zeno looked out the window and up at the pale blue sky. How often he'd wondered if Mr. Steiner had abandoned her or if she'd left him. But they'd stayed together.

"What happened," he said, steeling himself, "the night they left Budapest?"

"They were taken by train to Vienna and flown to Portugal."

"Portugal?"

"There were some last-minute changes. The details were never clear to me."

"So there was no arrest?" Kati said. "Apu was told the Gestapo arrested them. He assumed the worst."

"No, the escape more or less went like clockwork. German precision." Eva pressed her lips together and smiled. She turned to Zeno. "And how did you come to be here?"

Zeno turned back to look out at the pale afternoon while Kati told his story. The bellboy brought the tea. How odd to be in the presence of a Steiner in a hotel room and not be serving.

"What is it you want from me?" he said, interrupting them. "I've no money."

"Apu," Kati said. "This isn't about that."

"It's okay," Eva said. She turned to Zeno. "I wanted to meet my father. You can't deny that's who you are. All my life I'd looked at my father--at Sándor--and could see nothing of myself. I've Catherine's eyes, her hair, but Sándor... I've nothing of his temperament. A love of piano, perhaps. It wasn't till after she'd died that I found this."

Eva took a book from the table near the sofa. Zeno had never seen it before, its fabric cover worn and faded and battered.

"It's the only journal she had, at least, the only one I found. She writes sporadically, not in linear time but it details a period from..."

She opened the book. Zeno let his eyes drop to the page, line after line of Catherine's hand. He turned his face away, the shape of the characters too intimate to bear.

"It starts in, well, I think it's about June 1943. She was at Lake Balaton it would seem for the summer and was very discontent. Restless. She describes meeting you. Well, I assume it was you. In the lake, of all places. This book finishes just after we arrived in Israel. Once I'd read it all... Well, it was pretty obvious."

She closed the book.

"I want you to have it. I must warn you, the writing is intimate. The descriptions of her pleasure are—"

"You think I need to read this," he said, "to know she enjoyed herself?"

"I think she wanted you to have this. She knew she was dying. The last six months she threw out everything she owned. Except some clothes, a crucifix, and this journal. It was written for your eyes."

"She kept the crucifix?"

"She mentions it. You found it."

Zeno felt overcome and returned his gaze to the endless blue sky.

"You've an American accent," Kati said.

Intent on studying Zeno, Eva took some time before she spoke again.

"My education. It was in America, here in New York. I've lived here, over the years, on and off. My Uncle, Zoltán, lived here."

"Zoltán?" Zeno said.

Eva looked back at him. "He moved here before the war."

"I know." Zeno leaned back into the couch. He exhaled. "I'd forgotten about him. Completely."

"You knew him?"

He shook his head. "He'd left Hungary before I went to work for the Steiners."

How could Zeno have been so stupid? He'd never thought of Zoltán. In all the searching for Catherine, the answer he'd sought lived in New York City. He felt dazed, clouded.

"You lived here?" Kati said.

"Mother and Father… were often here. My husband and I came for his work. I bought tickets for Chopin's birthday--"

Zeno stood up.

"I must leave," he said.

"Apu."

Kati came to his side. He fought to clear his thinking. He wanted to be free of this room, this conversation. He needed air.

"I'm all right. I need to go."

"I'll come with you."

"You stay here, darling." He looked about him for Zsuzsi and then realized she wasn't there. "Zsuzsi needs a walk. You stay. I'm fine. I'll see you back at the apartment."

He turned and smiled at Eva, perplexed and confused.

"I'm an old man, Eva. I hope I'll find room in my heart for you. This is a lot for me. I just need to be alone."

"Of course." She started to cry. She took the journal and handed it to him. "I think it may help you."

CHAPTER TWENTY-FIVE

In the sun outside Schonberger's, he placed the journal on the table. His waitress brought him coffee, a bowl of water for Zsuzsi, and unwound a packet of cigarettes from the sleeve of her t-shirt.

"You okay?" she said.

He looked at her. He breathed deeply. He was still breathing so he must be okay. He nodded. She lit a cigarette and handed it to him. He dragged in the memories.

"Yell out if you want another one."

He smoked the cigarette. Had Catherine walked past this café with Mr. Steiner and Zoltán when he'd turned his head in the other direction? Had he looked at her and just not recognized her? Had she ever seen him, recognized him, and turned away? He stubbed the cigarette into the ashtray.

He turned the pages of the journal quickly. His heart constricted. Certain phrases stood out. '*You fill me.*' '*I resented your freedom.*' '*I made the right decision.*' '*I was wrong.*' Later she'd written, '*You completed me*'.

He stopped at the last page. Catherine had written at the top, *Haifa, March 19, 1954.* She'd underlined it twice. He ran his finger over the loops and circles and lines of the writing and felt her indents still evident in the page.

So this is where you end your book. This is *la petite mort* of our story.

Eva came from school today. Like every day, she enjoyed herself wholeheartedly, but she was very keen to show me what she'd learned. She took a tall glass and carefully filled it with water until it nearly overflowed. With a steady hand, she pushed a paperclip from the glass's rim, out onto the surface of the water. Like a little sailboat it floated, moved around, drawn to the edge of the glass.

"There's a skin on water," she said, a note of glee in her voice.

She made me look at the surface. Such things fascinate her. It bulged, rose up from the rim of the glass. I touched it. Immediately, the skin tore apart, the paperclip fell through the glass of water to the bottom.

We live on that skin. With all the security of our lives, we live on that skin. We all live on that surface. Ruffle it and we sink.

I followed you into the forest that day. I'd left lunch with those tedious women and I saw you walk into the forest, caught up so completely in your camera. So beautiful.

If you ever read this, now you know I stayed with Sándor. Don't let Eva tell you we were in love. We weren't. Fear is an odd anvil. It finally molded us to one another, the hewn rough, but we grew into one another. I was safe with him. In the end, after everything, that was all I needed to feel.

I wounded you. How deep the scar ran, I don't know. The depths of what you've thought of me since, I'll never plumb. With the force that had descended on Hungary, I was forced to make a decision. Yes, I betrayed you. Our plan to leave Hungary was so flimsy I thought you'd have seen through it in an instant. But you were naïve, too trusting in people. How sad I blemished that. As a child, I once stole an apple from the garden of my father.

You'll have survived. I'll have broken your heart. You'll have thought you'd never survive or feel that love again. And you won't have, that first love. I know this as you were mine and I miss you every hour of every day.

We would have grown familiar. As I grew older, you'd have wandered. My heart couldn't have borne that. You live on in my dream, beautiful, resplendent, green, perfect, and unimaginably sensual.

The journal dropped from his hand and hit the pavement. Zsuzsi stood and tucked her tail between her legs, flattened her ears, put her head on his thigh, and looked up at him. He ran his hand over her head. The waitress came, picked up the journal, and placed it on the table.

"Are you sure you're all right?"

He couldn't look at her. He nodded. She lit another cigarette, gave it to him and left him in peace. He dragged on the cigarette, looking at Zsuzsi. He'd remembered something, never thought of until now, a world and a lifetime away. In an instant, a change of tone in her voice, from rage and resentment and aggravation and grief to pity and interest and fear. He heard it only once, the day he was stuck in her bedroom and she argued with Mr. Steiner. He'd told her of two Slovakian men who escaped from Auschwitz and reported the gassing. After all these years, he could hear her mind work, as the disparate pieces clicked together and she saw the interconnectedness, the complexity, the difficulty, the danger, the fragility, and the impossibility of her situation. She released Zeno from her heart. She opened the door and he flew away. She said goodbye to him. She shot the cleanest arrow between herself and freedom. She'd followed him into the forest, he'd been her escape, but at that moment he ceased to be her survival.

"I thought you might be here."

Kati stood before the table. She sat down opposite him. He dragged on the cigarette and exhaled.

"You'd looked for her in Manhattan, hadn't you?" she said. "You'd forgotten about Zoltán in New York."

"She followed me into the forest."

"What?"

"In the film I showed you, she wasn't the actor at all. I wasn't observing her. She'd seen me and followed me into the forest. She was observing me."

"What do you mean?"

"She was thirty-nine years old. If she was going to get pregnant, she was running out of time. She planned it all. A young virile man was her best shot. If Mr. Hitler hadn't got in her way, she'd have continued to live in Budapest with Mr. Steiner and the child."

"That's a bit harsh, don't you think?"

"Is it? It would be, except for one thing; she fell in love with me."

"And you with her."

"I fell in love the moment I saw her."

He retreated into his thoughts. He may have put his camera away, but all his life he'd edited how he saw things. He'd choose what he now thought of Catherine.

"I don't care what Catherine did at the end," he said. "She loved me. I loved her. She broke my heart. You can't imagine what that passion meant to a young man—a boy, really. She taught me love. I met your mother, we had you, we worked and worked and worked and these things all made me frustrated and tired but happy. I was happy, Kati. It's obscene to think I could've been happier. It is a silly competition. I won't have it."

Kati sat back heavily in her chair. "I've not met one person who I'd be completely happy with, and you met two."

"You're too choosy."

"I'm not! I just haven't met the right one."

"You see too much. You must cut what you see." Zeno smiled and raised his eyebrows. "The war is long over, Kati. Perfection doesn't exist."

He looked away from her and thought of Catherine, of her intensity and artifice and questioning, of her delights. And then he thought of Panni, her practicality, her patience, her slow thorough way of going about everything, even love. And her mind, that trap which stored all information that came her way, shored it up, always ready for discussion. Their conversations never ended. Mostly her patience. The women were so different. And he was different with each of them. What infinite variety. One was his first love and the other his last. He wouldn't make them compete.

"I want to transfer your films to digital."

"Why would you want to do that?"

She frowned. "Lots of reasons. To preserve them, make them easier to view. But they should be archived. Researchers would hack off their right arm to see the streets of Budapest *during* the occupation. That small segment of Tibi attacking that man is unbelievable."

He thought of his one-time burning desire to film the world.

"So I become a famous director, at my age."

"You're my favorite."

He laughed and shrugged his shoulders. "You are what you are."

She slid her hand across the table, on top of his.

"Enough of all this," Zeno said. "Zsuzsi needs to keep moving. Let's go for a walk."

END NOTE

If you enjoyed *The Skin of Water*, please consider writing a review and posting it on shop websites, Goodreads, or your own blog. As an independent author, I'm reliant on word-of-mouth recommendations, dependent on the kindness of strangers, so if you feel you could oblige, I'll be eternally in your debt..

Please drop by my website www.gsjohnston.com. On *The Skin of Water* tab there are links to some of the music I've used, the films and much more. I've even read a couple of my favorite pieces. And I'll update it with more stuff.

If you are a book club looking for an author to meet with you via Skype, I never sleep so I'm on all time zones, truly global.

Also, please feel free to contact me, either via www.gsjohnston.com Contact Page or on Twitter - @GS_Johnston

ACKNOWLEDGEMENTS

As I said at the beginning, this novel wouldn't have been written if I'd not met George Perko who told me of a Hungarian Jewish manufacturing family, Weiss Manfred, who were so wealthy they were able to bribe the Gestapo to fly them out of German-controlled Hungary to neutral Switzerland. Two things boggled my mind; that a family could be so wealthy and that the Gestapo could be bribed to that level.

After a few years of thinking about this, weighing up many aspects of the story and many hours spent scouring libraries – God Bless The University of Sydney Fisher Library stack! – I'd found very little of the family, far from enough grit and grime for a novel. They'd existed and this escape had happened and that was about it. But in the course of this exploration, I'd read of other families who'd done the same or similar thing. One afternoon I made a leap of faith – I could invent a family and their drama, nestle them amongst history.

George provided me with great detail about life in Budapest during the Second World War, before and after the German occupation. Lily Wolfe also provided me with this type of information, even confirming many of my extrapolations and suspicions. And a new friend, Ann Major added a final sheen.

As a readable draft came together, my editors at The Editorial Department (http://www.editorialdepartment. com) Renni Browne and Shannon Roberts, were both very generous and guided me again with velvet covered gloves to the final draft.

And Beth Jusino put a bomb under my self-promotion.

My good friend Ian Thomson created the beautiful cover, his effortless eye distilling the fragments of the story to this impressive image.

Of course I have to thank Miss Mia and Reba who always sleep soundly while I write but especially Miss Mia who takes me on walks to the park where often two utterly contradictory plot points resolve.

And thanks to John who puts up with it all and always has something to say, something to add and often unwittingly tells me the exact thing I need.

AUTHOR BIOGRAPHY

G.S. Johnston is the author of two historical novels, *The Skin of Water* and *Consumption: A Novel*, noted for their complex characters and well-researched settings.

In one form or another, Johnston has always written, at first composing music and lyrics. After completing a degree in pharmacy, a year in Italy re-ignited his passion for writing and he completed a Bachelor of Arts degree in English Literature. Feeling the need for a broader canvas, he started writing short stories and novels.

Originally from Hobart, Tasmania, Johnston currently lives in Sydney, Australia with two cats – home-loving Reba and the wayward Rose – and Miss Mia, a black and white cuddle dog.

He would be impressed with humanity if someone could succeed in putting an extra hour in every day.

Visit him online at www.gsjohnston.com
or follow him on Twitter at @GS_Johnston

READING GROUP QUESTIONS

The need of survival is a major theme of *The Skin of Water*. How is this theme played in the text?

Given Catherine's need to survive, how much can she be held accountable to her actions?

How can the role of the Hungarian Government be considered in the course of WWII?

What themes does *The Skin of Water* share with GS Johnston's debut, *Consumption: A Novel*?

Also available from GS Johnston

THE CAST OF A HAND:
Based on a true story of love and murder in second empire France

http://www.amazon.com//dp/B015649EUG

CONSUMPTION: A Novel

http://www.amazon.com/dp/B0052YX8K8

A Novel by GS JOHNSTON

The Cast
OF A HAND

Based on a True Story
of Love and Murder
in Second Empire France

AUTHOR NOTE

The mass murder on which THE CAST OF A HAND is based took place in France, in 1869. Monsieur Antoine Claude, the celebrated Paris Chief of Police, led the investigation. Such was the height of the public's outcry, the case is often referred to as the first thunderclap in the fall of Napoleon III and The Second Empire.

PROLOGUE

Hortense came to.

The darkness caused her no fear, nor the pain or the bone creaking cold, so cold, not even the dirt about her mouth.

She couldn't hear the children.

She held her breath.

Listened. Listened to the sound in the fields.

A spade sliced the earth. She was sure.

The sound ceased. She could hear nothing now, not a solitary sound.

She dared to inhale a shallow breath. The air moved like molasses yet burned like whiskey all the way down her throat. She must breathe. Confine her breath to the apex of her lungs. That she could bear.

Her torn basque covered her head, a pocket in the earth. She arched her aching fingers, pressed them into the soil above her.

She tried to move her head but there was no room, just crushing pain. She opened her mouth, thrust out her tongue. Rotting vegetation in the dirt made her nauseous. She opened her eyes then closed them quickly, soil snared under the lids.

Where were the children?

What had happened?

Why?

What could she do?

She held her breath again, listened again but heard no cry. The slightest murmur would reach a mother's ear, attuned to the crib. The children were obedient to the last. But she'd failed to protect them, failed completely, utterly.

The loam sat heavy on her chest. She was going to die here.

Was she six feet down or thrown in some cursory grave?

Would anyone ever find her?

Would there be a marker with letters carved deep in gray stone?

> *Rests here Hortense Juliette Joseph Kinck*
> *née Roussel*
> *Deceased September 19, 1869*
> *Pray for her.*

Why was she forsaken?

Such thoughts were futile. She must find her children, press her hand to theirs. Touch warmth.

Not dirt.

CHAPTER ONE

It was already mid-morning when Monsieur Antoine Claude, the Paris Chief of Police, strode across the Pantin field on the outskirts of Paris—and stopped dead. Good God. Streams of women lifted their hems high through the rows of lucerne. Men in black top hats and business vests stumbled in the furrows. Away from them, patchwork crowds roamed the reaches of the field, covering it as if some great fête were in progress.

Damn them. This was murder, mass murder, a blood bath. Claude removed his hat. Evidence had surely been lost, traces of the crime trampled.

If only there'd not been a delay in the police prefecture's getting the news to him. Surely his superiors knew travel plans would cause him no hesitation in returning to duty. Catherine, bless her, had "unpacked" many a holiday without having left the apartment. *Damn them.*

He continued across the dewy field. Ahead of him a mob ringed a flimsy barrier erected at a small distance from the grave, people pushing, jumping to catch a glimpse.

"Who's done this, Monsieur Claude?" a voice yelled.

It was a journalist from *Le Petit Journal.* His question set off the pack, yapping quicker than any mind could follow. The police saw Claude approaching and parted, arms raised to deflect the journalists and let Claude through.

Officers, some down on hands and knees, combed the narrow periphery of the communal grave. The earth had been removed, the loam piled in a corner. He hoped someone had taken note of its state. Was it packed solid or loose? Moist from the dew or dry? Such details would help fix the time of the event. At the far perimeter, a young policeman vomited violently.

Claude took his pocket note book and walked forward. The grave was shallow. He drew closer. The woman was in her early forties. The children ranged from a small girl of two or three to a boy in his mid-teens. Five children. Four male. The woman had dark hair, her dress of dark fabric torn about the basque. She could be any middle-class woman in Paris. She wore a wedding ring. Her eyes were open, wide with unimaginable horror. Blood caked over her chin and across the white undergarment covering a huge belly. She must be the mother—a pregnant governess was unlikely.

The children were neatly dressed, well kept. One boy's mouth hung agape at a grotesque angle—he'd left life in terrible pain. Not that they all hadn't. The little girl's hair was dark and still coiled but her light smock was soaked in blood.

A photographer gingerly set a tripod on the uneven turf near the grave. Claude pointed him out to the nearest officer.

"Is he police?"

The officer scuttled towards the man, who had no identification.

"Get him out of here," Claude said. "And anyone who isn't authorized."

To the side of the grave, the farmer who'd discovered the bodies was recounting his story. Claude opened his note book.

"It were daybreak," the farmer said after giving his name. "I was walking to my plot."

"Why did you see this?" Claude pointed to the single rut track at the side of the field. "It's away from your path."

"I don't know, I guess… the furrows I'd ploughed had been disturbed. The mound caught my eye. I knew it weren't there yesterday evening. I was annoyed someone had been on the plot overnight."

"Annoyed?" Claude made a note.

"People come to the fields, gypsies and the like, help themselves to whatever they want. This is my living."

"Of course. What happened then?"

"I walked towards the mound, saw a trail of blood leading to a handkerchief so I went closer. There was blood on the handkerchief. I kicked about in the soil and ... and..." Claude made another note. "It were dark but I kicked... I found a hand." Again he stopped, and when he resumed speaking his voice shook. "A little human hand. And him."

He pointed to the far edge of the patch, where the smallest boy lay with his hand extended away from his body.

"He were stone cold and I ran to the authorities."

Claude thanked the man, then turned to an officer.

"Do any of the local police recognize the woman?" he said.

"No one knows anything."

Claude left the farmer as the police prepared to exhume the bodies. The crowd surged forward. An officer trying to push them back was forced into the grave, his foot barely missing the little girl's chest. He touched the woman's cheek.

"The flesh is warm!"

The crowd waved forward again.

"Stand still."

Claude's voice, a full baritone, dry and even, arrested the crowd.

"You must stay back," he said. "This isn't some fairground attraction. You're destroying evidence." He fixed the crowd with his pale gray eyes. "Come now," he said in a friendlier tone, "something terrible has happened here. We owe this woman and the children some respect."

There was a moment of standoff. And then, as if a sheep dog had motioned the right command, a small retreat waved through the crowd.

A doctor ushered to the grave lifted the woman's wrist. Claude squatted next to him.

"She's alive," the doctor said. "But only just."

The woman's eyes were open wide, as if stuck, but the iris contracted and relaxed. Claude felt her hand, warm yet offering no return of pressure. Her lower lip trembled. He moved his ear towards her mouth. There was no sound, just the faint warmth of breath on his cheek.

"Who are you?" he said.

He heard nothing. The doctor held the metal of his fob watch near her nostrils.

"Her vital signs are gone."

"But she's warm," Claude said.

"She was alive, undoubtedly, when she was first uncovered."

Claude sighed heavily. The poor woman. If he hadn't been delayed...

"Check the others."

As he walked from the shallow grave a man retched behind him. At least something was human in this field. Rows and rows of workers' cottages stood not a hundred meters away from it. The area was populated with Prussian and Alsatian laborers brought to Paris to work on Haussmann's rejuvenation. Surely someone had heard something.

"She wears a fine wedding ring," a male voice said. "She's not been murdered for her jewelry."

Claude recognized the voice. It was Adolphe Desbarolles, standing at the edge of the excavation. Desbarolles' work sought to link the characteristics of a criminal's hand to crime. Claude took this with some seriousness though many dismissed chiromancy as parlor entertainment, a judgment reinforced by Desbarolles's earning the major part of his living from reading bourgeois women's palms. On a normal day Claude wouldn't have minded his presence but he'd not authorized it and the laxity annoyed him. Still, Desbarolles was an acquaintance—a perceptive, highly intelligent acquaintance. He looked closely at the children's bodies, even more closely at the woman.

"What else do you see?" Claude said.

"All the children were alive when they were buried but died from injuries. Except the one who died from the single blow that pierced his forehead."

Claude could see that one boy was marked by an ugly mid-forehead gash.

"What leads you to that conclusion?"

"Their contorted bodies. They fought for air, fought to dig themselves free. An examination of their fingernails will confirm. And the woman was in labor."

Noting the pregnancy was one thing, but why had Desbarolles thought to look further?

"The mound has moved lower on her belly," Desbarolles said.

"If you continue with such clear observations," Claude said, "I may suspect you for being at the scene of these murders."

"I witness events but not in such a base manner."

"We may assume she's their mother, but we can't be sure as yet."

"But my friend, she is. They have the same inherited features in their hands."

Claude looked at the small hands of the little girl. She still held a piece of sausage, her little thumb pressing it to her palm. The hand of the boy next to her was twisted with what look like dislocated fingers, the other boy's hands were lacerated. But there *was* something, some commonality between them— what did Desbarolles's tuned eye see?

"There's a similarity," Claude said. "But I can't name it."

"And neither will I."

For a moment, Desbarolles's soft eyes rested on Claude. Then he nodded his head, clipped his heels in a salute, and left the enclosure. With his refined gait, he all but glided across the field—the starkest of contrasts to the rattling, cleaned but still stinking empty dung carts now arriving to remove the bodies to the Paris Morgue. Was no more dignified transport available?

Claude wouldn't watch the children being put into the carts. Best return to his office and commence the investigation.

CHAPTER TWO

"See that man? Take a break, take a look!"

Hortense stopped her sewing machine and looked up at Martine, who stood near the doorway, pointing to the shop. The other half-dozen women and their machines rattled on without missing a beat. Martine was a gossip. Who could possibly be so interesting?

But when Martine beckoned Hortense, she walked along the line of machines and joined her.

"I've seen him here before," Martine said.

The man in the shop was Hortense's age, in his mid-twenties, well dressed. In fact, he was trying on a long coat she'd stitched last week. He *was* handsome—dark chestnut hair and thick eyebrows, a high forehead and high cheekbones that gave him the appearance of nobility—but she'd not paid particular attention to his looks in the brief time they'd seen each other.

"He lingers to catch a glimpse of someone."

"He does nothing of the kind." Hortense couldn't stand tomfoolery. "You can see, he conducts his business with Monsieur Noël."

"He tried that coat on last week and it fit fine. Unless he's changed his weight in a week, he's here to see someone."

"He may linger, but what interest is it to me?"

Hortense returned to her machine. But the other, prettier girls fluttered around the doorway, passing and repassing it to catch a glimpse of the man.

Monsieur Noël appeared at the door and ordered them all back to their machines.

"Except for Hortense," he said.

Why should she be singled out when she wasn't caught ogling?

"You sewed that coat?" he said.

"The dark navy? I did, Monsieur."

"Then come with me."

She felt their eyes on her but seized her pins, scissors, and a marking block. The man remained standing on the plinth. He nodded his head, and she thought she detected the smallest trace of a wry grin before she averted her gaze.

"Monsieur would like the waist to sit a little more... comfortably." Monsieur Noël looked at her. "I don't think that's possible, now it's been cut."

The waist? It was already cut tight. Before she began stitching the coat she'd asked Monsieur Noël if the cut was correct—the proportion of shoulder to waist seemed extreme. Now she looked at the coat. She walked to the rear. The coat hung well, the fabric dropping from the man's square shoulders. And Monsieur Noël's pattern had been correct. The man had a fine figure, slender and taut, and the coat encompassed his waist most comfortably.

"If the waist is taken in, it will buckle here... and here." She pointed to two seams. "But if I increase the packing slightly in the shoulders, it would give the illusion of a tighter waist."

Noël looked at the man for a moment, then raised his eyebrows slightly and nodded.

A thunderous crash rang out from the workroom.

"Forgive me," he said and hurried away.

The man took off the coat and said something—she had no idea what—as she raised her hands to accept it.

"I'm sorry," she said.

He repeated it, his accent as thick as undercooked choux pastry. What did he want? He was a foreigner, not from Nord-Pas-de-Calais.

"Would-you-like-to-join-me," he began, then continued with each word individually placed, "at the Café Magot? Tomorrow evening?"

She gasped. Her face flushed. Though unsure what to say, she didn't want Monsieur Noël to hear. She'd long held a flame for Monsieur Noël, a flame he'd neither fed nor starved. The easiest path was to agree to join this bold man, if only to get him out of the shop and not give Monsieur Noël any cause for suspicion.

She nodded.

He smiled.

Monsieur Noël returned, apologizing, and she fled to the workroom.

"I knew it was you he wants to see," Martine said, her faced squeezed with delight.

Hortense was scowling.

"Who is he?"

"That's Jean Kinck," Thérèse said. "He has his own factory. Wealthy, very wealthy."

Jean Kinck was a fine-looking man, anybody could see that. And rich. He could have any woman. Any! So why on earth was he interested in her?

CHAPTER THREE

In the middle of Paris—in the middle of the Île de la Cité to be precise—Claude stood at the window of his third floor office at the prefecture of police. He gazed down on the square, busy with people, busy with the business of the day. He'd inhabited the same small office his entire career while one by one his contemporaries had been offered something larger, higher and quieter in the building. But he liked this small office, and not just for the view. It was filled with memories of triumph and disappointment, with the knocks of professional life.

From the corner of his desk, he took the dossier of recently reported cases. It was a ritual when he entered his office, the dossier updated through the day, a quick way of keeping abreast of new cases. And there it was; Woman and Five Children Slain in a Pantin field. If only one of those fools had noticed that poor woman was breathing. If only he'd been called to the field earlier. Children. Five murdered innocents. He sighed deeply. Mutilation was one thing, but he'd not been prepared for what he saw. Who were they? The farmer had walked past the site close to sunset and returned just after sunrise. At this time of year there was just under eleven hours of dark. Six murders, eleven hours.

He opened his notebook: *Why were they in the middle of a farmer's field in the middle of the night on the outskirts of Paris? Mother and children? Then, where was the father?*

Pierre Souvas came down the hall—Claude recognized the sound of his assistant's gait, irregular in its rhythm when he rushed.

"I'm sorry I'm late," he said. "I only just got word of this."

Souvas, a tall man in his late twenties, flopped a pile of papers on the desk. Claude looked at the clock. It was nearly midday.

"There goes your holiday," Souvas said.

Claude had told the prefecture he and Catherine were going on a walking holiday but in fact they were going to the Auvergne to look for a small parcel of land for his retirement in the not too distant future.

"My wife is disappointed." Claude shrugged. "What do we have?"

"Somewhere here…" Souvas rifled through the pile of papers. He was normally organized but the case notes were in a mess. He pulled a sheet from the pile, unfolded it, and leaned his large frame over Claude. The drawing detailed the grave site, three metres long but only half a metre deep, an outline of each body, the positions of the bodies, their limbs. Claude briefed him on what he'd observed.

"The bodies have been searched," Souvas said. "There's nothing to identify them." He opened another paper. "In the children's clothes we found seven francs in copper coins, three clay marbles, and a small doll." He looked up at Claude. "A wooden rosary was in the earth sifted from the grave."

"The mother had no bag of any kind?"

"Nothing. We've searched the field."

"And she wasn't robbed." Her wedding ring, a not ungenerous collection of diamonds around a ruby, hadn't been taken. "There's no obvious motive."

"What motive could there be?"

"Rape is unlikely, with the children present. Robbery is possible but we have no idea what was taken or why the thief left a valuable ring. And why kill her and the children? Evil for evil's sake? Revenge? It's all guesswork at this point."

Why let his mind run on motivation? It *was* all guesswork.

"One other thing," Souvas said. "Some distance from the grave, we found part of a small photograph."

He handed the remnant to Claude. It was a portrait shot of a person with dark hair and a high forehead, the type kept in a locket or wallet. But it was ripped in half above the level of the eyes.

"The hair on the top is thick and wavy," Claude said. "The person may be young." He pointed to the side of the head, above the ear. "It's cut close, do you see? It's probably a male." Souvas nodded. "No one of that description among the cadavers?"

"It mightn't even be related to the murders," Souvas said. "Dropped by someone else."

"A photograph is expensive."

"Her dress was silk, very well made, same with the children's clothes."

Claude sighed. Whomever they were, they were bourgeois. He couldn't remember a case starting out this frustrating.

"Police have been to the surrounding cottages," Souvas said. "No one can report any disturbance."

"Good lord! There must be fifty laborers living within earshot."

"They often don't want to get involved. This occurred at night. Or perhaps the bodies were killed elsewhere and brought there."

"There would be evidence of a cart. Or movement across the field. Damn those crowds. If only the whole area had been cordoned off..."

Now Souvas sighed. "The autopsy has started. They'll work all night to finish a draft. The lack of an adult male... "

"I know. If they're a family, we need to find the father."

A junior came into the office.

"The bodies were followed to the morgue," he said. "The place is over-flowing, surrounded, nearly a riot."

The Paris Morgue was open to the public to view unidentified bodies. Distraught relatives, English and American tourists, searched for friends or family members, bloated bodies dragged from the Seine, the poisoned, hanged, shot, or stabbed. But a much larger band of ghouls came in droves. Chaste bourgeois women tittered at the naked corpses. And the men? God knows what perversion drew them. The whole business infuriated Claude, who'd long advocated closure even though the Paris Morgue was listed in American tourist guidebooks. Damn it, these mutilated woman and children deserved privacy.

"Close the morgue."

"You can't," Souvas said. "They must be identified. And there'll be ramifications—"

"There always are. Close the building to the public. Anyone who thinks he—or she—knows them must supply good detail as to their suspicions. Then they'll be allowed to look."

The junior officer said, "The woman's black silk bore a tailor's label, Thomas du Roubaix."

Roubaix was a small manufacturing city in the area of Nord-Pas-de-Calais.

"Many garments are made there," Souvas said. "Sold all over France."

"We've got little else to go on," Claude said. "Dispatch a message to the police prefecture in Roubaix. Tell them what's happened."

What else could be done?

With no forewarning, Joseph Piétri, the Prefect of Police, stood at the door. How long he'd been there, how much he'd heard, Claude didn't know.

What the devil did he want?

Unannounced.

By instinct, the junior officer slipped away. Souvas remained. Claude stood, nodded and then turned to Souvas.

"When missing person reports come in," Claude said. "Any at all, we're to know immediately."

Souvas gathered some papers and left. The two men watched the door as his swift, uneven gait echoed away in the hall.

"We don't often see you down here," Claude said.

Piétri, younger than Claude, a small knotted man of fifty, continued to stand. His eyes, deep set and dark, moved slowly over the few documents on the desk.

"Damn, ugly mess," Claude said, returning to his seat. "The fields of France reduced to a shambles."

Piétri closed the door. "What have you got?"

"A woman and five—"

"I've been briefed. Where are you starting?"

Claude detested his tone. Piétri had risen to his position through astute political ability rather than good policing practice.

"This must be solved…" Piétri considered his next word. "Swiftly."

Claude waited for some more edifying remark but nothing came.

"Of course," Claude said. "Swiftly. And accurately."

Piétri grimaced. "Perhaps you're not completely grasping the situation."

"Then, perhaps you could enlighten me?"

"When the evening newspapers run the story, this vicious-ness, in a laborers' neighborhood, will send the populace mad."

"Why does the neighborhood increase the spectacle?"

"The woman was clearly bourgeois and odds on she was attacked by a laborer."

Piétri had heard his discussion with Souvas.

"I don't see that's necessarily so. And what makes you think it was one person?"

Piétri withdrew slightly, pulled his expression tight. "What makes you think it's more than one?"

"I've made no such conclusion. But the sustained savagery points to many hands."

Piétri slowly shook his head. "Will this happen again?"

"Another murder? I can't see in to the future."

Piétri breathed out slowly and moved to the office door.

"I support you closing the morgue," Piétri said. "Souse the public outcry."

He stepped in to the hall but turned back to face Claude.

"Swiftly," he said. "For everyone's sake, execute this swiftly."

He left the door ajar, his heels firm and determined in the hall. Claude sat back in his chair.

What the devil...? Of course, unless the culprit was apprehended there was great chance of another attack, or set of attacks, but why on earth wouldn't he solve this as quickly as possible?

This wasn't going to be easy. The newspapers would wind people wild, the resulting dervish reporting all manner of people missing, all manner of culprits, all manner of crimes. They'd have to sift through the chaff. But he wouldn't play second fiddle to the newspapers or anyone else in the police prefecture. Damn them. Damn them all.

Made in the USA
Middletown, DE
30 December 2016